SINGLE DAD on Top

By JJ Knight

Copyright © 2017 by JJ Knight. All rights reserved.

No part of this book may be used or reproduced by any means, graphic, electronic, or mechanical, including photocopying, taping, and recording without written permission.

All the characters, organizations, and events portrayed in this novel are either products of the author's imagination or used fictitiously.

FIRST EDITION
ISBN: 978-1548482916

Also by JJ Knight

The UNCAGED LOVE Series
The FIGHT FOR HER Series

www.jjknight.com

For all the single daddies

Chapter 1: Dell

I love women.

The smell of them. Their skin.

How their hips fit against mine. The spread of their thighs.

That perfect sensation of slipping inside their bodies.

Exquisite.

But I sure as hell wouldn't want to live with one of them.

Thankfully, I don't have to choose.

Last weekend was Camellia Walsh, a winsome redhead who wasted no time in the back of the limo after we left the ballet.

And next up is Meredith Sing, a southern belle who just came on as an attorney in one of my company's legal divisions. I don't bother worrying about the fact that she works for me. Her position is far enough removed from my office that our paths will never cross again.

Our positions will cross plenty on Friday night.

But today is only Wednesday. I review my choice of attire, set aside by my butler. Navy suit. Pale gray shirt. Burgundy Yves Saint Laurent tie. Simple and precise.

As I dress, I consider the two critical meetings taking place today. Both are sick companies I will purchase and make well. Then sell for a profit.

The first appointment will begin in precisely seventy-two minutes.

I will be there in thirty.

My tie slides into place as I walk through the master bedroom toward the hall. I only moved into this penthouse six months ago. Prime real estate in Manhattan is hard to come by with a billionaire on every block. Eventually, I had to buy an entire building to acquire a living space that met my standards.

But I had succeeded. And the busty blonde who got me the place broke it in properly.

We made use of the pristine marble countertop of the kitchen island. My lips still twitch in a smile when I spot Bernard, my butler and cook, preparing a meal in that particular spot.

When I reach the breakfast room door, Bernard himself greets me, tall and gray-haired.

"Good morning, sir," he says with a slight nod. He is impeccably dressed in a charcoal shirt and pants. This man is a godsend.

The only other creature allowed to take up residence in my home is Maximillion. This sleek greyhound once held all the leaderboards at the Birmingham Racetrack. He has been my pride and joy since I purchased him after his retirement.

Bernard holds out the heavy silver bowl with Maximillion's breakfast. I take it, part of my morning ritual.

The space I enter would have been a sunroom for other people. It boasts a bright atrium with glass walls and wicker furniture. For us, this is Maximillion's domain.

He bounds toward me. But after a quick cluck of my tongue, he stops short.

When I say, "Here, boy," he approaches with lean, muscled poise.

Maximillion is a real beauty, pearl gray and long-nosed. Exquisitely behaved. Each command has been perfected by his obedience trainer.

He is my favorite thing in this world. Possibly the only thing I truly adore.

"Your breakfast," I say, setting the bowl in the custom cabinet with his name etched in steel.

Maximillion gives me a handsome nod. I lavish him with precisely three scratches between his ears. Then he turns to address his meal. I stand, arms crossed, watching him for a full four minutes before turning on my heel. My free time is at an end.

I will breakfast myself at the office as I review a few figures before my first meeting. I pass Bernard, who holds out my attaché case. Barring a traffic condition, I should arrive at Brant Financial Industries within my preferred time frame.

It has been this way every day since I opened the Manhattan office. Six years. As punctual as my childhood paper routes. Only a tad more lucrative.

"Have a good day, Mr. Brant," Bernard says.

I press my hand to the security console next to the heavy oak door. The seal opens with a small pop. Bernard pulls on the handle and steps aside.

But I don't move.

There is an object blocking my way. A lacy frilly *thing*.

I peer down the hall to the elevator. I occupy this entire floor. No one can approach my penthouse without approval by the doorman, who would have alerted Bernard.

The gleaming wood floor is silent and empty.

I take a few steps, peering at the plants on either end of the hall. No one is hiding anywhere.

My face turns back to Bernard.

"Perhaps it is a gift, sir?" he suggests.

Who would give me this odd cart, layered in ruffles and lace?

"Dispose of it," I tell him. "Perhaps the doorman will know where it was supposed to go."

I'm about to stride away when I hear a sound.

A strange, tiny cry.

I freeze.

Bernard's lips form a grimace. "There's an odor, sir."

I check my watch. My driver is waiting down below. "Just handle it, Bernard."

Then the sound again, louder.

Against my better judgment, I approach the mound of fluff and bows. It's a blanket, I see now, embellished with all manner of feminine bling. It covers the opening of the cart.

I peel a corner of the blanket back. *Shit.*

It's an infant, quite young, its red squally face scrunched up in misery. It makes another terrible sound. This one is more distressed than before.

"It's a baby?" Bernard takes another step back.

He looks ready to slam the door.

"Apparently," I say. There's a large card resting on the pink blanket where the child's body is wrapped in a mummy fashion. I don't even have to look closely to read it. The type is outrageously large, like a tabloid headline. The words are few and simple. They shrivel my loins.

Dell Brant,
Do the DNA. She's yours.

Chapter 2: Arianna

The day has barely begun and already I'm strung out to the nines.

One of my baby room employees has called in sick. None of my backups are answering their phones at seven a.m.

I juggle a four-month-old on my hip. He's got a fist full of my rather delicate silk blouse, and no doubt any second it will have spit-up on it. That's not his fault. I didn't dress for baby holding today, even though it's one of my favorite things in the world.

I'm supposedly in charge of the women who do hold the babies.

I hire them. Train them. Help them love these children as I do.

But today my well-oiled machine is stuck in the mud.

I'm waiting for Mrs. Andrew P. Shilling III to

stop texting her yogi and discuss potty training her son.

Of course, she's only twenty-five and the fourth Mrs. Andrew P. Shilling. I wonder if the former ones still call themselves Mrs. Andrew P. Shilling.

These are the things I think about when trying to remain patient with the rich and clueless.

The baby in my arms, Titus, lets out a big yawn and thunks his head on my shoulder. Within seconds, he lets out a little snore. Thank goodness. Still, I can't put him down. Until I get an extra worker in the baby room, I don't have the guaranteed three-to-one ratio that my upscale day care promises its über-wealthy parents.

And there are several of them who will walk through the rooms to count.

Every day. They count.

"Mrs. Shilling," I say. "About little Drew."

She waves her coral-manicured hand. "I'm sure you've got the piddles under control, Arianna," she says, as if her child is a dog. "I trust you." She gives me a long meaningful stare before glancing back down at her screen.

"What I mean is that it's helpful to follow through at home as well," I say. But she's already turning away. I'm dismissed.

I shift Titus to my other shoulder and pull out my cell phone again to see if anyone has returned my message. I'll have to contact a service to help with my shortage if I can't get anyone to come in. Or I'll end up in the baby room myself all day. I don't mind usually. It's just I have so much else to do.

I pass the check-in display in the hall. The last babies are here. There's no point in carrying Titus around. I'm off ratio. I better get in there before one of the parents raises a fuss.

I may be the founder, director, and owner. But today I will watch the babies.

Del Gato Child Spa is the gold standard in child care. I have two baby rooms, four toddler rooms, and a preschool. We have indoor and outdoor playscapes, baby massage, our own kitchen to prepare individual meals for each child, and a splash pad.

The facility is impeccably organized, and two staffers have the sole responsibility to keep things tidy so that no one ever peeks in on a toy-strewn room.

Wait. Maria.

She's one of my Organization Experts.

I could ask Maria to tend the baby room for the day. She's been asking to move up. She's almost done with her child care certification. She's proven trustworthy and reliable.

I shove my phone in my ample bra. I have plenty of boob to squish around to conceal it.

And Maria is perfect. She raised three kids of her own. I couldn't bring her on as a baby teacher right away, as she didn't have the credentials. But she's been here two years and she's close enough.

I wander down the hall, looking for her. I spot her in the changing room, a bright white facility as sterile as a hospital. It's her job to make sure everyone is stocked with their preference of disposable, cloth, organic, hemp, lined, or fully custom diapers.

The rather handsome monthly fees cover everything. No one tours my facility without feeling amazed and impressed. It's designed to do that. It's not for the budget conscious.

I pop my head in the changing room, holding on to Titus. "Maria, you ready for a different assignment today?"

She turns, her elaborate black braids twisted in coils on either side of her head. She's a little over forty, with a broad happy smile and cheerful demeanor.

"What would you prefer I do?" She stands and pats the pockets of her elegant slate blue smock with the Del Gato Child Spa logo stitched over her heart.

"I'm just thinking — would you like to work the

baby room today? Elena is out, and I think Shelly can handle the organization duties for today."

Her eyes light up. "None of the subs could come?"

"I can't get them to answer, and I'd like you to get some experience."

She squeals a little, then quiets when Titus stirs. "Room A or B?" she asks.

"A. You can take Titus. The co-teacher is Dot. She's already there."

Maria expertly transfers Titus to her shoulder without waking him. "I'm so happy, Miss Arianna! I've been waiting for this day!"

"Have fun," I say. "I'll check in regularly."

Now that this is settled, I resume my morning walk-through. All the children are already here despite the early hour. Their parents bring them the maximum time, seven to six, leaving maybe an hour or two of parenting duties for themselves.

My clients are wealthy, driven, and successful. They expect to continue the work that got them where they are, unhampered by the time-consuming duties required by their offspring.

I'm here to make sure their sweet babies get what they might otherwise be missing. Love, hugs, Band-Aids with kisses, and a nurturing environment.

My website, brochures, and marketing all push the things the parents want to hear. Getting ahead. Testing above peers. Excellence, school prep, quality. But for the day-to-day, I know what these kids need the most. Someone to gaze at them. Tell them they are precious. To really *see* them. I charge the fees I need to ensure I can keep that standard. The one that counts.

My footsteps are light as I turn the corner toward the preschool. Genevieve is reading a story while Nadia organizes the art tables. All is well for these children.

I don't really judge the parents for where they've ended up. I get it. Their work is important. They keep Wall Street humming and new companies funded. I do what I do because all this happened to me. My father managed global funds and spent his days in London, Zurich, and other far-flung places.

My mother was a professional charity volunteer. She organized galas, helped the hungry, made the world a better place. Everywhere, of course, except the place where she was needed the most. With me. So now, I do this.

A low tone sounds, the signal that someone has entered the foyer. I take another glance at the check-in panel on the wall, wondering if I missed someone coming in late.

But all the children are confirmed as arrived.

My phone buzzes. It's Taylor at the front desk. She needs me up front.

Must be a new prospect. They will be disappointed to learn we don't anticipate an opening for six months, and there is a long waiting list for the spot. I don't just have pregnant women on the list. I have clients who plan to get pregnant in the next year on it as well.

I press the security code that separates the classrooms from the foyer and step through.

Then immediately pause.

A man is standing there, impeccably dressed in a navy suit. He's mid-thirties and the level of handsome you only expect in magazine ads. Dark hair. Chiseled jaw. Broad shoulders. My cheeks heat up.

"Can I help you?" I ask.

He pushes a baby carriage at me. It's draped with ribbons and lace and covered with an exquisite blanket. I take a deep breath. Does he think this is a baby drop-off?

Still, I must be professional.

"Who is this?" I ask brightly, peeling back the blanket.

The smell hits me first. "Oh!" I say. "You need a

change!" I glance up at the man. "Did you need to borrow our diaper room?"

His lips — oh, wow, those lips — press together into a deep frown. "I haven't the slightest idea what to do about the stench." His voice has a low sexy rumble, edged with annoyance.

At the sound of his irritation, the baby puckers up her face and lets out a howl.

"And how do you make it stop?" he asks. "I tried the mouth plug that was in the carriage, but she keeps spitting it out."

Behind the desk, Taylor's eyes get big and she has to cough to hide her laugh.

I'm not rattled. He isn't the first father to walk in completely clueless about the basics of baby care. Most of the men of his stature have a nanny for these things.

I lean down and scoop up the baby. "Sweet girl," I say. "What is her name?"

The man fumbles for a moment, then admits, "I haven't the slightest idea."

Now my alarm bells go off. "Did you find her somewhere? Was she abandoned?" I pat her back and turn to Taylor. "Please buzz Penelope to come up."

"No, no," the man says. "The baby is mine, allegedly." He mumbles something else.

Now I'm angry. "Is she yours or not?" I'm about to have Taylor call the police when the man holds up his hands.

"Look, her mother left her with me. I guess she doesn't want her. She did not tell me the child's name, only that I'm supposedly the father. I will do a DNA test to be sure."

Penelope bursts through the security door. "Is everything okay?"

I pass her the baby, my mind racing. "Can you change her diaper?" I ask her. I rummage through the carriage.

Sure enough, there is a canister of formula and a baby bottle in a side pocket. Several disposable diapers in another. I pass her it all. "And prepare a bottle?"

"Let me get a bag," Taylor says, tugging a Child Spa tote from our swag drawer. She drops the items in it to make it easier for Penelope to carry everything.

"Thank you, Taylor," I say.

When Penelope is through the door again, I turn back to the man. "What are you going to do?" I ask him. "You obviously have no idea how to manage a baby."

"But you guys do," he says. He looks around. "This place looks perfect." He pulls out his wallet.

"Just tell me what I owe you and you can keep her all day."

"I'm sorry. That just isn't possible," I say. "I have a six-month waiting list and the baby rooms are full. Taylor might be able to make you some referrals."

I don't mention that without a birth certificate, paperwork, and a pediatrician, he isn't going to get in anywhere I know of.

He glances at his watch, and it's my turn to lift an eyebrow. He's not going to bully me into keeping her, even if, technically, state licensing standards say I'm allowed four babies per caregiver. Del Gato Child Spa is not about minimum standards.

"This is a huge inconvenience already," he says. "I have a meeting in ten minutes." He pulls out his cell phone and holds it up as if that should convince me he is important.

Now I'm really angry. I snatch the phone from his hand. "This is not an inconvenience," I say. "It's a child."

"It may not even be my child," he says. "I need to find out how to schedule a test."

"Then why don't you call Child Protective Services and let them handle it?" I say. I don't add that I'm pretty sure he isn't fit to be a father anyway, trying to dump the baby wherever he can.

"Foster care? What if she is mine? I won't have my child in foster care."

I let out a long sigh to avoid punching him in the gut.

Chapter 3: Dell

This woman cannot be reasoned with. I extend my hand so that she will return my phone. I'd rather stab myself in the eye than work with her, but I'm out of options.

Bernard threatened to quit if I tried to leave the infant even for five minutes. And that I can't handle. I need to frame this is a way she understands.

"I'm sorry, what is your name?" I ask. I'll backtrack, bring on the trademark Dell Brant charm, the sort that got my real estate agent naked on my newly acquired kitchen island.

"Arianna," she says. Her hand is a fist on a curvy jutted-out hip, a stretchy mauve skirt smoothed over it just so. She is a pain, but definitely an attractive one.

Her white silk shirt is sheer enough to show a hint of the line between the edge of her bra and her skin. I spot the rectangular outline of her phone lodged in that sweet, sweet space.

Her honey-brown hair is short and spun into curls that frame her face. She's gorgeous and looks like a spitfire. Despite her maneuver with the phone, I feel my cock stir a little.

Then I remember the child, and it's like a splash of cold water.

"Okay, Arianna," I say. "I can see you run a great business here. I'm sure there is a dollar figure that will convince you that this baby can remain temporarily. Until the test proves she isn't mine and CPS can be called."

One arched eyebrow lifts. Damn, that's sexy. The cold water evaporates.

I turn to the girl behind the counter. "What is the fee for an infant? I'm sure she won't be here long, but I'll compensate you for whatever is necessary."

The young woman, her hair pulled back in a sloppy twist, fumbles for an answer. I get the distinct impression she's been staring at my ass. "Twelve thousand per month," she says.

I turn back to Arianna. "Can't I get my own babysitter for that?"

The two of them gasp.

"What?" I ask. "You guys are seriously difficult."

"Babysitters are teen girls," Arianna says

carefully, as if I'm some sort of idiot. "You are looking for a professional nanny. A good one is hard to find. It's not as easy as placing a want ad and Mary Poppins showing up."

Smart-ass.

I'm about to retort when the other woman returns with the baby.

"Here she is," she says. "All clean. And her bottle is prepared."

She approaches, holding the child out toward me.

An unfamiliar heat rises in me. Panic? I haven't felt that emotion in a decade. I take a step back. "What are you doing?"

"You'll want to feed her," she says.

Despite my efforts to avoid it, the woman places the baby awkwardly in my arms. I'm not sure where my hand should go, or my elbows. The child isn't screaming, at least, and looks up at me with solemn eyes.

The woman, Penelope, judging from the name stitched on her smock, adjusts the infant until she rests more securely in the crook of my arm.

"Here you go," she says, holding up the bottle.

I'm not sure how to free up one of my hands to accept it. After a bit of shifting, I manage to take the plastic bottle, startled to feel that it is warm. Shouldn't milk be refrigerated?

Still, these are the experts. I stick the nubby part of the bottle in the infant's mouth and am surprised to see her suckle on it greedily. This isn't so hard.

The women all look at me, their expressions softened. Suddenly I'm father of the year.

But my problem is far from solved.

"So that's it, then?" I ask. "I pay a month in advance and she can stay?"

Arianna's mouth opens in an "o" and I flash with an image of what those lips could wrap around. A quick glance at her ring finger assures me she is not married. Surely she can be charmed.

"Not possible," she says. "I have several babies waiting already."

But as hard as her words are, I sense a tenderness as she steps forward and presses down on the collar of the infant's dress. "You need a bib," she says. "Taylor, is there one back there?"

The girl produces a small cotton garment with a neck hole and passes it to Arianna. It bears a logo of a cat with its tail shaped in a heart surrounding an infant, the same as the one on the smocks. This woman has her brand well established, certainly.

I haven't gotten where I am in this world without being bold. I'm about to anger them, strategically this time. I *will* get a spot here. I *will* get to my meetings.

I pluck the bottle from the infant's mouth and tuck it in the carriage. "That should be enough," I say and set her down on the blanket inside. "Don't want you getting fat already."

The child howls. I figured this would be the case.

"Oh, hush now," I tell her. "I'll find a mouth plug that suits you. You can sit in my office. I'll have the receptionist look after you." I glance up at the horror on the three women's faces. "She has a headset," I tell them. "She can push the carriage with her foot while she takes calls."

I demonstrate with a perfectly polished shoe pressed against the wheel. I didn't plan this part, but the carriage rushes forward and winds up rolling across the tile floor.

"Oh my gosh!" Arianna cries, hurrying after it.

I actually feel a bit of chagrin as she flies across the room, her luscious breasts bouncing from the effort, to grasp the handle before the carriage bumps into the wall.

She plucks the wailing infant from inside and holds her high on her shoulder. "I should call CPS myself, Mr. — what is your name?" Her cheeks are scarlet and her eyes flash with anger.

This is when I know I have her. That trump card

I've been holding.

I extend a hand. "Dell," I say. "Dell Brant."

Arianna pales. "*The* Dell Brant?"

From behind me, I hear the young woman at the counter breathe the word "Shit."

Penelope, who has gone for the bottle, is the one who actually states the problem aloud. "You mean the Dell Brant who renamed this building Dell Brant?"

"That would be the one." It was the publicist's idea. For establishing *my* brand. Thirteen buildings in Manhattan were now Dell Brants.

Arianna takes the milk from her employee and expertly shifts the baby in her arms to finish the feeding. "Nice to meet you in person, Mr. Brant," she says. "I'm sure you will understand that I must fulfill my obligations to my current clients."

"What about this one?" I ask, pointing at Penelope. "Can you spare her for a few days?"

Arianna bites her lip. "I don't know."

"Oh no," Penelope says. "I'm not going to work for no bossy rich man. I like *you*. I work for *you*." And with that, she heads through a secure door.

Arianna looks down at the infant. "Taylor, call all the usual places and ask for a preferential spot. Also call our subs and see if anyone wants a temporary nanny position." She looks up at me. "I assume you will pay well."

I nod.

After a moment, she sets the bottle back in the carriage and shifts the baby to her shoulder. With a few pats, the child lets out a belch more likely to come from a drunk sailor.

Both the women laugh.

"Is that normal?" I ask them. "Is the child ill?"

"Perfectly normal," Arianna says. "Come on. Let's get you some supplies so you can handle her until we find you a place to keep her."

"But I can't handle her at all!" I protest.

"I'm not going to ditch you with her until you can handle it," she assures me.

I let out a long sigh. I can call the office and reschedule today's meetings. Probably both companies will assume I'm playing hardball. Who knows, it might even get me a better deal in the end.

Hopefully by the end of this wretched day, I will have someone to take this child off my hands until I can figure out if she's mine. And make some inroads on who her mother might be. I haven't even given that matter any thought. Which one of those vixens was heartless enough to abandon a child at my door?

Chapter 4: Arianna

I lead Dell to the supply closet. Surely someone like Dell has a staff member who can pick up some necessities this afternoon. Until then, I load up the storage net beneath the bed with whatever I can spare. I guess I'll be babysitting for a billionaire today. I can't leave her.

Only when we exit the child spa and turn right back into the main entrance of the building do I realize he lives upstairs. He nods at the doorman, who keys in his floor automatically. I know this because I live here too.

"There's a back way into our facility from the inside," I tell him.

"You mean I could enter from the rear?" he asks, his eyebrow raised, his intention clear. He thinks he can rattle me with a sexual innuendo.

"Only if you pull my hair," I shoot back.

His startled expression is priceless. He didn't

expect that from me.

My heart hammers for saying this to him, but I don't run a facility like I do without having a comeback for most things. A lot of the wealthy fathers are used to scouting for their next ex-wife. I've been propositioned a lot of ways.

It's jaded the hell out of me, truth be told. Their wives have just had a baby and they're already bored. There is no bond. No cuddles in bed with the three of them. Just another line item on their tax return. One more dependent. And eventually, another divorce decree.

We ride the elevator in silence. We pass my floor. I don't think I'll let him know I live downstairs. The child spa will run fine without me for a few hours. Surely by then, Taylor will have come up with some options for Dell.

Dell Brant. Right here in this elevator with me.

I peer into the carriage. The baby is sleeping now, her hand curled against her cheek. She's beautiful, every perfect feature you'd expect. Fat cheeks. Nubby nose. Fine down hair.

Dell looks down at her too. "How old do you think she is?" he asks. "I have no experience in these matters."

"I'd say about three months," I tell him. "She's

filled out. Newborns tend to be scrawny. And she has some muscle tone in her neck."

He nods. "So almost exactly a year ago."

I assume he's trying to figure out the mother. "She didn't leave a note?" I ask.

"Just one that said to do the DNA."

"You have any ideas?"

Those perfect lips purse together, and my heart skips. I'm annoyed by this feeling and squash it immediately. Here is a man in a ridiculous predicament, no doubt caused by his own crappy behavior.

But there's an unexpected intimacy in the moment. It's just the three of us in the elevator. We're gazing on one of the sweetest sights there is. A sleeping baby.

"I'll have to refer to my message history," he says. "What are the parameters? The margin of error?"

"What do you mean?"

"If it was born prematurely, would it still look like this at three months?"

"She's not an *it*!"

The elevator glides to a stop. "Never mind," he says. "I'll hire an expert. I suppose I will need to find a child doctor for her."

I don't even respond to this, still angry that he

called the baby an "it." I push the carriage into the hall.

There is only one door. As we approach, it opens. An elderly man stands to one side. "Welcome back, sir," he says. Then his eyes fall on the carriage. He frowns. Then they lift to me. "I see you found some assistance for your problem."

"She's a baby, not a problem," I say. Seriously, what is wrong with these men?

I'm instantly blown away by the size and elegance of Dell's home. I grew up with the rich and famous myself, but this is right up there. The entire back wall is filled with bay windows looking out on Central Park.

I have a trust fund that is nothing to sneeze at, but my apartment's view is to one side, with another building just feet away from the glass.

Everything gleams in variations of black and gray. Marble floors. Black leather furniture. An occasional red accent breaks the monotony. A rose in a vase. A small pillow.

A woof sounds from farther back.

I turn to Dell. "You have a dog?" He doesn't seem like a pet person.

"Yes, a greyhound," he says.

"Greyhounds aren't good with small children," I

say. "You'll have to monitor them carefully until you know how he will behave."

"She's not going to be here that long," Dell says.

"The dog or the baby?" I spit out.

He sighs. "The child."

"What if she's yours?"

The man who opened the door looks horrified.

There's another woof.

Dell turns to the man. "Maximillion is out of control. Can you please quiet him?"

The man heads out of the room.

"Out of control? Two woofs to let you know he'd like to see you?" My anxiety is rising by the minute. How will he manage a crying baby if two woofs by a dog is "out of control"?

I look down at the sleeping child. Her arms fly out, startled by her own dreams. Poor little bub. She really has nobody.

"She has to have a name," I say. "Every hospital requires all the paperwork to be filled out. Name, parents, application for a social security number."

He pulls out his phone and scrolls through screens.

I wait for an answer, but he provides none. I don't even know what he's looking at. Probably work.

I'm out of patience, but I can't leave. He won't

have the least idea of what to do with her when she wakes up. I push the carriage close to the windows and settle on an armchair next to it.

"I'm trying to get a time of conception," he says. "I need to narrow down the possibilities."

My gaze stays on the beautiful view outside. It's the height of summer, and hundreds of people mill around the park. I can see the pond and one of the arching bridges.

"Are there that many possibilities?" I ask.

"Can we assume there are legitimate papers somewhere but the mother didn't want me to see them because I'd know who she was?"

"Probably. But she won't file the baby as missing."

"Somebody has to know she had this baby."

"That somebody has to speak up." My body shifts in the chair. Dell shrugs off his jacket and lays it across the back of the sofa. Almost instantly, the man who opened the door slips in to whisk it away.

"Is he watching everything you do?" I ask.

"He pays attention."

"Who is he?"

"Bernard, my butler." Dell sits on the black leather sofa, still scrolling through his phone.

I watch him for a moment. "Maybe you should

have kept a spreadsheet," I say.

"Would have come in handy," he says absently.

I make a disgusted noise and turn back to the view. I'm not sure I can stand being in his presence another minute.

But the baby stirs, her body shuddering a little as she stretches. Her eyes open and she watches me quietly a moment before drifting back to sleep.

My sympathy surges again. What will happen to her? If Dell is her father, she's doomed to a life of caregivers and boarding school. If he isn't, she goes into foster care.

I reach into the bassinet and feel around. There is a pacifier, as Dell mentioned. Mouth plug indeed. He has to be an intelligent man. He should know these things, or at least figure them out. He must have been desperate to simply bring her downstairs. The image of how panicked his face must have been as he pushed the stroller to the elevator makes me laugh with a little snort.

"I'm glad you find my predicament amusing," Dell says.

I straighten my expression, still feeling around the edges of the bassinet. There's nothing else. Just the cushion and a cover, and the pink swaddle blanket.

I finger the soft cloth, looking for a tag.

Interestingly, there is none. No indication of manufacturer, and no evidence of one being cut off. Maybe it is handmade.

I check the elaborate blanket draped across the top. It is festooned with an outrageous amount of bows and ruffles and frills. My fingers run along the edges. No tag here either.

I drop it on my lap. The baby still wears the Del Gato Child Spa bib, so I can't examine her outfit without removing it. I roll the stroller out a little and bend down to sort through the side pockets. The mother left a bottle, a canister of formula, and a few disposable diapers. All of those could have been picked up at a store nearby.

Otherwise, the pockets only contain what I placed in them. No change of clothes. No note. Nothing for the child to keep or remember her mother by.

I shift the carriage back and the baby stirs again. This time, her forehead crumples. She's about to cry. Rather than let that happen, I pick her up.

"Sweet baby girl," I say, lifting her to my shoulder to pat her back.

She presses her head against my neck. This warmth flows through me, peaceful and calm. I close my eyes, relishing the feel of her, the weight of her body against my chest.

"I've narrowed it down to twenty-five," Dell says, startling me.

"Twenty-five women?"

"Once we speak to a doctor, I bet I can get it into the teens." Dell pockets his phone. "Do you know one who can see her?"

"Taylor has a list."

"Could he administer the DNA test?"

"I don't know about that," I say. That's one thing that hasn't come up at the child spa. Paternity is established by the time they arrive at my door.

Dell stands and paces the room. "I'm not going to let her do this to me," he says, his voice hard. "You can't just dump something like this on a doorstep."

"You should give her a name, at least for now," I say. "Stop calling her *it* and *this*."

"Sure. Fine. My grandmother was Grace. She was a good woman."

"That's lovely," I say. The baby shifts and I bring her down to rest in my arms. "Hello, Grace. You are a precious baby girl."

Her eyes are open again. She seems worldly and wise, looking into my gaze.

I know how important this position is, this eye contact. I won't have her miss important developmental moments. Not if I have the choice.

Damn. I'm already involved. I can't stop looking in the baby's eyes. Will he do that? He didn't even know how to hold her.

Although he did give her the bottle. The image of him with the baby in his arms is etched in my brain. When I think of it, another part of my body heats up.

And this feeling is definitely not the same as the other.

It's uncomfortable and alarming that I have even the smallest soft spot for that womanizing jerk who got himself in this mess and can't narrow the candidates below twenty without a doctor's help.

So I do the only thing I can. I tell him exactly how I feel.

"I don't trust you with her. Let's call CPS now."

Chapter 5: Dell

Jesus Christ. Did this curvy little spitfire really say she didn't trust me?

I can feel the anger rising up. This is why I don't keep cute little playthings around. They get not-so-cute really fast.

I tower over her and the baby in the armchair. "I'm entrusted with billions of dollars in capital and the viability of at least one hundred start-ups, so I think I can handle an infant."

Arianna stands up at that. Her nose doesn't even reach my chest, but her spine is as stiff as a board. Her palm pushes at my shoulder.

"Oh, really?" she says. "Then handle THIS."

She presses the baby against my belly and I have to fumble to figure out how to fit her in my arms. The child's eyes fly open and a terrible retching cry escapes her mouth.

When Arianna is sure I have a good grip, she backs away. "Let's see how you do."

I try to put the squirmy bundle up on my shoulder the way I saw her do before, but this only makes the baby cry louder.

My knees bend, and I straighten, down and up, trying to jiggle her enough to stop her noise. This works for a moment, so I do it more, and faster, trying to stay ahead of her breath. I feel like an idiot, a puppet tugged by a string, up-down-up-down, and spot Arianna hiding a laugh.

Then it inexplicably quits working, and the infant howls directly in my ear.

"How do you make it stop?" I ask Arianna.

She shrugs. "You could try the mouth plug again." She holds up the brightly colored plastic knob. I can't for the life of me remember what they are called.

I take it from her, shifting the baby into a lying position in my arms, like we did downstairs. Still, she howls.

The rubbery nub of the mouthpiece goes in and for a moment, the baby sucks contentedly on it. Her watery eyes look up at me.

"See, not so hard," I tell her.

Then the thing falls out of her mouth, slides over

my arm, and hits the floor.

Arianna bends over to retrieve it. I want to admire the healthy cleavage I spot on her way down, but this blasted infant won't stop the noise.

"I'll just go wash this," she says saucily and disappears toward the kitchen.

Great. Just great.

I plunk down on the sofa. This joggles the infant and she starts crying again. "What is it?" I ask her red face. It's most unattractive, nothing like the smiling babies on billboards.

She pauses a moment to take in a breath. In a fit of brilliance, I get the idea to place her own fist near her lips. This interests her, and she chews her gummy mouth against her own thumb. The silence is blissful.

"All right, then," I say. "Now we can talk like rational people." Her fist pops away, and I set it back before the howling can start up again.

"I don't smell anything, and the fact that you want something in your mouth seems to indicate you are hungry." I give her my best disapproving stare. "You just took a bottle before the nap on the way up. Are you going to eat me out of house and home?"

Arianna has been gone too long. Is she sterilizing the … damn. What IS that thing called?

It's driving me mad, and the infant is calm, so I

pull out my phone with my free hand and type in "baby mouth plug."

I get an alarming set of links of children who were electrocuted. I switch to images and see many content babies with these plastic bits in their mouths, like horses.

But I get names. Binky. Pacifier. Yes. I let a long breath escape. I hate not knowing things.

The child's eyes are drooping again. She sure does sleep a lot. I hope she isn't ill.

I want to leap up with the realization. Of course. That's why some errant ex deposited the child with me. It's dying.

I examine her legs and arms. All seems normal. Ten fingers. She's in a frilly dress that doesn't seem all too practical or comfortable. Dainty socks with frills at the ankle cover her feet.

I glance around to ensure the room is still empty, and pull them off. Ten toes.

I don't know how to tell if an infant isn't well. I do hope this employee of Arianna's comes up with a list of doctors. Perhaps I should phone my own physician.

The click of shoes can only be Arianna, as Bernard is silent as a mouse. She leans over the back of the sofa and hands me the pacifier. "She seems all right now," she says.

"The young cannibal feasted on her own fist and drifted off to sleep again," I say.

Arianna laughs, a low throaty sound I could definitely get used to. She comes around the sofa and sits beside me.

"Taylor has a work-in appointment with a pediatrician about six blocks down for this afternoon as well as three nanny prospects arriving this evening."

My body sinks into the sofa a little more. "Thank you."

"I'm not sure you have enough formula and diapers to last until tomorrow. I highly recommend someone on your staff picking up more."

My blood chills. "You're leaving?"

"I showed Bernard how to mix the formula. He said you would have the diaper duties, but I'm sure you can figure out what goes where."

She stands up.

I pop up next to her. "You can't go. I haven't the least experience."

"I have a business to run," she says.

"I have many! And I'm here!"

The baby stirs, and I snatch the binky from where I left it on the sofa. This time, the baby takes it, thank God. I hold a finger on the handle to help keep it in place.

Arianna gives me a sympathetic smile. "See, you're figuring it out. I stand corrected." She takes a step for the door.

"I'm begging you," I say, then bite my own tongue. I don't beg. Not for anything.

But this gets her attention.

"Dell Brant is … begging?" A smile flirts on the edges of her lips.

I've never seen a single vision more critical to me than her. She's beautiful. She's luscious. And most importantly, she can save my ass right now.

"Think of the children," I say, holding the baby out for a second. Baby Grace takes that very moment to make a very unsavory noise from her frilly little bottom.

Then, the stench.

"Ah, that's why she was fussy," Arianna says. "Gassy belly. She'll need lots of burping after every meal. If it continues, you can try Mylicon drops."

I want to pass her away, but I'm afraid to take my finger away from the binky in her mouth.

"I have no clue how to change a diaper," I say.

Arianna continues to the door, and I follow her like a puppy.

"Surely you can spare a day," I insist. "Just until we have a nanny."

She turns around at that and looks me up and down. Her gaze takes in everything. My tie, scrunched under the baby, my shirt, totally wrinkled, my hand on the binky. Then she looks around the room.

She lets out a long sigh. "All right," she says. "But only until you get a nanny in place." She leans in to touch Grace on her fuzzy head.

"Great," I say quickly. "I'm sure you can manage while I make a quick stop by my office."

"Oh no," she says. "I'm not your employee or your token female. If I stay, you stay. Otherwise, you're on your own."

Damn.

"All right," I say. "Can you at least take her while I call? I had two huge meetings today and I'll have to deal with the fallout of missing them."

Her eyes narrow. She takes out her phone and sets a timer for five minutes. "You have exactly this much time before I leave here if you're still conducting business."

She's bluffing, I can tell. But I nod and hand her the baby.

"Let's get you changed again," she says to Grace. She holds her differently than I do, more turned in. I make a mental note to adjust my positioning next time and quickly stride to my home office to make the call.

This will be a hard one to explain.

Chapter 6: Arianna

The nerve of this guy!

Just to spite him, I lay Grace out on the Italian leather sofa to change her diaper. When I'm done, I tape the disposable into a neat ball and set it smartly on the center of the coffee table.

I've just picked up the baby when I hear another soft "woof." I decide to see this dog. If I think he's a problem, I'll get this baby out of here.

I never had the opportunity to have a pet growing up. Too much travel. We spent summers on the French Riviera, Christmas break in Aspen, and every three-day weekend in the Hamptons.

By "we" I generally mean me and my nanny, when I was small. My parents would be with us, of course, but they had grown-up things to do.

I remember well my various caregivers. Kind-faced Miss Lucille, who was dismissed when I became school aged. Terrifying Miss Beatrice.

My last one, Miss Camille, was soft-hearted and saw me through high school. She taught me how to wear mascara and French-braid my hair. I stay in touch with her even now.

But still, no dogs.

I peek into the kitchen where I showed Bernard the formula. Empty. It's enormous, the size of an apartment by itself, steel gray and black. Everything gleams. On the kitchen island, the monotone is broken by a glass bowl filled with red apples. The formula canister is by a coffeemaker that looks like it could land aircraft.

"This is a lot of space," I say to the baby.

Her eyes stay on the ceiling, taking in all the sights.

A noise off to my right makes me turn. There's a breakfast area with a round table inlaid with stone. Beyond it, an atrium. That's where I hear sound. Shuffling. Maybe a bit of a snort.

My steps click on the floor and I wish I'd taken off my heels. As I approach the door, a flash of gray jumps against the glass, and I leap backward, startled.

I clutch the baby to me. What sort of monstrous dog is in there? Is this a guard dog? Is he trained to attack? My fear flashes with a vision of the baby in those big jaws. This will not work!

I'm about to turn away, my heart hammering a million beats a minute, when the dog comes up to the glass door. This time he sits. His ears prick up and his warm eyes look into mine.

He's beautiful. I pull my hand out from beneath the baby and press it against the glass. The greyhound approaches slowly and pushes his nose opposite my palm. He whines a little, as if sad we are separated by the door.

Despite his wild dash, he seems well trained. "Nice to meet you, Maximillion," I say.

The hound dips his nose as if he's acknowledging my greeting. Huh.

I head back to the living room to stand in front of the windows. I understand now how lonely being a mother can be. These long periods with a sleeping infant, just waiting for the next thing she needs.

Suddenly, the front door opens, and I'm startled to see a stout woman holding a caddy with cleaning supplies. "Oh!" she says. "Excuse me." Then she spots the baby. "Who is this?"

I have no idea what Dell wants people to know

about the child. "It's Grace," I say.

"Lovely sweet bairn," the woman says. "I'll just be on my way to the guest quarters." She pauses. "Unless you are staying there. Mr. Brant does not usually have guests overnight, but I reckon you're here, so I thought I should ask."

"I'm just here for a few hours," I say.

She nods. "I'll be on, then."

My anxiety settles with the presence of this woman. At least not everyone here is so stiff. When I taught Bernard to warm a bottle, he acted as if I'd asked him to scoop poop.

I picture the staid, straight-backed man cleaning up after the dog, and it makes me smile.

Grace mimics my expression with a gurgling cooing sound. I squeeze her little chin. "Baby sounds," I say. "Three months for sure. Maybe four?"

The idea that we don't even know the poor baby's age makes me frown. How could her mother leave her here with nothing to identify her? A birthday at least. A name.

I turn Grace to the window. "This is Central Park," I tell her.

The light makes her seem translucent, like an angel. She really is a beautiful child.

Her face is too round, too baby-like, to be able to

compare it to Dell's strong masculine features. But something in her eyes makes me think of him. Maybe I'm trying too hard.

I tug at her little ears. They lay flat against her head. She smiles at that, her attention still on me. I make crazy expressions, then glance around the room. If Dell has a photo of himself anywhere, I can compare them more easily than trying to stare at the real him.

We walk the room, taking in the elegant fireplace and mantel. Above it looms an enormous painting in black and white with a dash of red. A heavy wood door must lead to an office. Dell went that way. I lean in, trying to catch his voice. Nothing. What's he doing in there?

I picture him climbing out a window on a knotted length of bedsheets and laugh again.

Grace gurgles with glee. I glance down, finding her mimicking my expression. "I hope he gets a happy nanny," I tell her. "Or you'll never see another smile again! Not with those two!"

"I'm that serious, then?"

The rumbling voice is so close that I almost jump out of my shoes. The door is open.

His nearness makes my chest tight, so I step away. "I met your dog. He's lovely."

"Maximillion is the best-behaved dog in Manhattan."

"He was running around like mad at first. You should be careful." I lift my chin. Dell glares straight down at me, and I don't budge an inch. "I'm just worried about Grace."

"Well, don't. Maximillion has his own part of the house."

This does make me relax. "Do you ever visit him?"

"Every morning for breakfast and in the evening for a review of his training commands."

"You know a baby isn't going to have a schedule like that, right?"

He sighs. "When is the doctor appointment?"

I glance at my watch. "In an hour."

He nods. "What about these nannies? Are they good? Available now?"

"I have good people," I say. "I can't promise they'll drop everything for you, though."

Grace squirms in my arms, so I walk across the room, patting her back. "Most people secure their nanny during pregnancy. We'll have to take what we can get at first."

"Should I choose a business like yours instead?" he asks.

"Not unless you want to handle the middle-of-the-night feedings."

"It doesn't sleep?" he asks.

"She's Grace," I shoot at him. "And no, babies do not sleep all night. When they start eating solids, they will sleep all night."

"When is that?"

"Your pediatrician will advise you. Normally around five or six months."

"So she isn't going to sleep all night for another three months?"

Dell's expression is so shocked that I have to laugh.

"Welcome to fatherhood."

He paces the floor in front of the fireplace. "I suppose I will have to prepare a room. My African tribal mask guest room will probably give her nightmares."

"It might give me nightmares," I say. "Do you have space for a live-in nanny?"

He waves his hand. "Probably. I don't really wander around."

I shake my head. "It's your home."

"There are some bedrooms down the hall. Probably more bathrooms." He braces his hands on the mantel, his head down. "Damn, this is unexpected."

Grace has fallen asleep again, so I shift her more securely in my arms and approach Dell. He looks like a lost kid himself right now.

"Look at me," I say.

He turns, and I have to quell the stirring that heats up inside me once again. He's beautiful.

"Let's see if there is a resemblance," I say.

I examine his ears. "Both of you have detached lobes and your ears lie flat."

He laughs. "Is this an expert opinion?"

"Yes!" I reach out and touch his jaw. My finger sparks where we connect. "The chins don't match, but then she is a girl. Yours is rather manly."

Dell grunts. "Her eyes are blue. Mine are brown."

"Most Caucasian babies are born with blue eyes," I say. "She won't show her true eye color for several months yet."

"That's inconvenient," he mutters.

"Babies are rather inconvenient beasts," I say. My arm is starting to fatigue with her weight. I'm not used to carrying babies for more than a few minutes here and there.

I walk over to the carriage to set her down, but Dell says, "Give her to me."

This is a surprise. I turn back to him. "You want

to hold her?"

"I don't want to look completely incompetent at the doctor," he says. "No sense setting off any more alarms than they will already have."

He's right. "Are you afraid they will take her when you don't have any paperwork?"

"I already have my lawyers working on this," he says. "I plan to keep her a secret until the test is done, but we might get spotted with it." His eyes pop to mine. "Her. Grace."

I nod. "Well, let's work on this, then."

Dell steps close, his arms all elbows as he tries to recreate the position he took at the child spa earlier.

"Relax your arms," I tell him.

He doesn't make a smart remark this time, just drops his hands to his sides.

"Move your arms to the baby, not the baby to your arms," I say.

As I move Grace near, Dell's arms lift to receive her. This time she nestles against him more naturally.

"See, your body knows what to do instinctively, if you don't overthink it," I say.

"She didn't wake at least," he says. He walks across the floor, his dress shoes much quieter than my heels. I sink into the sofa, suddenly exhausted from the tension of the past hour.

I watch him pace the floor. I know a little about him. I looked him up after he bought the building six months ago, worried that he would change the terms of my lease.

It didn't take long for me to realize how powerful he is. Or how cliché. A different woman at every function. Professed bachelor. Bloodthirsty investor. He's thirty-six, if memory serves, and that seems about right. He's got just the right amount of age on him to make him look distinguished as well as handsome.

His black hair is perfect, other than one errant curl that has fallen from the wave over his forehead. I sense him wanting to fix it, but he's stuck. He's still struggling to figure out how to hold Grace with one arm.

After some careful shifting, he gets his hand free. But he doesn't fix his hair or straighten his shirt or check his phone, or anything else I expect.

He touches the baby's cheek. Gently, like a proud father.

I'm a goner.

Chapter 7: Dell

The time arrives to take Grace to the pediatrician. I refuse to feel anxious. If the pediatrician feels as though she must take the child to protect it, then that is just the way it is.

I've made fifty circles of the living room. I've mastered holding her.

Arianna stands by the window, checking over the carriage. She isn't sure it is roadworthy.

"This silly thing is more like a decorative rolling bed than a stroller," she says.

"Stroller?" Half the time this woman is speaking Greek.

"Normally you walk with something a lot more sturdy and a lot less frilly." She sets the baby in the cart and pushes it back and forth, bending to look at the wheels.

I force my gaze away from her sweet ass and examine the useless object along with her. "It's only a few blocks, you said. I suppose she can just be carried."

Arianna stands and twists her lips in the most adorable way. I squash the urge to run my thumb across her mouth, and ask, "Is that terrible?"

"It's just hard to carry a baby free-handed very far."

"She weighs less than my briefcase," I say.

"Your briefcase has a handle," Arianna quips. "Babies get fussy if they are handled too roughly, and walking through a jostling crowd isn't easy."

"It will be fine," I tell her. "Once we settle the situation, we'll stock everything we need."

Or let it be someone else's problem, I think, but don't say it. I have to tread carefully, lest I piss this woman off enough that she abandons me.

But her concern persists. I can see it in her posture, her hand on her hip.

"How about we just take a car?" I suggest. It's more private anyway. I prefer to avoid being spotted with an infant. Particularly by anyone with a cell phone and Twitter. I'm not often a target of the tabloids, but occasionally they decide to shine their glaring light on me. An unidentified baby in my arms would definitely grab their attention.

Arianna takes Grace, holding her high against her neck. "Without a proper car seat, it's not legal for her to ride in a car."

Right. Car seats. I hadn't even thought of that. The whole baby business is a racket. I wonder if I own any companies in this market. Perhaps I should.

Then I shake my head. No doubt all this will be straightened out shortly. Either the child will not be mine, placed by some desperate building worker who had access to this floor. Or the mother will be located and forced to reclaim her offspring.

I see no scenario where the infant finds a permanent home here.

"If we're walking, we should probably head out soon," Arianna says. "I'm sure you like to be punctual. We can stop by the child spa on the way down."

"Do the five minutes of working apply to you as well?" I don't mean for my voice to have a hard edge, but it does. Arianna turns to me, startled.

Her reply is measured, as if she is holding her temper. "I'm just going to pick up a baby wrap so we can carry her more securely."

I don't respond to that. She knows more about

these matters than I do. But my chagrin is pricked. I feel bad for upsetting her. She is going out of her way for a stranger.

"Hey," I say, reaching out to touch her slender arm. "Thank you."

She pats the baby's back. "I'm not doing it for you," she says. "It's for her."

"Fair enough." I turn to the carriage. "What do we need to bring?"

"Have Bernard fix another bottle. And whatever diapers are in there. We absolutely have to pick up more. The way she's going through them, we won't last the evening."

I like the way she says "We," as if the two of us are in this together. I suppose we are. I'm not sure what is keeping her here, other than perhaps fear that I will cause harm to the child.

I pick up the bag from her child spa. Arianna continues to hold Grace. I have to hope everything else today works out.

Hope. It's an unfamiliar feeling. I'm accustomed to everything turning out the way I plan. Foresight. Expertise. Competence. In most things, I can force the issue if necessary.

But nothing has prepared me for this.

We ride the elevator down in silence. Grace

makes gurgling noises on Arianna's shoulder. She seems happy finally. Arianna pats her absently, her mind clearly on other things.

We exit the elevator and turn down a side hallway I've never noticed. It's a service corridor with entrances to the coffee shop, a clothing boutique, and then finally, Arianna's spa.

She swipes a security card and we enter a small break room. A long cabinet holds a microwave, coffeepot, and other items.

We pass through, and I follow her down another hall. A large digital screen displays a list of names and rooms. She pauses at it and nods with satisfaction.

We pass the woman who changed the baby's diaper that morning. She seems surprised to see me again, but just says a quiet hello to Arianna and walks on.

Several rooms are filled with children engaged in various activities. Art. Dancing. Singing. Another is darkened, a woman in a rocking chair with an infant. Other cribs line a wall.

Arianna pauses here to watch. For a moment I sense something is amiss, then another woman enters the room with another baby. Arianna sighs and moves on.

"It's Maria's first day in the baby room," she says.

We enter another door. This room is bright white and filled with drawers.

"The diaper room," Arianna says. "We store everything for the babies here."

She passes all the drawers and opens a tall cabinet in one corner. She pulls a purple swath of heavy fabric off a hook.

"What is that for?" I ask.

"A baby wrap," she says. She lays Grace on a smooth pad. I expect the baby to wail, but she doesn't. She just watches Arianna expertly twist and turn the fabric and tie a knot.

"The baby goes in that?" I ask.

Arianna just smiles as she picks up Grace and tucks her securely in the folds of the fabric. Within seconds, the baby is yawning and closing her eyes.

"Incredible," I say, but I get it. She's snuggled up against Arianna's chest. I could get lost there myself.

As we walk through the facility, I have to admit to being impressed by the scope and quality of what I see. Babies. Toddlers. Small children. Everyone is calm and happy. Everything is perfectly organized and clean.

"You run a solid business here," I say.

"I do." She presses a code on a door and we're back in the foyer where we met.

The girl behind the desk looks up, her expression also giving away the shock of seeing us together. These people would never make it in a boardroom. The infants have better poker faces.

"Let me know if anything is amiss," Arianna says to her.

The girl simply nods.

Then we're out in the warm air of a Manhattan summer.

I've come to appreciate the lack of searing heat you find in the south. Nothing in these months compares to the shimmer off the asphalt on a hot Alabama day.

I do not remark on this out loud. No one knows about my upbringing, not here. Everyone says they love a rags-to-riches story. A poor shit-shoveling kid hitting the big time.

In reality, they like tradition. Old money. Pedigrees. So I changed my name at age twenty-three. My past remains a mystery.

The sidewalks aren't too packed, so Arianna and I walk in companionable silence along the city streets. We pass small businesses, a bakery, a florist, a jeweler. I picture her inside each one, examining a necklace, sniffing a rose, choosing a pastry.

I don't make small talk. I'm not able to categorize

her properly, so I don't have a script. She's not a date or a conquest. Not a business partner. Not an employee or service provider.

She's just... Arianna. The sun glints on her hair as she walks, occasionally looking down at the baby's head peeking out from the bright purple wrap. An oddly contented feeling washes over me, looking at the two of them. There's no strain here. No push-pull of conflicting interests.

Just a walk. A baby. A woman.

My loins stir and I drag my attention away from her. We pause at a crosswalk, and the exhaust of taxis brings me back to the New York I know.

This is just a walk to a doctor. The fate of the child will be decided by a test. Only if she is actually mine do I have any additional decisions to make.

And the likelihood of that is virtually nil.

Chapter 8: Arianna

"This is it," I say to Dell as we approach a tall brownstone that has been converted to a medical office.

He holds the door open for me. I'm hit with the smell of antiseptic. A couple other mothers glance up at us. The waiting room is colorful and neat, cushioned chairs lining the walls.

We approach the front desk, where a bright-faced young woman looks at us expectantly. "And who is this?" she asks, standing to peer at the baby.

"Grace," I say, then decide to shut up. I don't know what to do about a last name. I'll let Dell handle that.

"Hello, Grace," the girl says, then sits again.

"Date of birth?"

Dell and I exchange glances.

"This one is a ... situation," I say.

Her eyes get big, and I sense other mothers in the waiting area shifting in their seats.

I lean forward. "I believe my assistant spoke with your office manager about this."

The girl pushes back in her chair. "Just a moment."

I straighten and turn back to Dell. His face is an iron mask, his jaw clenched.

"You okay?" I ask.

He nods in a small tight gesture.

The girl comes back and drops into her chair. "Just fill out what you know," she says, passing us a clipboard. "I assume this will be self-pay since she isn't currently on insurance as far as you are aware?"

This is horrible. I glance around the room. The other mothers are pretending not to listen.

Dell leans in to her. "Is your office always such an illegal breach of privacy?" he hisses.

His powerful body, angry jaw, and low voice would scare the spots off a cheetah. This girl is definitely affected.

"I-I'm sorry," she stammers. "Th-these are standard questions."

"Ask them somewhere else," he says. His anger is palpable. I can feel it in my belly.

He has a point. This girl has just outed our situation and piqued the curiosity of the room. But these are standard doctor questions. Dell just thought he'd be different here.

He takes the clipboard and covers the distance from the desk to a quiet corner of the waiting room in several long strides. I toss a sympathetic smile at the girl and follow him, patting the baby, more for my comfort than for hers.

Dell stares at the page, making occasional hard scratches of writing across its surface. I have no idea what to say. I do feel for him. He's been thrust into this situation against his will. He could have just dumped the baby on CPS and been done with it.

I sit beside him. "Anything I can help with?" I ask.

He grunts, crossing off big swaths of the page and flipping it over.

Baby history. Birth history. Age. Place of birth. We know so very little.

He gets to the guarantor section. "Can't I just pay cash and not put my name to this?"

"I think they have laws about privacy," I say. "They can't tell anyone."

He jabs the pen in the direction of the front desk. The girl there carefully avoids looking our direction. "Oh, like the privacy we just experienced?"

"Probably fewer people care than you think," I say. And that part is true. A man as arresting and handsome as Dell would draw attention no matter what he did. The fact that he seemed to be clueless about his own baby is just a bonus.

A door opens and one of the other children is called. Dell crosses through the last section of the paperwork and sits back. "I should have had my office manager come do this," he mutters.

The baby stirs and yawns. I stroke the downy hair of her head.

"Will her hair change too?" Dell asks. "Like the eyes? Go from blond to something else?"

I shrug. "Lots of small children stay blond. My hair didn't turn until my twenties."

He examines my face and hair, and I feel a flush of warmth. "So you were blond as a child and a teen, then it got darker?" He lifts his hand and takes a few strands between his fingers.

"Yes," I say, breathless now at his nearness. I feel completely out of my element. I'm used to holding randy married men at arm's length.

Not having a single one, and a killer specimen at

that, touching my hair.

"Is it safe to say that her hair won't ever be black?" he asks.

I'm still looking at his face, so it takes a moment to register his question. "Black?"

"Yes. It won't turn from blond to black, right?"

He lets go and tugs his phone out of his breast pocket.

Right. His list of potential mothers.

The chill that follows the withdrawal of his attention makes me shiver. "I don't think so. Her hair will stay fair and never go much darker than medium brown. If it were going to be black, it would have shown up that way by now."

He nods, scrolling down his list. "Given that my hair is so dark, that should eliminate quite a few more."

I've recovered from his touch now and sit up straight. "Not necessarily. Recessive genes can show up anytime. My parents both had dark hair and brown eyes."

He looks at me again, this time focused on my eyes. "They are almost green. Are you sure you aren't adopted?"

Anger flushes through me. "You don't say things like that!" I whisper harshly. "I got my hair and eyes from my grandmother!"

He holds up a hand. "Sorry, sorry. I didn't mean to offend your tender sensibilities." He laughs. "Growing up, I was desperately hoping I would turn out to be adopted."

As soon as those words are out, his face darkens, as if he is angry he said it. "Never mind. I'm sure a simple test will clear me of all this."

But I'm too angry now to let any of this go. "Maybe if you didn't sleep with every woman that came within striking distance of your snakebite, you wouldn't be in this predicament at all!"

He drops the phone back in his pocket. He's comfortable now, as if my disdain is what he expected and he's back in his element. "Careful, now, or I'll bite you next."

"As if!" I groan as soon as I've said it. I sound like a teenager.

Thankfully, a woman in pink scrubs comes out and calls for Grace. I stand up in a huff, then get hold of my composure and smooth my skirt, one hand still on the baby's back.

Inside the hall, we turn to a scale on a small table. "Place the baby here," the nurse instructs. She's mid-fifties and rather no-nonsense.

I tug Grace from the wrap and place her gently in

the curve of the scale.

"Fourteen pounds, two ounces," the woman announces. She picks Grace up and stretches her out on a small counter next to a measuring tape. "And twenty-two inches. All good."

She slides the tape around Grace's head and marks down the measurement. "Perfect."

We move on to a room and I rewrap the baby. Dell hands the mostly empty clipboard to the nurse and settles in a chair near the exam table.

The woman closes the door and frowns at the paper. "So what are we here for?" she asks.

"To assess the infant's overall health and do a DNA test," Dell says. "We need to establish paternity."

The nurse snaps to me. Great, now she thinks I'm the mother that Dell is questioning. "I'm just here to help," I say. "The mother is unknown."

"So no vaccine records, birth information, nothing?" the woman asks.

"Not a clue," Dell says. "The heartless beast left the baby at my door."

The nurse bites her lower lip. "I may have to call social services on this," she says.

Now Dell stands up, towering over the woman. "I'll call social services myself once we've concluded the test. This isn't the time or the place to involve outsiders."

The nurse takes a step back. "I'll bring in the doctor."

"Thank you," Dell says curtly. He settles back in the chair.

When the door is closed, he glances over at me. "What are you so smug about?"

"Being friendly is going to get you a lot further than being Dell Brant," I say. Grace has fallen back asleep in my arms. "If she thinks this child is in any danger, she's obligated to call the hotline."

Dell leans his head against the wall. It's an amusing pose due to a school of silly painted fish behind him. I have to stifle a giggle.

"Are *you* obligated to call?" he asks.

"Yes," I say. "Anyone in contact with children like we are is supposed to report anything suspicious."

"Have you already done so?" His voice is hard-edged.

"No," I say. "I'm curious to see if the baby is yours."

Now he frowns. "Is that the reason you've stayed? Morbid curiosity?"

I sense the subtle power shift. "There is that, certainly. But mainly I'm here because you asked for my help."

This mollifies him. We sit in silence, listening to the sounds in the hall. Handwashing. Murmured greetings. At one point, a child's lusty scream pierces the quiet.

Dell's eyebrows lift.

"A shot," I say, and he nods, relaxing.

When the doctor steps in, Dell's entire demeanor changes. He stands to shake the woman's hand. "Thank you so much for helping us today," he says to her. "I'm so anxious to confirm that this child is my daughter."

This is an entirely different Dell. I guess he took my lecture to heart.

"Let's see this little darling," the doctor says. She turns to me. "I'm Lilluth."

Lilluth is in her sixties with a cotton-candy head of gray hair, and a grandmotherly expression usually only seen in children's books. I adore her instantly.

"Arianna," I say, sliding the wrap around to release the baby. "I run the Del Gato Child Spa down the street."

"Ah, yes, I see many of your wee clients," she says. "I hear lovely things about your business."

"Thank you for getting her in so quickly," I say carefully. I want to place a little distance between myself and the situation since she knows me. "Mr. Brant came in quite concerned about the proper steps to take once the child was left in his care."

"You are good to help," Lilluth says. She takes the baby from me and holds her in the crook of her arms. "Nice weight. Good skin tone. Let's wake you up now," she says. "I want to hear that healthy cry!"

She lays the baby on the exam table. "Wake up!" she says, then asks, "Is Grace her name?"

"It's what we're calling her," Dell says. "For my grandmother. We weren't given any paperwork."

"So we don't know if she has her immunizations or a confirmation of her age," Lilluth says. "Let's take a look."

Grace opens her eyes sleepily, then closes them again. Lilluth pulls on her legs, opening her knees and checking her hips and ankles. Then she slips the disc of her stethoscope inside the frilly outfit to listen to her heart and lungs.

"All seems well," Lilluth says. She plucks gently at Grace's cheeks until Grace is more fully awake. "Let's look at those gums!" she says.

The baby finally gives a hearty cry and Lilluth examines her mouth. "Three to four months for sure," she says.

I nod. I thought so too.

"She's right in the center of the growth chart for three months, which we would expect with no sign of teeth erupting." Lilluth straightens. "I'm tempted to inoculate her since she'd be due for a second set anyway." She glances at Dell. "Are you on board with that?"

"If your professional opinion says it is in her best interest, then yes," Dell says.

Lilluth picks up the baby and places her on her shoulder. "So let's talk about the DNA test."

"How quickly can we get results?" Dell asks.

"Three days," Lilluth says. "But since today is Wednesday already, you're looking at Monday before we'll get back to you."

"There is no way to speed the process up?" Dell asks.

"I think there are one-day clinics around, and some of the home kits will get you results the next day," Lilluth says. "But you want a court-admissible test. Ours will be one you can take to a judge to establish custody."

"But if I could know in a day, I can call the child agency if she isn't mine," Dell says.

Lilluth pats Grace on the rump. She's asleep again. "I don't think I would rush this process if I were you," she says kindly. "Once the baby is in the system, it's a lot harder to get her back."

Dell stares at the ceiling a moment, then says, "Let's go ahead and do yours. I can decide about the other later."

Lilluth nods. "Here you go," she says, passing the baby to Dell. I can see in her sly smile that this is on purpose.

Dell handles her well, holding her gently and angled toward him. She doesn't wake.

Lilluth smiles with satisfaction. "She looks good on you." She pushes up from the stool. "I'll send the nurse in with the vaccinations and the DNA swabs." She pats Dell's arm. "Good luck to you." Then to the baby, "I hope to see your pretty face again soon."

When she's gone, Dell says, "I like her."

"She doesn't take many new patients," I say. "But she had a cancellation. Lucky for us."

The stern nurse re-enters the room and Dell instantly tenses up again. I'm not fond of the woman either.

"Sounds like we have a few items to take care of," she says cheerfully.

"Are you going to be the one giving her the shots?" Dell asks.

"I am. Now if you'll just lay her down here."

Dell hesitates, but steps forward to set Grace on

the exam table. She looks so small and vulnerable, spread out on the flat gray cushion covered in wrinkled paper.

His eyes meet mine. I try to convey calmness in my expression.

The nurse opens a round Band-Aid and sticks it on one finger as she pulls out a syringe. As soon as Dell sees it, his face loses color.

I stand up, alarmed at how quickly he changes. "You okay, Dell?"

He nods curtly.

"Hold the baby in place," the nurse says. "She'll take the first one fine, but the second one won't be as easy."

Dell and I glance at each other again. He presses a palm on the baby's chest. I fold in close in case I can help.

I may have run a day care for several years and dealt with all manner of child situations. But I've never been a parent, and I've never watched a baby get stuck with a needle.

When the syringe goes in and Grace snaps awake with a blood-curdling cry, Dell and I reach for each other's hands at the same time.

Chapter 9: Dell

"That was pretty tough," Arianna says as we walk down the sidewalk back to our building.

I don't answer. I'm holding the baby now. I may never let another person touch this child.

"These are the hard parts," Arianna says, her voice insistent. She won't stop saying the same thing over and over. "Some things just have to be done."

Finally I stop cold, right in the middle of the sidewalk. "I'm not taking her back to that horrible nurse."

"Maybe you can ask Lilluth to do it next time," Arianna says.

I can only grunt. Probably it wouldn't have gone any differently with the doctor. It's barbaric, sticking needles in their legs. I'm not thrilled about my role in her misery, holding her down, having a cotton swab stuck in her mouth. The woman practically gagged me with it herself.

We take off again. My stride is punishing, fast and long. Arianna is keeping up well enough, though. She must do cardio in some form. Grace is still howling. She hasn't calmed down since she got stuck. I don't blame her.

"Shhhh, little one," I say to her. "Nobody is going to hurt you again." Not if I can help it. I'll buy the damn pharmaceutical company. Force them to come up with another method to vaccinate. This is outrageous.

We're halfway back when my ears prick. Something familiar. Something I don't want to hear.

Arianna nudges me. "That woman is calling out to you," she says. She points into the street.

Traffic is nose to nose, barely inching along. A black Mercedes has its back window down. Leaning out, waving madly, is none other than a woman I went out with a couple weeks ago. Camellia Walsh.

This day just keeps getting better.

"Dell, oh Dell!" she calls. "I've been texting you!"

I keep walking, refusing to acknowledge her.

"You ignoring her on purpose?" Arianna whispers, practically a hiss.

I don't see any reason to answer her either. It's obvious what I'm doing.

But Camellia is damnably persistent, and the slam of a car door is quickly confirmed to be her. She catches up and pulls at my shirt sleeve. I realize for the first time since leaving my penthouse that I'm without my suit jacket. Or tie. Damn it all.

"Dell! Couldn't you hear me?"

Her red hair is ridiculously bright in the sun, almost lurid. Her eyelashes are like spiders fighting with every blink. What did I see in her?

Then I spot the rack. The tiny waist. The tennis-honed thighs flirting beneath the hem of her crazy short dress.

And I remember.

Arianna has taken several steps away from me, walking as if we aren't really together. She frantically tries to tame the flapping bits of the purple wrap. She has no idea how classy she looks compared to Camellia's fake facade.

"Dell! I'm right here!" Camellia calls.

She seems to notice the child finally and crosses in front. "Stop! Stop right here! What is that you are holding?"

I'm forced to halt or run her over. There aren't enough four-letter words for how pissed I am that she's seen me with Grace. I have no way of explaining her. And I don't want to speak to this woman anyway.

Despite my reputation and my absolute clarity that we were not a couple, she has insisted on seeing me again.

Our sudden jolting stop causes Grace to stop crying for a moment, her wet eyes taking in Camellia's vivid hair.

Arianna stops as well, her face etched with uncertainty. There's a tree between us, circled with a small wire fence. I want her to come out, not hide.

But I don't need saving. I'll deal with Camellia.

"It's nothing that concerns you," I say coldly. "Now please get out of my way."

Camellia looks around, as if certain there has to be some explanation for the presence of the baby. She spots Arianna standing by the tree.

"You there," she says. "Are you the mother of this child?"

Good God. "Camellia, get back in your car," I order her.

I take a step around her and carry on with the walk. I can't tell if Arianna has followed or not.

I know Camellia in her kitten heels will never be able to keep up with me. I can see the building two blocks down. I will get there, and I will calm this baby.

Although she's not taken up her cries again. She has her fist in her mouth.

I can feel the way I'm jostling her as I walk. Arianna was right. I should have a wrap or carrier. I see why people use strollers. If nothing else, you can force people out of your way.

I sense someone following me. I have no idea if Camellia is showing more spunk than she did on our dates, or if it's Arianna or a random New Yorker. I'm not particularly interested in turning around to look either. My eye is on the building.

But I'm stopped at the crosswalk and I'm not about to dodge taxis with an infant in my arms. So I wait. After a few seconds, Arianna stands next to me. "You lost her," she says. "Shoe disaster."

I huff a sardonic laugh. "Broken kitten heel?"

"Worse," Arianna says. "Strap blowout."

I turn to look then. Camellia is a block back, hopping on one shoe, one bare foot, back to the Mercedes.

The light changes and I charge across the street. Arianna keeps up easily now.

"So who was that?" she asks. "She sure tried to boss you around."

"Just someone I used to know," I say.

"She saw the baby. Will that be a problem?"

"I don't know yet." Camellia's warped brain is probably already trying to figure out a way to use the situation to her advantage. But she can't know anything about Grace, and there isn't anyone anywhere who could inform her. Even my office staff and the executives whose meetings I canceled were not told anything other than I couldn't be there.

Still, of all people to run into. It was no coincidence. She's probably had her driver circling my block all afternoon.

Damn.

"Can I help?"

I glance over at Arianna. The curly brown-gold hair is lit up in the early afternoon sun. She couldn't be more different from Camellia Walsh. Or most all the women on that list of twenty-five potential mothers. Who is she? How did she end up running a day care?

"Just help me settle this child," I say.

"Pass her over to me," Arianna says. "Since you'll have her until Monday, have your people buy some things. A stroller. Some sleepers. More diapers. Maybe a changing pad. Probably another blanket or two."

We approach the front of our building. The doorman nods as we enter.

I hear what Arianna is saying, and I agree. But now I'm not so sure I want anyone in my employ to buy the baby things. I suppose I could pretend they were gifts. I won't have the child be the subject of gossip.

We step into an elevator. "I'm not sure anyone on my staff is particularly well versed in baby gear," I say.

"Oh, surely someone has had a baby," Arianna says. "With as much staff as you have."

"Perhaps I could get a personal shopper from one of the boutiques," I say.

Arianna makes that adorable scrunchy face with her lips. "The boutiques who have personal shoppers will only have high-end fussy stuff. You need basics."

"Where do you get that?"

"Honestly, with what we need, I'd just go straight for the superstore." Her expression is pained, as if this is the worst suggestion ever.

"You don't seem thrilled."

She shifts Grace to her shoulder and pats her frilly bottom.

"Those places are a little impersonal and some of the inventory is just total crap. But we don't want to have to drive all over Manhattan."

There goes that "we" word again. It makes me smile for the first time since Nurse Evil jabbed this poor baby's thigh.

"Are you suggesting we get the items ourselves?"

She grabs my arm and twists it to look at my watch. "We have a couple hours before the first nanny interview. Why not?"

I can think of a million reasons. Camellia Walsh. The public at large. Being spotted by literally anyone.

But she's grinning now, like shopping for the baby is her idea of a winning afternoon. She lifts Grace with both hands, up in the air. "We're going to get you some sleepers! And some blankets! And some toys!" She pumps her up and down.

Grace's face lights up like nothing I've seen since she arrived this morning. Her eyes are like little stars and her mouth curls into a magic smile. Then she giggles.

"You like that idea, don't you!" Arianna says. "Or getting to fly!" She lifts her up and down again.

More giggles.

Something unfurls in me. Something that was so tight for so long, I had no idea it had gotten lodged into the lock position. I can't put my finger on it, chest muscles, abdominals. Shoulders.

But I'm relaxed. Like really relaxed.

And the joy of this little baby is like a drug.

Chapter 10: Arianna

We give Grace another bottle. Well, I do. Dell mostly paces the living room, running his hands through his black hair until he looks like he's been electrocuted.

His shirt is wrinkled, and he's given up on the tie altogether.

It looks good on him. Like he's a real human.

"Can you fetch me a dish towel or a hand towel or something?" I ask him.

He nods. He heads toward the kitchen but Bernard intercepts, holding a beige towel.

Spooky.

"He's like Big Brother," I whisper.

"He can hear that," Dell whispers back.

"I can!" confirms Bernard from the other room.

"Shouldn't he be losing his hearing by now?" I ask.

"I'm only sixty-two!" Bernard adds.

"Cheeky, isn't he?" I say to Dell.

"He can be," Dell says.

"Who else is here with you?" I ask.

Dell drops onto the sofa beside me, spreading the towel across his thigh. "Just Maximillion. The others come and go to do their work."

"I saw a cleaning lady, I think."

"Probably," he says. "I don't pay much attention unless they annoy me."

I glance down at the baby at that. I imagine most people probably annoy him.

Grace has almost finished the bottle and I decide to burp her so she can drop off to sleep. The outing to the baby store will go a lot easier if she's down for the count.

I reach for the towel and my fingers graze Dell's thigh. It's rock hard beneath the smooth pants leg.

My hand jerks back without the towel. I don't know why I'm startled. I guess I figured a billionaire workaholic investor would be pale and soft.

"You missed," Dell says, passing me the towel.

I throw it over my shoulder. His expression

doesn't reveal anything, if he's amused or annoyed or thinking of something else entirely.

I lift Grace to my shoulder and she immediately lets out her trademark drunk sailor belch. We both laugh.

"I should have named her Popeye," Dell says.

"She's definitely got the baby burp down." I pat her back a few more times to see if anything else is in there.

But her head drops to my shoulder. She's done for.

"We should probably go while she's sleeping," I say.

"But we still have the car seat problem," Dell reminds me.

Shoot, he's right. "Taxis are exempt from the car seat law, but I can't really condone letting her ride without one," I say.

Dell snaps his fingers. "I bet there's a service somewhere that comes with one. Bernard?"

"On it," the man calls out.

"Good plan," I say. I should have thought of that myself.

"You probably don't need to buy one yet since she might…" I trail off. What if Grace isn't his? What will happen to her?

"We'll buy one," he says. "It can go with her. We'll get her all set up no matter what."

I relax against the back of the sofa, carefully shifting Grace's heavy head.

"Is she asleep?" I ask Dell, turning my shoulder to him.

"Out like a light," he says.

Bernard steps into the room. "I have a black Lexus SUV arriving in ten minutes with an infant seat installed."

"Thank you, Bernard," Dell says.

He leans forward in his position on the sofa, his elbows braced on his knees. He still seems a little uncertain. The Dell that walked into my child spa that morning wasn't uncertain about anything.

"What's getting you?" I ask.

"Oh, just bullshit," he says. "It doesn't matter."

"You don't want to baby shop," I say. "Nobody does. I could leave her here with you and go."

His eyes pop. "No, no thanks. I'll go."

"You're still thinking about somebody seeing you."

He shrugs. "It's stupid. I just don't like people speculating about things they know nothing about." He frowns. "Nobody needs to know she was left here. That her mother…" He stops.

"I understand," I say. "But hey, you've got a LOT of hair out of place. You're halfway into your anti-Dell disguise."

He cracks a hint of a smile. I stand up, holding Grace carefully. "Let's go through your closet. I bet you have some not-so-Dell-ish things in there to wear. You can go all Hollywood on them. Sunglasses. Big hat."

I can't picture Dell in even a ball cap. But maybe something that isn't a suit. I doubt the clientele at the superstore would be people who would know him anyway. None of my parents from the child spa will set foot in there.

Which makes it perfect.

Dell stands up, and I follow him out of the room, careful not to jostle Grace.

We pass the front door and walk down a long hall of closed doors.

Finally, we get to the last one. When he opens it, I realize — I'm going into Dell Brant's bedroom.

It's as enormous as you'd expect from a penthouse. My entire apartment would fit into it. Four arched windows fill the back wall. A giant bed is angled in the corner, all dark wood and navy stripes.

There's a reading nook with a window seat, two armchairs, and a table. Near the front corner is an entertainment center with a large flat-screen television and an overstuffed leather sofa.

Two more doors stand open. One leads to a bright bathroom in navy and white. The other is dark, a closet, I presume.

I transfer Grace to a cradle hold. She lets out a little snore and I have to smile.

"Still out?" Dell asks.

"Still out," I say.

He heads toward the closet, unbuttoning the wrinkled shirt as he goes. My heart hammers a little more than I expect. He's so confident. The feeling is effortless to him. It shows in his stride. The nimble tug at each button. The movement of his shoulders.

I've had to work hard for years to make sure I project competence and strength to the families who entrust their children to my spa. Dell looks like he was born knowing his place in the world.

He strips off the shirt, then the undershirt.

I force myself to control my sharp intake of breath. Dell Brant works out. His shoulders are cut, the biceps pronounced. His back is a case study in musculature.

I tear my gaze from his body as he moves inside the closet. Just beyond the door is a swinging panel built into the cabinet. He shoves the shirt through it. I wonder what other items of Dell's are lying there. I imagine for a moment burying my face in them.

Then I snap out of it as Dell flicks on the light inside.

The room is astounding. Ties in every color, carefully hung in a case. Shoes, shined to brilliance, all lined up on an angled shelf.

Then the shirts, from pale pastels to deep rich tones, perfectly spaced in two long rows.

And the suits, pants nestled beneath the matching jackets, all along the back.

But then, that's all there is.

"Where are your regular clothes?" I ask Dell. "Jeans? T-shirts? Shorts?"

Dell presses a corner of a drawer and it slides out. Inside are high-tech moisture-wicking shirts and short sets, warm-ups, and wind suits.

"I guess you could wear some of this," I say uncertainly.

"I have jeans," he says. He closes the drawer and pauses, as if not certain where they are.

"Don't dress down often?" I ask.

"It isn't called for," he says. "I live a very formal life. And Bernard usually gets things out for me."

I want to make a joke about mothers picking out clothes, but bite my lip instead.

He opens another large drawer. It is filled with undershirts and boxers.

My face flushes.

Dell pushes it closed.

"What's in this one?" I ask, pushing on a smaller drawer.

Silk handkerchiefs like a rainbow. "Wow," I say.

"Bernard keeps it very organized," he says.

I close it and choose the one below. "How about this?"

I see Dell's mouth open as if to stop me right as I press the corner to spring it open.

I don't expect what is in there.

"Birmingham Bulls?" I ask, pulling out a red and blue ball cap. "What are they?"

He takes the hat and drops it back in the drawer. "Just an old defunct hockey team."

Next to it, though, is an Auburn University sweatshirt.

"Are you from Alabama?" I ask. I can't picture someone like Dell being from the south.

He frowns. "There isn't anything suitable in there," he says. He closes the drawer with his knee.

"There's nothing wrong with being southern," I say. My interest is definitely sparked now.

He clearly doesn't want to talk about it.

"Jeans are here," he says curtly and opens another drawer, snatching the first pair on top.

"It's summer, so maybe just a workout shirt," I say. I back out of the closet with Grace. He's so touchy! I totally plan to do a thorough search for him and his connection to Alabama when I get a chance.

He doesn't respond, just opens another drawer.

I walk back through his room to the bed. I sit down on it, realize where I am, and pop up again like a jack-in-the-box. I'm not sitting on that bed.

I picture the one-shoe redhead sprawled on it and grimace. No telling who else has been there.

Bernard enters the room, sees me in it, then backs out quickly, eyes wide.

"Sir, do you need assistance locating a suitable change of clothes?" he calls from the doorway.

Dell emerges from the closet, bare chested, bare footed, in just the jeans.

I catch my breath but can't quite look away now that I get to see him from the front.

His chest is muscled and smooth. His pecs bulge. And speaking of bulge, I can spot his in the jeans. It's sizable.

"I'm fine, Bernard," he says. "Just trying to find something less conspicuous to go baby shopping."

"Baby shopping, sir?" Bernard's voice catches.

"How long do you anticipate the infant remaining here?"

"Until Monday," Dell says. "The doctor will call us then with the official DNA results."

"But surely this is just some sort of prank," Bernard insists. His controlled expression is utterly lost now, full of horror and distaste.

Dell pulls the shirt over his head. "I don't think people prank with small children," he says. "There are a few laws concerning their welfare."

I hold Grace tightly by the bed.

"Is she staying to assist in the nighttime?" Bernard asks. "I understand they can make quite a commotion at odd hours."

I open my mouth, then shut it again.

"We're interviewing some nannies tonight," Dell says quickly. "I'll select one who can start immediately."

Fat chance of that, I think, but don't speak my opinion again. Dell already knows.

"Do they know who they are interviewing with?" Bernard says. "We might get a number of unsuitable candidates."

This time I chime in. "Taylor was very discreet about the inquiries," I say. "She is used to dealing with clients of stature."

Bernard takes me in as if my assurances are insignificant.

"It's your business, sir," he says, watching Dell shove on socks and running shoes with definite disgust. "Would you like me to find a pair of proper leisure shoes?"

"Don't worry about it. This is fine. I'm sure that car is ready for us by now," Dell says.

"Indeed." Bernard steps aside. His eyes cut to me as if to blame me for Dell's state of dress.

I shrug and cradle Grace carefully. "Did you make another bottle?"

"Yes," he says. "It's in that *sack*."

He means my Del Gato Child Spa tote. I guess it isn't up to his standards.

I could be offended, but honestly, he reminds me greatly of my father. When I pass, I shock him by kissing his cheek. "Thank you, Bernard. You're a good baby butler."

He pinches his lips together, his placid face spotted with pink. Ha, I got to him.

Now to see if we can turn this uptight billionaire into a proper father by Monday.

Chapter 11: Dell

When Arianna and I walk into the bright, overstimulating explosion of baby goods, my first instinct is to shield my eyes.

But, if I'm honest with myself, it reminds me of Wal-Mart. And after growing up in Birmingham, Alabama, it's practically home.

I feel myself slipping into my old way of walking, more casual, arms swinging. It's the jeans, the tennis shoes, the lightweight shirt. And the store.

Arianna adjusts the baby in the purple wrap. She looks comfortable here despite the work blouse and skirt. Just a career mom picking up a few things.

I wonder if she plans to have kids.

"Grab a cart," she says. "We'll be getting some big boxes for the stroller and car seat."

I'm about to counter that we can have things sent back to the penthouse, but then I just roll with it. A silver cart breaks free of the line with a sharp tug. I push it, Arianna walking beside me with the bundle in her wrap like we're any couple with a newborn.

Everybody smiles at us. There is zero recognition of me in a place like this. It's mostly harried mothers with a baby in padded seats, holding another toddler by the hand. Their carts are full of diapers and little jars and usually a toy or two. One small boy crosses our path with a truck under each arm.

"Nice negotiating," I tell him. His brown eyes glance up at me for a minute, then turn back to his mother.

"Generally it's more emotional blackmail," Arianna says.

"What do you mean?"

"Oh, generally the child will ask for something. Mom will say no. Then the kid will scream or kick or make such an embarrassing fuss that she caves."

"I've seen boardroom meetings go much the same way."

Arianna laughs and the way her face lights up teases another level of relaxation for me. This is enjoyable. The store, the lights, her company.

She points us in the direction of an open aisle with dozens of padded seats like the one in the Lexus. There are so many choices, sizes, colors.

"Are there salespeople to tell us what to buy?" I

ask.

"Good luck finding anyone," Arianna says. "But this is a good brand." She points to a navy blue seat that allegedly works for infants through larger children.

"But the other mothers have those buckets."

"You're observant," she says. "If you get one of those, you just have to buy a whole new seat when she's a year old."

"Why do they buy the buckets, then?" I glance around. Virtually every woman with an infant has one tucked in the front section of her cart. I push on the flimsy metal cart. I can't imagine trusting it to hold your child.

"Because you can take a baby in and out of a car without having to wake them."

I look around for the boxes of buckets. "I'm sold."

She laughs again. "It is a good feature."

I find a box and load it into the cart. "I've already figured out that if she is sleeping, let her be."

She glances down at Grace's head. "That might be the most important lesson for the early days."

"So I'm not hopeless," I say.

She tilts her head, her grayish green eyes on me. "I can't imagine anyone trying to tell you that you are hopeless."

She didn't talk to my father, I think, but I don't say that. She's already learned more about my past than anyone else. My lawyers have had all photos prior to my name change purged from the Internet. There is no connection between my new name and my old. I'm a man without a history. No references to my kennel cleaning. My terrible upbringing. My lack of pedigree. And that's the way it will stay.

I'll get on to Bernard for keeping those silly clothes close at hand. I had no idea they were anywhere that could be found. Maybe it's time to just get rid of them.

But just the thought of that last connection with my childhood stabs me, so I push the thought away. I won't have anything to do with this Arianna woman after today, so it doesn't matter. She claims to be discreet, so it will be fine. Serves me right for allowing a woman into my bedroom. I should have known better.

"Oh, there's the strollers," Arianna says. "You think we should pick one up? You'll be taking her back to Dr. Lilluth on Monday."

"Will she have to go with me for the results?" I ask.

"I guess not." Arianna twists a bit of her hair.

"Sure, you're right. But the nanny might want to take her to the park."

We walk along the aisle. "Why do there have to be so many kinds?" I ask. "You just need something to push the kid in."

"There's jogging ones. And ones with more storage. Bigger wheels for different terrain." Arianna keeps listing the various qualities.

"I like this one," she says finally. "Narrow enough for stores but big enough wheels for a smooth ride."

"Works for me." I heft a box into the cart. The two items almost fill it.

"Let's get the small stuff," Arianna says. "Maybe we can make a run out to the car and come back in for more things."

We head to the diaper aisle and I pile more boxes on top. Then formula and bottles and little scrubbies to clean them. Bibs and blankets and burp cloths. Baby soap and brushes.

"This is a crazy racket," I say to Arianna. "Why does she need her own soap? Do you really need a bib AND a burp cloth?"

She laughs. "You'll see."

An employee spots our precariously stacked cart and offers to take it up front and bring us another.

"Huh, you can get service here," Arianna says. The baby yawns at the sound of her voice and opens her eyes.

"Uh-oh, the tyrant awakes," I say.

"Your turn," Arianna says.

Just as the baby starts to fuss, she pulls her out of the wrap and hands her to me. She digs through the tote I've slung over my shoulder and produces a bottle. "You can take this one."

Arianna stretches out her arms and unwraps the purple cloth. Her silk blouse clings to her from the warmth of carrying Grace. I'm momentarily distracted by the depth of her cleavage and how the fabric hugs her body.

Then Grace brings me back with a wail.

Arianna laughs and uncaps the bottle. "Here you go," she says.

The employee comes back with an empty cart. Arianna takes it. Grace greedily gulps the bottle as we head toward another section of the store. Clothing.

"Sleepers," Arianna says, holding up a soft pink number.

"Does it have to be pink?" I ask her. "Anything with proper girl things? Like 'I'm the CEO' or 'Glass ceilings are for people without hammers'?"

For this I get another throaty laugh. "You might

have to custom-order those," she says. "Baby clothes aren't quite caught up to feminism."

She holds up a frilly dress with "Princess" etched across it.

"I'm okay with Princess," I say. "Just some balance." I spot a shirt with "Genius" written across the front. "What about that one?"

She turns to look. "That's for three-year-old boys."

"Bullshit," I say. "Put it in the cart."

She rummages through the rack and locates a smaller one. "Okay, okay. Let me find something to go with it."

She selects some blue tights with hearts on them to match the color of the letters. "We can make this work."

We pause in front of a display of one-piece outfits in animal themes. They all have hoods, complete with ears.

"Let me guess," I say. "The pink kitties are for girls. And the lions are for boys."

"Pretty much," she says.

I glance down at the baby girl fiercely downing the formula. "If anybody ever calls you a pussy, I will kill them with my bare hands."

Arianna slides the lion outfits along the rack and

pulls one out. "Her size."

"Done," I say.

She watches me as she pushes the cart over to packages of little accessories like socks and hats. I focus on tilting the bottle the right way as it empties so Grace doesn't suck empty air. Arianna drops more things into the cart.

"You are going to take every dime of mine, aren't you?" I say to Grace. I realize my voice has automatically taken on a higher, lighter tone and clear my throat. "Just like a woman."

Arianna looks up from a package she's examining and lifts an eyebrow. "You want to buy her 'Genius shirts and then accuse her of fleecing you like a trophy wife?"

I have nothing to say to that. Arianna is far more combative than my usual companions. It's refreshing, even if infuriating.

The bottle empties. I stick it in the tote bag and lift Grace to my shoulder like I've seen Arianna do several times now. "Here comes the sailor belch," I say.

Arianna reaches out.

"I wouldn't do that on your —"

I hear the burp. "That's right, baby."

Then I feel it. Hot and wet and sticky.

"What the hell?" I ask, lifting Grace from my shoulder.

A torrent of white goo streams from her mouth. It splatters on the front of my shirt, my shoes, the floor.

"Yeah, that's why you need burp cloths," Arianna says. She breaks open a package and wipes the baby's mouth. "Here, I'll take her."

"No, just get the…whatever it is."

"Spit-up," Arianna says. "Sometimes when they burp, the milk comes back out."

"So this is normal?" I ask.

"Very normal." She wipes my shoulder. I hold the baby high so she can get the front of my shirt.

She's close. Real close. Her hand glides down my chest to my belly.

Despite the situation, the baby, the store, the mess, I feel it. And it's not just the physical thing. Her touch. It's all of it. The family feeling. The ability to laugh at yourself. The closeness and rolling with the spit-up.

"I think I got it," she says. "Good thing your shirt is moisture wicking."

"Yeah, good thing."

She rolls up the towel and shoves it in the front section of the cart. "I'll let someone know about the floor." She heads off toward the main aisle.

I bring Grace down. "I guess it's just you and me," I say. I tuck her in the crook of my arm.

She gazes up, all awake and happy now that she's caused her chaos.

"You think it's funny, don't you?" I ask her. That tone has crept back in. The lightness.

I know where it comes from. I remember my dad, talking to my little sister that way. I'm sure he also did it to me. I hadn't consciously thought about what he must have been like when we were small.

That man decided I was worthless later on. But just now, with this little sprite in my arms, do I realize that maybe, before all that, he did something right.

Chapter 12: Arianna

When I get back to Dell, he's tossed half a dozen more outfits in the cart. Race car romper. A sleeper with a math equation. A sailboat onesie. He also managed to find a couple girl outfits that he liked. "This princess will end up saving YOU." And a dress. A beautiful pale yellow number with ribbons and ruffles.

"One of these things is not like the other," I say, holding it up. He's gotten the right size, even.

"Well, she is a girl," he says. "She can be all the things. Pretty and tough. Sweet and smart."

This amuses me. So there is more to Dell Brant than meets the eye. I had assumed so. Nobody gets where he is by being an asshole all the time. Even Bernard has a soft side in there somewhere.

"I think we've done enough damage here," I tell him.

We sidestep the spit-up as an employee arrives

with a mop. I'm sure it happens a lot. It definitely does at the child spa.

When we head back to the main aisle, we pass a nursery set, complete with crib, changing table, and rocking chair, all on a soft gold oval rug. It's lovely, the mahogany wood, the sweet olive green sheets with swirls and stars.

"We don't have any of this stuff," Dell says. "Where will she sleep?"

"The carriage she came in is good enough for that," I say. "Maybe after Monday you can look into more permanent things."

He frowns, and it's as if a spell is broken. He stands more stiffly, back to business. "Makes sense," he says.

I trail my hands over the smooth polished wood. A soft stuffed star in the corner of the crib matches the pattern on the sheets. Beside it is a little lamb of the same fluffy wool.

I pick it up. "She should have something of her own," I say. "Not just necessities. I can't believe her mother didn't leave a single sentimental item for her."

Dell frowns. "She's three months old. Seems like she should have had an entire trove of things. Clothes. Bedding. Mouth plugs — pacifiers."

"We should pick up a couple more of those!" I

say. "They come in handy."

I drop the lamb back into the crib. Grace's permanent mother, whoever she turns out to be, can pick out the sweet items. It's not like she's old enough to notice them right now.

We stop by a display of pacifiers on the end of a row and choose several more.

"What is that?" Dell asks.

He points to another display. It's one of the new state-of-the-art baby swings. It has a million modes to rock the baby in every direction, plus light-up toys at the top. It looks like a space pod.

"Lots of moms like baby swings to help the baby sleep during the day," I say. "This is just a souped-up version."

Dell fiddles with the buttons, making the round white oval of the bed move side to side, then front to back. The lights and music come on and he stands back. "Cool."

Of course it would appeal to him. It's totally impractical.

"If you want a swing, there are a lot of traditional ones," I tell him, pointing a couple aisles back.

"This one," he says, already looking under the display for the boxes.

I sigh. Let him have his way. Maybe the more he

connects to the baby world, the more accepting he'll be if Grace turns out to be his.

As we walk toward the checkout, I don't even know which way I want this to turn out. Dell is ill equipped for single fatherhood, for sure, but he has money to make sure she is cared for.

The foster system is risky, but for a baby like Grace, she'll have dozens, if not hundreds, of adoptive families all vying for her. She'll find a good home. And maybe even be raised by her actual parents, not nannies and au pairs.

So I guess if I'm honest with myself, maybe what's best for Grace isn't Dell Brant.

But as he jokes with the checkout lady about the spit-up incident and shows off Grace, I wonder if maybe he doesn't have fatherhood in him after all.

Chapter 13: Dell

By midafternoon, we're back home surrounded by an outrageous amount of stuff.

Arianna goes through my spare bedrooms, finally choosing the most neutral one for the baby. It's pale green and light brown and has a bathroom that connects to another spare bedroom, which can be for the nanny. Nobody has to be traumatized by the African masks.

Bernard helps us shove all the gear into the room. I open the baby swing first, connecting the base to the stand and attaching the accessories.

When Grace lies in it the first time, her face bright and happy as she reaches for the light-up toys, I get a sense of satisfaction that is unfamiliar.

I think about this. I've done much bigger, more important things. Acquired sinking companies and made them profitable. Built an empire of investment start-ups. I even snatched a clever little animation firm right from the clutches of Pixar, just because I could.

But pleasing this child provides a pleasure from an entirely different space. It's curious, and somewhat unsettling.

Arianna sits on the floor and unpackages the clothes to be washed. Bernard has already called in help to clear all the debris and prep everything. The housekeeper, a bright Scottish lady in her sixties, is here, as well as the woman who does the shopping, a tall energetic brunette in her forties.

Grace's presence has changed the demeanor of pretty much everyone in my employ. Before today, the few times I've crossed paths with the housecleaner or the shopper, they've been formal and serious.

Now they cluck over the baby, kneeling down to make faces and silly noises. The housecleaner holds up all the little outfits as she prepares to launder them.

"How long until the first nanny arrives?" I ask Arianna.

She glances at her phone. "Ten minutes."

The room is mostly clear of boxes and trash. I want it all to look good for the nanny, like this won't be a difficult gig. I need one of them to step in immediately.

"How many are coming?"

Arianna frowns. "There were three, but one

asked to reschedule until tomorrow. So two."

"I guess keep the third in case I can't handle the one I choose by morning," I say.

"You probably want to give her more of a chance than that," Arianna says. "She'll be settling in, trying to figure out a routine. Things might not go smoothly."

"No," I insist. "I'm very good at learning people. Like that Penelope woman you have. She's good. But when someone is not going to work out well, if they are not confident and communicate clearly, you know that within minutes."

"I disagree," she says, her expression set. "I have a few employees who blossomed over time. Take Maria. She started out in housekeeping, did great, and moved up to organization. Now she's in the baby room."

"It doesn't matter if they clean floors or buy airlines, it's all in that first impression." I believe this completely. It's never steered me wrong.

Arianna won't let it go. "I think there is an entire subset of people who don't interview well, and relating to someone in a position of power doesn't come easy. But they are still great to have on your team."

The housecleaner and shopper make their

excuses and leave the room. We've obviously spooked them with our argument.

"You're wrong about that," I tell her. "If a skill is critical, like interviewing, you learn it. You master it. If you don't, then you're not going to succeed."

Arianna picks up the little bucket of baby shampoo and washing items near her feet. "You do what works for you, Mr. Brant," she says. "I'll do what works for me."

And she disappears into the bathroom.

I look over at Grace in the swing. She's still awake, but her eyes are heavy.

"That's why your friend here is stuck with a single business that she has to micromanage," I tell the baby. "She can't confidently delegate to her substandard workers."

"I heard that!" Arianna calls out.

Grace's eyes snap open.

"You woke the baby!" I shout back.

"You started it!" she says.

Bernard appears in the door frame. "Sir, a Helen Montgomery is here to see you."

"Send her in," I say. "Let's see how she reacts to the baby."

When Bernard steps aside, I realize she was right behind him and probably heard the entire exchange between Arianna and me.

I jump up from the floor. "Hello, Ms. Montgomery. Welcome."

The girl is barely twenty, wisp thin, with blond hair down her back. She wears a pair of jeans and a striped shirt.

Not generally interview gear, but maybe she was already in the city when she got the call. I decide to overlook it.

We shake hands. Her grip is light, just the fingertips. I let this go as well. This is not a business transaction.

"Nice to meet you…" she trails off.

I realize she still doesn't know my name. This is for the best. I don't fill it in. No use having her spread gossip if she isn't hired.

"Nice to meet you as well," I say.

She spots the baby and makes a small ooooh sound. She kneels beside the swing to touch a white socked foot. "Such a pretty dress," she says.

"Thank you," I say. "So what work have you done with children?"

"Are you the father?" she asks.

I do not have an answer for that. Thankfully, Arianna saves me.

"Helen?" she says, stepping from the bathroom.

"I'm Arianna Hart, owner of Del Gato Child Spa. My assistant Taylor contacted you."

The girl seems relieved to see Arianna. "Yes. Thank you. I've subbed for you a few times. In the preschool. I'm getting my degree in early childhood education."

"Wonderful," she says, taking a seat on the bench again. "Has your experience working with children been a good one?"

"Oh yes," she says. "I have six brothers and sisters. I'm the oldest." She rolls her eyes and flutters her hands. "So it was like job training from when I was old enough to hold a baby."

I sit back. It's interesting to watch Arianna take charge.

"Is that what motivated you to seek an early childhood degree?" she asks the girl.

"Sure," Helen says, turning to look back at the baby. "It's what I know best."

Now a sense of annoyance rises in me. "Don't you want to branch out?" I cut in. "See what else is out there? There's more to life than spit-up and diapers."

Both women look up. I'm towering over them, arms crossed, like a damn prison warden.

Arianna looks like she wants to ask me to leave,

but technically, this is my interview.

"Oh, I agree," Helen says. "But this is a good place to start."

"Where can you go from here?" I ask. "Run a kiddie spa like Arianna here?"

Arianna stands up from the bench. "Mr. Brant has this interview under control." She leans down to shake Helen's hand. "Good luck."

And she storms through the door without a backward glance at me.

Well, damn. "For the record," I say to Helen as I also head for the door, "I didn't say it was a bad thing. It was just a question."

I take off down the hall, catching up with Arianna near the front door. "I didn't mean that as an insult," I say.

"Oh, really?" she shoots back. "Is my 'kiddie spa' too low a net worth for you? Are the only important people in your world the ones who are arrogant, rich, and total jerks?" She jabs my chest with each of the last few words.

I take her arm and pull her across the living room and into the study to avoid the sound carrying down the hall. "Arianna, you're saving my skin today. I would not insult you."

"You just did!"

Her color is high, cheeks flushed pink. I wonder if this is what she looks like after an orgasm. I have to shove that thought in a box to get it out of the way.

"All right. Then I apologize. I'm not used to being surrounded by people like you."

"Oh my God," she says. "People like me. Underlings. Lower class. Working Joes." She turns to leave the study, then stops and whirls around. "I'll have you know I vacation in the Hamptons! I went to Brown! And my family has a building named after it too!"

"Arianna, wait." I reach out to her again. I'm totally captivated by this version of her. Strong. Unyielding. Mad. And I had no idea she had a background like that, although it makes sense now. The classic look. The confidence. Instilled by her parents, no doubt.

She lets out a long breath. "You're in good hands. I think you see that the Helen girl is fine. So you're all set!"

"She's in school, Arianna. What do I do with the baby during classes?"

"Maybe she's taking a break. Maybe it's online. Ask her. It's an interview." Arianna reaches for the study door, and this time she opens it.

"Good luck," she says over her shoulder. "I hope

the answer you get on Monday is what you're looking for."

She storms through the living room, picking up her bag as she passes the sofa. Bernard is waiting by the door. He bows a little as Arianna passes.

When he closes it again, he says, "Well, that's done, sir. Now what are you going to do?"

"I'm probably going to hire that girl in there. Can you keep her entertained while I interview the next one? I don't want to let her out of my sight, really."

I sink on the sofa. At least I have someone here. She's probably still sitting by Grace, cooing her silly noises. For the first time today, I can totally relax. I prefer employees, people I pay. Not those doing favors who tend to argue and do as they like.

Bernard pinches his lips in an unhappy line. "That is unfortunately not possible," he says.

"Why?" My body rushes cold.

"She left. Said she didn't get a 'good vibe' but to thank you for the opportunity."

"Shit." I leap from the sofa and barrel to the door, praying Arianna is still at the elevator. Or Helen. I can buy her out. Pay for her college. She'll stay.

But the hall is empty. Both are gone.

Damn.

Stupid penthouse. I'd run down the stairs but no

way I'd catch them. It's forty floors.

I don't have Helen's number. But I know where Arianna is.

"Um, sir?" It's Bernard standing by the door.

"Yes, Bernard?"

"I think you are forgetting something."

"What?"

"The child. It is wailing."

"Can't the shopping woman do something? They were all fawning over her earlier."

"She isn't here. Wanted to get some dishwasher insert for the bottles."

"What about that housecleaner?"

"Went with her. Wanted to get some special detergent for the baby's clothes."

I glance over at the elevator. It's down around the sixth floor. Why doesn't this damn penthouse have a dedicated elevator?

"Can't you watch her just for a minute? I'm trying to save our skin."

Bernard stands a little straighter. "It's not in my contract, sir. You know that."

Shit.

I reluctantly head back into the penthouse. I can only hope the second nanny shows and she's a winner.

Chapter 14: Arianna

I'm tempted to stop by my own apartment on the way down and make sure I'm put together. But it's already coming up on five o'clock, and the exodus from the child spa will begin shortly. Plus I want to check on Maria and also find out from Taylor if she found any more candidates for Dell.

Scratch that. I've done enough.

The elevator arrives at the bottom floor. I'm about to step out when I spot a woman who has caught the attention of everyone in the foyer.

She wears a fire-engine-red dress with a sweetheart neckline that dives deep into her cleavage. Her skinny waist and perfectly curved hips are the reason Photoshop was created for everybody else.

To top it off, her shoes are adorable, wedges with red straps that crisscross her ankles.

She's the sort of girl that crushes my self-esteem. I could never be that bold or beautiful.

As I hold the door while she enters, I turn and look to see where the elevator is going. When I see the penthouse has been programmed in, I head right back into the elevator.

"Forgot something," I say.

She nods and steps back. She holds a glossy red purse and a slip of paper. I hit the number for my floor and steal a glance at the handwritten note.

It's Dell's address. And "Nanny job. 5:00."

WHAT?

I look at her again. I don't like to think I'm judgmental, but why is she going to a nanny interview in that getup?

Unless she was tipped off. She knows it's Dell Brant.

She's not after the baby job. She's after him.

The elevator stops at my floor, but I press floor 39 instead. I have to buy some time.

"So you know Dell Brant?" I ask.

Now her eyes narrow. "Why do you want to know?" she asks in a low voice.

I knew it.

I picture Grace crying while he's bending this girl over his navy striped bed, and I press level 30 just before we get to it.

The elevator stops.

The woman's perfectly groomed eyebrows lift. "Confused?"

I grab her arm and drag her into the hall.

"What are you doing?" she insists, but she can't fight me too well in the tall shoes and tight skirt. When I shove her toward a chair, she sits.

"Are you his ex or something?" she asks.

"No, I'm …" What am I? What should I tell her? "I'm helping him hire the nanny."

"I don't care about the job," she says. "I have every intention of being next on his list." She tries to stand up, but I block her.

"What list?"

"His just-fucked list, honey. Don't worry about the baby. A friend of mine works at Honey Bear Kids, and she'll take care of it. I just want the man."

I'm still stuck on the idea of his list. "You just want to sleep with him?"

"Everybody wants a little time on his arm," she says. "He won't stick with anyone, but once Dell has chosen you, doors open. Lots of doors."

This is wild. What doors? Should I ask her? Would she say?

I decide to crush her dreams instead. "He already hired some young college girl."

Her face pales. "He went all Christian Grey?"

I shrug. I realize that now she's out of the elevator, she can't get access to the 40th floor again. I'll go down, tell doorman Harry that someone is trying to get to Dell, and she'll never make it.

Her face rearranges into resolve. "I'm going anyway," she says. "I'm okay with competition."

"Do your best," I say. I move to the elevator and hit the down arrow.

She's placated and pauses by a mirror to check her hair and lipstick.

The doors open. I step in. By the time a rising elevator comes and she realizes she's screwed, I'll have tipped off Harry.

My work here is done.

Except to figure out how she got the interview in the first place.

When I arrive at my spa, parents have begun to arrive. I greet as always, smiling and shaking hands. I stop by the baby room, where Maria is handing over a baby and charming his mother. She's going to work out perfectly.

Dell is wrong about people. Maria totally botched her interview, but I gave her a chance anyway. Sometimes people just need an opportunity to prove themselves.

Finally, there is a lull, so I head to the foyer to

talk to Taylor. She's waving good-bye to one of the families.

"Did Dell find a nanny?" she asks.

"I think so. Helen, the college girl, was great."

"She sounded nice. I sort of remembered her from a few sub days she did. I'm sorry the third one couldn't come tonight."

"It's fine." I lean close over the tall desk. "Who was the second one? The 5:00?"

"I didn't get her name. When I called the other child-care places like you asked, someone at Honey Bear Kid Care said they had the perfect girl."

"Did you give Dell's name?" I ask.

Taylor's eyes get big. "I may have accidentally mentioned that he owned our building."

So it wasn't too hard to figure out.

"I'm sorry, Arianna." She twists a piece of blond hair as if she's worried I will fire her.

"It is what it is," I say.

She's just a girl. She shouldn't have sensitive information. Dell was the one who walked in here himself. Although he really didn't have a lot of choice at that moment.

I picture all the different versions of him I saw throughout the day. Stiff, perfectly dressed Dell from this morning. Frantic, anxious Dell when he realized he was stuck. Angry, protective Dell after Grace got her shots. And fun shopping Dell at the baby store.

But the one that still sticks with me is the last one. Condescending, judgmental Dell. Assuming his accomplishments were greater than mine or anyone else's.

Good riddance.

Chapter 15: Dell

Five o'clock comes and goes and no nanny.

The baby swing has worked amazingly well, and Grace has either slept or stayed mesmerized by the light-up toys ever since Arianna left. Best purchase I made today, despite that woman trying to talk me out of it.

I'm not sure what to do. Night is coming and I'm Googling "How to take care of a baby" to make sure I know all the salient points.

Bernard has contacted a few nanny agencies himself, but no one is sending out anyone for interviews before tomorrow.

"Late night baby care" got us no hits other than hospitals.

I can only sit in the chair near her and wait for her to wake up. Then figure out what's wrong. Then how to fix it. I pass the time reading the Wiki on "How to change a diaper."

It's oddly specific.

The house is quiet. Bernard does whatever Bernard does while not assisting me. Maximillion is probably napping. It's his retirement.

Is this parenting? Hours of boredom punctuated by fifteen minutes of being frantic?

The housekeeper arrives with stacks of clean, perfectly folded baby clothes. I've never been more relieved to see a woman in my life. She's perfect, a grandmotherly sort, stout, friendly faced, dressed comfortably. Her hands are strong. She obviously doesn't fear messes.

I stand up, putting on my most charming smile. We've never spoken more than five words before today, but I need her more than I've ever needed anyone.

"Chenille?" I say.

"Shannon," she corrects patiently.

"You have been amazing," I say. "Just amazing today. What I need, and I really mean *need*, is for someone to stay the night here tonight and help with the baby."

When her forehead crumples, I plead harder. "I thought I would have a nanny. But I don't. And I've never even been around a baby. I have no idea what to do."

She holds out her plump hands. "Mr. Brant, I would love to watch the sweet bairn, but my husband needs me. He can't get around the house. I have to feed him dinner, help him to bed."

"I see," I say. I can't exactly ask a woman with an infirm husband to abandon him. "I just don't know the least thing about feeding or cleaning an infant."

"Oh, it's not so hard," she says. "Just give them the bottle and burp 'em real good. If they dirty the diaper, wipe 'em down with a soft cloth and fasten on a new one." She glances around the room. "You've got everything you need."

Then she frowns. "'Cept a rocking chair. You really could use one of those. Isn't anything that'll settle a crying baby better'n a good rock in a pair of loving arms."

Right. Rocking chair. We should have picked one up at that store. They had that set that Arianna loved so much.

Arianna. Her spa. That baby room had rocking chairs. Maybe I can borrow one for the night. Then buy one tomorrow.

"Thank you, Chenille — sorry, Shannon. I'll try to pick one up."

She pats me on the arm. "You'll do fine. A father's instincts kick in just like a mother's."

Shannon turns and heads out, and I'm alone again.

I head for the door. I can tell myself that it's just the chair I want, but if that were true, I'd send Bernard after it. Or call one of the doormen to fetch it.

I know better. It's Arianna herself that I need. I've screwed up. I'll own it. I'll make it right.

I'm all the way to the elevator when Bernard calls out.

"Sir?"

I punch the button with aggravation. "What is it, Bernard?"

"You've forgotten something again."

Shit. The baby must be awake. Is she going to cry every single time I leave the room?

I hurry back inside the penthouse and down the hall.

She's still in the space pod swing, her face red. She gives out two or three good cries, then pauses to take in a breath before starting another set.

I unbuckle the belt and lift her out. "What is it, Grace?" I do the up-and-down bob thing again, but it doesn't work this time.

I cradle her in my elbow, turned in at the proper angle, and move her fist to her mouth.

This does nothing.

"Bernard!" I call. "Can you bring a bottle?"

My butler is as slow as he's ever been in the history of my employ. After long excruciating minutes of blood-curdling cries, he appears with the formula. I snatch it from him.

The nipple slides into her mouth, and for a moment, there is blessed silence.

I sigh in relief. That's all it was.

But within seconds, she's pushed the bottle out of her mouth, milk dribbling down her chin. It soaks the lacy collar of her dress. I forgot the bib.

I try to put the nipple back in, but she won't let me, shifting her head from side to side. The cries begin again, working their way back up to an ear-splitting howl.

I set the bottle down and put her on my shoulder. Arianna said she was gassy. I'll have to burp her. I remember the moment at the store and snatch up one of the newly laundered cloths. Yes, I have it. I'm on this. I can do it.

The cloth slides over my shoulder and I bring Grace up. I pat her back.

Nothing happens. No sailor burp.

I increase the pressure a bit more.

She continues crying, now at a headache-inducing

decibel so close to my head.

I can't pound the child. Didn't Arianna say we'd need something to help her? Some sort of drops?

I head into the bathroom and sort through drawers, scattering pacifiers, baby wash, baby powder, baby lotion, baby shampoo. Did everything come in baby form? Seriously?

But no drops. I guess we forgot to get them.

Meanwhile, Grace continues her cries, now jagged and punctuated by gagging coughs.

She's sick. I knew it. I'll sue that doctor for incompetence. She has pneumonia. Or whooping cough. Or consumption.

She'll die right here. It will be a scandal. The mother will show up with a lawsuit. They'll arrest me. Maybe that was their plot all along.

I hold Grace up in the air to look at her. As soon as she goes up, she stops crying. I bring her down, then back up, like Arianna did at the store in that magic happy moment.

And she giggles.

I do it again, down and up. Grace laughs again, her arms waving.

Okay, so she's not dying.

I bring her back down in my arms, and within seconds, she's back at it. Her cries echo off the tiled walls. Oh my God. What will make it stop? I run through the list. Hunger. Gas. Wetness.

Is it the diaper?

There's a curved pad on the counter with a soft cover. I'm guessing that's where I'm supposed to set her down.

When I place her there, it's like she's been put on the rack to be drawn and quartered. The wails intensify. I can barely stand it.

I soldier through and pluck at the elastic edges of the little undergarments she has on under her dress. Do I take it all off? Can I get it back on again if I do?

Instead, I stretch the elastic to the limit. Beneath is another layer of plastic. The diaper.

It doesn't stretch as easily, so I hold up her leg to get a look.

I've only moved it a small amount when a strange mustard-yellow substance leaks out.

God. What is that? She really is sick.

That's it. I can't take another moment.

I scoop her in my arms and rush out to the hall.

I don't stop to tell Bernard what I'm doing. I dash straight for the elevator.

I'm not sure where I'm going. The ER, maybe. Is there a children's hospital in Manhattan? The taxi driver will know.

Or maybe not.

The elevator is blessedly close to the top.

We only go down a few floors before we stop. Then again. And again. It seems everyone is headed out for the evening.

It's crowded and everyone stares at me and my wailing, dying child with her mustard-yellow privates.

Jesus, it's my building. I am seriously going to install a goddamn private elevator for the penthouse.

When we finally get to the foyer, I realize I haven't called my driver. No telling where he is. I'll have to just hail a taxi.

But I don't have the car seat. It's still upstairs.

Grace has unexpectedly quieted, her interest caught by all the new people and sights. But that doesn't change what's happened to her bowels. I knew that mother abandoned her for a reason.

I rush out onto the sidewalk, looking right and left. Traffic is bumper to bumper, and none of the taxis have their lights on.

I'm contemplating paying someone to abandon theirs, if I can get them to open their window, when I hear a soft voice.

"Mr. Brant?"

I turn. It's Taylor, from Arianna's child spa. I'm standing in front of the windows.

"Is there a children's hospital in Manhattan?" I ask her.

Her jaw drops. "Is the baby sick?" Then she motions me inside. "Come in here."

"You're still open?" I ask. The interior is dim.

"The teachers just left," she says. "I was about to lock up. What's wrong?"

"The baby. I checked her diaper. It's awful. I think she's sick."

Taylor bites her lip to hide a smile, and that's the first indication I have that maybe I'm wrong about this. She sets her purse on her desk.

"What makes you think something is wrong with her diaper?" she asks.

"It's — it's not normal."

"Is there blood?" she asks. She tries to be subtle, but I see her push a button on the edge of her desk.

"No," I say. "It's just…it's just not normal stuff."

The door to the back opens and Arianna comes out. "Is everything okay?"

She stops short when she sees me.

"Mr. Brant," she says. She glances at Grace, who looks around at the colorful walls.

"He thinks Grace is sick," Taylor says.

"Oh?" She's not the least bit concerned. "What are her symptoms?"

Now I'm starting to realize I'm wrong. But I've got Arianna back now, and there's no way I'm letting her go again.

"He says it's her poop," Taylor says.

Now Arianna takes a turn biting back a smile. "Her poop," she repeats.

"There's no blood in it," Taylor says.

"It's yellow," I say, less frantic now.

"It was that way earlier," Arianna says. "Probably the formula. It's not uncommon."

I fumble with my words. "But poop is," I can't believe I'm saying this, "brown."

Now both the women are biting their lips.

Yeah, I get it. I'm stupid.

"Bring her back," Arianna says. "Let's change her." She glances over at Taylor. "You can go on home."

Taylor picks up her purse. "Bye, Mr. Brant," she calls.

I follow Arianna to the quiet halls of her child spa. She flips on the light of the bright white diaper room.

"What happened to the nanny?" she asks.

"She left," I say.

"She couldn't stay right away?" Arianna pulls a diaper from a closet.

"No, she didn't take the job. Apparently our argument gave her a 'bad vibe.'"

Arianna turns around. "So you don't have anyone?"

"The second one didn't show."

Her eyes flit downward at that. "Set Grace here," she says.

I lay her down on a curved pad like the one upstairs.

Arianna lifts the dress out of the way, and peels down the frilly underpants.

"How is Grace?" she asks in a gentle voice, her face down low. Grace reaches up for her and touches her cheeks. "Have you been a good baby?"

She unsticks one tab on the diaper, then the other. When she peels it down, I take a step back.

"See?"

Arianna holds both of Grace's ankles with one hand and reaches up with the other to tug a wipe from a dispenser on the wall. She makes this look effortless.

"This looks perfectly fine." She cleans up most of it with one wipe, then pulls the diaper away. She sets the wipe on the diaper, cleans Grace more carefully with a second wipe, then brings the clean diaper beneath Grace.

I study this like it's a law exam. Tab. Tab. Peel. Lift. Wipe. Move. Second wipe. New diaper.

Within seconds, the fresh diaper is on and the undergarment back in place. Arianna rolls the old diaper into a perfect ball around the soiled wipes and drops it into a sealed container. "There you go," she says, moving to a sink to wash her hands.

Grace lies on her back, happily kicking her legs. Her face is all normal colored now. She smiles up at the ceiling.

Great. All that fuss for nothing.

Arianna dries her hands and watches me. "Seems like my *kiddie spa* has saved you twice today."

"I'm sorry about what I said," I tell her. "I was an ass. I'm lost here. Completely and utterly lost."

I pick up Grace and prop her against my shoulder. "I'm stuck. I need you. I'm an idiot. You are the genius. Can you please have pity on a pathetic stupid man and help me tonight?"

She tosses the paper towel in a trash can. "You assume I'm free tonight to do that."

"I don't. I'm sure you are canceling epic plans with amazing people. But it's for a good cause." I turn Grace around so she faces out and hold up her hand for a floppy wave.

Arianna makes that scrunchy expression I'm

already getting used to. "All right. But I have to get a few things. I can't wear this one more hour." She gestures at her silk blouse and mauve skirt.

"Are you far from here?" I ask. "We could grab the car seat and go for a drive." I hastily add, "I have a limo."

She laughs. "Limos don't impress me. And actually, I live in the building."

This is news.

"Really? So I'm like your landlord?"

She laughs again and pushes a combination on a keypad to pop open a cabinet. She extracts her purse. "You going to beat on my door demanding rent? Because I have it automatically drafted from my bank account."

"Ah, so I have no excuse to try and arrange some other form of payment?" Only after I've said it do I realize what has just slipped out.

She looks away and closes the cabinet with deliberate slowness. Then, quietly, "Do you do that?"

"No!" I say. "No. Sorry. That just. Came."

She lifts an eyebrow.

"Out! It came out!" God, I'm like a high school freshman today. Gone is the Dell Brant who got up this morning. I'm a sniveling, spit-up-covered, frantic mess.

She relents. "Let me stop by my place and I'll be up. Is there any way I can go straight to your penthouse without having to come all the way to the ground for Harry's approval?"

"Sure," I say, shifting Grace so I can reach for my pockets. I'm not used to jeans. Normally I keep everything tucked inside a suit jacket. It's a much more elegant way to extract necessities.

I pull a card key out. "There's an invisible sensor above the button panel. Wave this and the 40th floor will light up. Only the far-right one goes to the top."

"Wow," she says. "I feel privileged."

I've got my bearings back now. "No, I do," I tell her.

There is no way I'm going to screw this up again. Whatever I thought was important at 7:15 this morning has been completely upended.

She is what matters. She's getting me through this day from hell.

Chapter 16: Arianna

I get off at my floor, still holding the key card Dell gave me. He was right. You wave it and the 40 button lights up like Christmas.

He heads on up with Grace while I rush to my apartment to prepare for a night away.

I can't believe I'm doing this. I was really mad at him.

But he's trying. Really trying. And I had no idea Helen would ditch him.

I don't feel bad about sending Red Dress away, though, even if they did have a spot for him at that other child-care place. It wouldn't have solved his problem tonight.

Although maybe she would have stayed over.

Ick.

It was the right thing for Grace, I tell myself as I kick off my shoes and unzip my skirt.

And so is going there tonight.

I try not to giggle as I picture his panic at seeing the yellow in the diaper. At least she did the spit-up while we were together. No doubt seeing that would have sent him into a tailspin too.

It makes sense that he knows nothing. He's a professed bachelor with a wicked streak when it comes to women.

I ponder what to wear. Something I can sleep in? Or something casual now, then change?

I admit to feeling a little wicked myself as I slide a pair of boy shorts and a stretchy spaghetti-strap tank into an overnight bag. To cover my bases in case that seems too sketchy in the end, I toss in some pajama pants and a normal T-shirt.

As for now? I go with jeans and a pretty off-the-shoulder top. It's cotton, beige with small red flowers. Practical enough. Easy to wash. It seems motherly but still youthful and sweet.

I pause in the bathroom. Motherly. I've never really thought of myself as that. I didn't really intend to be twenty-seven and not dating. It just happened. Running your own business can do that. I have no peers, only employees. No men work for me, not that I would date them anyway. My college friends paired off and married years ago. We've been relegated to Facebook acquaintances.

"You're still young," I say to the mirror. And it's true. I have plenty of time.

Just not plenty of fish in my current sea. The couple of times I tried using an app to find men, it was horrible. I can't even think about it without wanting to flush my phone down the toilet.

"You'll prioritize this eventually," I say, then frown at my hair. The wild curls are out of control after the long day. I pin as many of them back as I can tame and twist the length into a knot. Curls still spill around my face, but it goes well with the shirt, like I'm about to go on a picnic.

Good enough. It's not like I'm trying to get Dell interested. His type is clear. Leggy, big-boobed, and tottering on crazy shoes. Just to prove I'm not even considering it, I slip on a pair of ballet flats. So there.

I drop a toothbrush and my face cream in the bag. Then, just because morning *is* going to come, some lip gloss and mascara.

And because I don't want to look like I'm taking a walk of shame, a different shirt for tomorrow.

Now I'm ready.

If anyone can be ready for this.

In the elevator, I'm grateful for the card key. I'd really rather not have to speak to Harry at the desk and tip him off that I'm going up after insisting he not let Red Dress access the penthouse.

It would really seem like I was just trying to take out the competition.

I wasn't. Was I?

When I arrive at the penthouse, Bernard is waiting to let me inside. "Good to see you again," he says, but it's just a formality, given in monotone. He probably blames me for losing Helen.

I move past him down the hall to the baby's room. Dell is there. Grace is back in the space pod swing, eyes on the lighted toys up top.

"She probably needs more visual stimulation," I say, dropping my bag on the floor. "High-contrast toys, things that light up and make noise."

"We'll get more," Dell says. He's still watching her. "It's interesting, seeing what catches her attention. I turned on the ceiling fan in the living room, and she couldn't take her eyes off it."

"Makes sense," I say, kneeling beside them. "When did she last eat?"

"Bernard is making a bottle," he says. "I figure when she smells our dinner, it might make her hungry too."

"There is no telling when she last had a bath," I say, tugging at the frilly sock. "You up for tackling that now or after dinner?"

"Let's eat first," he says. "I think we skipped lunch."

My stomach suddenly growls and we both laugh. "I think we did!"

"Totally my fault," Dell says. "We were at the doctor, and then the store."

"I think it happens a lot to new parents," I say, then catch myself. We're not new parents. We're watching an abandoned baby until we figure out where she belongs.

I stop the swing and slide Grace out of the seat. "Let's see where you are developmentally, baby girl."

The rug is soft and clean, so I lay her on her tummy, arms and legs sprawled.

She immediately holds up her head for a second, then it thunks on the rug.

"What does that mean?" Dell asks.

"Just wait."

She lifts it again, bobbing up and down for a few seconds before thunking again. When she starts to fuss, I pick her up.

"Definitely closer to three than four months unless she's delayed," I say.

"Delayed?"

"Not hitting her developmental milestones on time. It could help us figure out how well she was cared for before coming here. She might have just been lying in a crib all day for all we know."

Dell's face is etched with worry. "When we find out the mother, she is going to hear from me."

I hold Grace upright and lower her until her feet touch the floor. She immediately pushes back, standing and squatting. She loves this, her laugh filling the quiet of the room.

"Is that good?" Dell asks.

"Really good," I say. "It's possible she was held a lot, but not given tummy time." I set her in my lap, facing out. "Or maybe she has trouble on her belly because she has a really big head. Like her father."

"Hilarious," Dell deadpans, but he is smiling. "I haven't eliminated the possibility that someone who works in the building left her. A Moses baby to be picked up by somebody rich."

I lift Grace and let her test her legs again. More giggles.

"That carriage is at least five hundred dollars," I say. "That fancy blanket, another hundred. I can't imagine someone who would leave a baby also being able to buy those."

"Good point," Dell says. He sits casually, his legs kicked out in front of him. His hair is nothing like it was this morning, curled up and wild instead of perfectly in place. I like it.

"Do you have pictures of any of these women to compare to her?" I doubt we'll find anything of use in looking at them, but my curiosity is high.

"I don't take photos," he says. "I suppose we could find press images."

It pleases me that he doesn't have private shots. "We'll have the DNA test," I say.

"It won't tell us anything about the mother," Dell says. "There is no real registry for that."

"How do you aim to find her?" I say.

"As soon as we know she's mine, I'll hire a private investigation firm. They'll figure it out. It shouldn't be too hard to determine which one of the twenty-five was pregnant or in hiding."

"Actually, can't we rule some out with press photos?" I ask. "If you see a photo from, say, five months ago and she's not hugely pregnant, then she's out."

"I'll put someone on it," he says.

I look down at Grace. She has no idea what is happening on her behalf. Only that she's in a new world, full of different people, smells, and sounds. At least we knew what formula to feed her. Which diapers to buy. They are small comforts.

"You think this will scar her?" Dell asks. "Is she

going to need a therapist all her life?"

"That depends on how things go from here," I say. "I see a lot of kids who get moved from home to home as divorces are filed and mothers remarry. Children are pretty resilient."

Dell frowns. "I won't have her abused or neglected, even if she isn't mine."

My heart squeezes. "That's good of you. If she goes into foster care, though, you won't have any say."

His frown deepens. "Maybe we should manage the adoption privately, with our own lawyers."

I'm amused again at his "we" and "our." As if I'm a part of this.

I pick up Grace and turn her onto my shoulder. "Got any trademark burps in there, baby?" I ask. I pat her back.

"Let me see her," Dell says, his strong arms out.

Interesting. Voluntarily taking her. I pass her to him.

He shifts her to his shoulder. "So I was doing this earlier, and I wasn't sure how hard to go." He pats her lightly on the back. "Is this enough?"

"To start," I say. "Some babies actually like to be burped very firmly. It can feel like you're pounding them. But if you're trying to work out some gas, it's important."

I take Grace back from him and stretch out my legs. I lay her little body across my thighs, facedown.

"Let's see if there's anything in there," I say. I flatten my hand and bring it down lightly, then increase in intensity.

"Whoa," Dell says. "That's a lot."

But Grace's eyes close, as if she's blissed out. Then a big sailor belch comes out.

"Huh," Dell says. "It works."

"Like I said, she's a gassy baby."

"We forgot those drops you talked about," he says. "I searched all over for them earlier."

"Shoot," I say. "We did. Well, one of us can make a run out if we decide she needs them." I rub her back. She's falling asleep. "But she's burping pretty well. I think we can do it."

We watch her, one hand curled up to her mouth, the other arm dangling off the side of my leg. We're doing it again, having these conversations like we're a couple. It's nice. Right now, Dell is nice too.

I glance up at him and catch him staring at me. A zip goes through my body and I find it hard to swallow.

He takes me in, my pinned-up hair, the collarbones and shoulders that are bared above the shirt. He lingers on my breasts.

He doesn't care that I know what he's doing. And I'm seeing why women swoon for him. Even with a baby lying across my lap and a pompous butler down the hall, he's making me feel like we're the only two people in the world.

Chapter 17: Dell

I've seen a lot of sights in my life. Debutantes. Society women. Models.

But right now Arianna tops them all.

That blouse cuts straight across her chest, revealing creamy shoulders and an elegant collarbone.

Her hair falls in little circlets around her face, the rest pinned up, leaving so much skin that it takes a fair amount of willpower not to lean over and press my lips against her neck.

The exposed shoulders leave me wondering about a bra. Did she skip it? Is there something strapless under there? The possibilities are killing me. If her breasts hold that perfect shape despite their blessedly incredible size, it's going to be a Christmas miracle. In July.

When I drag my gaze back up to her eyes, I see she's noticed me watching her. I'm not ashamed of this. We hold each other's gaze a beat longer than just acquaintances, and I see her catching a little breath. Good. I want her to feel it too. Maybe we can make these five days until Monday a little more interesting.

I'm glad we didn't hire a nanny. She's here. She's perfect.

I look at her some more, since it seems it's arousing her. Her tender ears, back to those shoulders. I take in those luscious breasts another moment. This time I see a clear delineation of a nipple.

Shit, no bra. My body stirs now, my cock pressing into my jeans, thickening, waking up to her presence.

Admiring her body has become a drug. It's hit my bloodstream, and now every heartbeat is her. The bottom of the blouse is loose over the tops of her jeans. I can picture my hand there, sliding beneath the hem and rising to cup those glorious tits.

I come back to them yet again. I'm a breast man. I know it. And I don't play favorites. Large, small, soft, firm. I don't even mind implants. I take them any way they come.

But I can tell Arianna isn't the sort of woman to augment. She isn't fussy about those things. She'll be all natural. And I absolutely will find a way to convince her she wants to reveal her body to me.

The thrill is in convincing her that she wants

what I want.

Because that's the way I play it. Yes, I'll push her against the wall. Tie her wrists. Strap her down. But the first time, the intense new discovery, will be all about her coming to me. Willingly. Insistent.

Then I'll learn every inch of her. Take her beyond anywhere she's ever gone.

My eyes slip down to her belly, but the sleeping child reminds me this isn't a normal conquest. Grace covers key areas of Arianna's body. Hips, thighs. That incredible hot center.

And she won't sleep through the night.

Shit. I break my line of thought and refocus. Arianna hasn't spoken a word, just waited, watching me.

"You done gawking?" she asks.

I'm a little taken aback. "It's a lot of beauty to take in," I say.

I think she's about to make another smart remark, but she stops herself and takes a deliberate pause before saying, "Well, thank you, but I'm just here to help with the baby."

She bites her lip, which she only seems to do when she's guilty of something. I wonder what crime I've missed.

But Bernard appears at the doorway.

"Dinner, sir."

I jump to my feet. "Great. Should we put her in her bed?" A little wine with dinner might loosen Arianna up a bit more.

She shifts, trying to lift Grace carefully.

But it's no good. As soon as she's moved, Grace stirs, looking around with sleepy eyes.

And then, she's wailing.

"Poor bub," Arianna says, shifting to her knees and pulling Grace to her shoulder. "You're okay. You're just fine."

She repeats these words over and over as she stands, then rocks back and forth in place. I don't want to notice the luscious sway of her breasts, but they are right in front of me.

I can see all of her now. Her belly is flat, hips curved. There's a nice round ass accentuated by the pockets on her jeans. She's not very tall, but nothing is dainty about her. She's exactly right.

Grace settles again.

"You going to try for the bed now?" I ask.

At my words, Grace lifts her head to look at me with an expression so angry and annoyed that I have to laugh. Then she flops down again.

"I don't think she's really sleepy enough," Arianna says. "It will probably take a bottle to settle her in for the night, or whatever part of it she'll sleep."

"Bottle it is, then," I say. Bernard leads us back down the hall, through the kitchen to the formal dining room. Only when I see the crystal and china at two places do I realize the breakfast nook would probably have been more appropriate.

Arianna's frown at the arrangement seals its fate.

"Bernard, please move us to the smaller table," I say. I won't make him scrape the amazing-looking cut of veal and garlic roasted potatoes off the plates, but at least we can sit someplace casual.

When we're back at the breakfast nook, Arianna sinks onto one of the cushioned spinning chairs that surround the round stone table. I can tell she's relieved to be someplace comfortable while holding Grace in the crook of one elbow.

The chairs are very mobile, and soon she's turning hers from side to side, keeping Grace in her almost-sleep mode.

Bernard places the plates in front of us and there's a clear problem. Arianna can't cut her veal with only one hand free. She tries separating a bite with the edge of her fork, but it doesn't quite work.

"Here, let me take her. You eat," I say. "You had the rumbling stomach."

She looks at me suspiciously, as if she wasn't expecting chivalry. But she passes Grace to me. I hold her as Arianna did and rotate back and forth on the chair. "We should have bought that rocking chair," I say.

"You didn't want anything permanent," she says, swiftly cutting the meat.

I don't reply to that. It's true. Still true. I can't send furniture with social services.

Arianna takes a bite, then makes a swooning face as she chews. "So good," she says. "We had a cook like this when I was around ten." She spins in her chair to face Bernard. "This is amazing."

He nods from his place between the kitchen and the breakfast nook.

Behind the glass door to the atrium, I spot Maximillion sitting and watching us.

"Bernard, can you go and fix up Max's dinner? He's not used to watching us dine in here. I don't want to torture the poor boy."

Arianna turns to where the dog waits patiently for our attention. "He's a beautiful dog. Did he race?"

This is a topic I can warm up to quickly. "Yes. He started as most greyhounds before the age of two. He soon proved himself a worthy racer and commanded the leaderboards at four facilities. His home track was Birmingham."

Arianna takes a long pull from her glass of red wine. She closes her eyes, as if overcome by all the flavors. It is true that Bernard is a master of food and wine pairings.

I pick up my glass to take a sip myself. My dinner will get cold, but I don't mind.

"You're missing out," she says. "I'll cut this for you."

She leans over and slices several generous bites. "Is it always this good? I might move in."

I smile, feeling unsettled at the familiar gesture of her cutting my food. "Bernard is very consistent, although I still have him working on a lasagna as good as my mother used to make."

Arianna grins at that. "He'll never achieve it," she says. "Or so I hear. My mother never cooked a meal in her life."

"Power parents?" I ask.

"The worst," she says. "I think I only saw them both together once the entire time I was in high school." She spears another bite of veal, and I am fairly certain she's actually stabbing the memory.

"That must have been difficult," I say. I had a different sort of upbringing, but I'm not about to enlighten her on that.

She doesn't seem to want to discuss parental shortcomings either, so she changes the subject. "So how long did your dog race?"

"The full five years that is expected of a greyhound. He was bred six times, and then I was allowed to bring him home."

Arianna perks up at this fact. "Is that a lot of breeding?"

I cannot suppress my grin. "He got more than his share."

"Did you always want to adopt a greyhound?"

"It was sort of a tradition at my house," I say, then stop. I do not talk about my past or my family's position at the Birmingham Racetrack. I spent hundreds of thousands of dollars getting it purged.

One particular image was nigh impossible to get erased. Me, in mud-covered overalls, holding a shovel, with the grand champion racer whose kennel space I managed. I had this huge grin and naive air that made the image hit the papers and later persist on the web.

She continues to eat, and I take a few bites as well. I am used to the quality of Bernard's cooking, but after Arianna's delight, I notice it for the first time in a while. He really is quite gifted.

She pushes the plate away and takes a long drink of wine. "That was amazing. I've gotten in the terrible habit of curry takeout and breakfast cereal."

This amuses me. "Favorite cereal?"

"Cap'n Crunch, hands down," she says, then shoots me a warning look. "Don't be dissing the Captain. I'll ditch you with a baby."

I hold up my free hand. "I wouldn't dream of it, I swear. I was always partial to the 'all berries' version."

She scoffs at this. "Too much of a good thing. And what about that worthless 'no berries' version? What is the point?"

"I believe that was the original version," I say.

"What? No way. They took them out."

"You can look it up."

She narrows her eyes. "Are you a connoisseur of Cap'n Crunch?"

Bernard arrives at the breakfast table with four boxes. "Evidence," he says dryly.

Arianna bursts out laughing as she examines them.

"My butler betrays me," I say.

"Look at these! The plain kind," she shoots me a look. "Then, berries, the good stuff. And 'Oops' with all berries." Another shake of her head. "And peanut butter?" She picks up the peanut butter box and holds it out accusingly. "This is an abomination."

"No, it's delicious," I tell her.

She sets it back down. "Well, Mr. Brant, it seems we at least have the berry version in common. I'll overlook the others for the sake of friendship."

"I shall leave the berries to you," I say. "I only eat them on occasion."

She ducks her head. "I only eat them…every day."

This makes me laugh. "I have been known to stash a bag in my desk drawer at the office."

Her head pops up. "Really? Because I keep a box at the child spa."

Our mutual smiles both warm my chest and unsettle me a little. What is this? Bonding over sugar cereal?

I straighten my expression and glance down at Grace. "Should we wake her to feed her?" I ask.

"You're forgetting rule number one," Arianna says.

Right. "Never wake a sleeping baby," I say.

"Exactly. But I'd have it ready. She's going to be so hungry when she wakes. Here, give her to me so you can finish in peace."

I pass the baby over to her. Grace stirs a little, but once settled on Arianna's chest, she is out again.

I think about this interplay as I attend to the meal, watching Arianna rock the baby in the springy chair. How easy it feels. How natural.

It should come hard to me. The messiness. The wild schedule. The grand consumption of fourteen hours with nothing to show for them. And this woman, just being here. Helping me and letting me help her.

But somehow, it's working.

Chapter 18: Arianna

She's asleep.

The last bottle did the trick.

After dinner we adjourned to the baby room. Dell moved to one of the breakfast nook chairs since it swiveled and rocked. A bottle, a warm sleeper, dim lighting, and the chair were the winning combination.

She's in her carriage, breathing heavily. Dell and I stand close together, watching her. Neither of us want to move, in case the spell is broken and she cries again.

I feel the heat of him next to me. It's pretty crazy to think I'll be sleeping here tonight.

In Dell Brant's penthouse.

If only my Brown sorority girls could see me now. They would never believe "frizzhead" Arianna would even step foot in a place like this.

They were all social climbers, of course. And I got some begrudging respect for my family name. But

I didn't fit in. I couldn't master the ability to find everything boring. To push aside all emotions other than disdain.

I hung out with scholarship girls, which got me panned by the old-money crew. I'd probably have been kicked out of the sorority if I hadn't been a legacy plus my father funded a renovation of the house.

And I did date then. I knew I was expected to find the right sort of boy during those four years and get engaged. Have a brilliant career until the maximum age of thirty-two, when I would be expected to have popped my first progeny.

I could have two, three if there was an "oops," but any more was "unnecessary." I needed room to grow in case I got dumped for a trophy wife in my early forties and had to squeeze out another kid with another man to seal a union.

Okay, so I got a little jaded along the way.

I dated. There were boyfriends. But they weren't right, and I knew it. When I pushed them away one too many times without consummating the relationship, they moved on.

So yes, I have hang-ups. One of them being having sex for love, not because it's an expectation. The other is having kids you adore, not just to carry on some family plan you've forced on them.

Maybe if I'd had brothers and sisters, things would have been different. A shared misery might have been pain halved, like they say. But it was always just me. Mom tried, but I came after they'd given up, and it never happened again.

For all I know, having a baby will be just as hard for me.

So standing next to this man in the most prime real estate in Manhattan is a mixed bag.

A neener neener on all those Brown girls.

A sneak peek into a life I may never have with a husband and a new baby.

And a scary lion's den of salacious sex.

I didn't miss how he was looking at me earlier. Like my boobs were his first meal after a famine.

And he's undoubtedly the sort who expects sex. He assumes I will fall at his feet like Red Dress, or that poor woman with the broken shoe on the sidewalk. Or the twenty-five possible mothers of Grace.

God. Twenty-five. I hope he was making a big margin of error on the birth, like six months' worth of women. But I have a feeling he wasn't.

Still, he's standing right there, and the seconds are ticking.

"You think it's safe to leave?" he whispers.

"You go first," I say.

He turns in slow motion, like he's moving through water.

It's so ridiculous, I can't help it, I laugh.

Grace shifts on her bed.

We both hit the floor like we're soldiers who just heard the word "Incoming!"

I'm down on my belly, breathing hard. Dell is opposite me, his face just an inch from mine. If I shifted forward, I could kiss him.

Not that I would. That's just how close he is.

It's really close.

"You think she saw us?" he whispers.

"I don't know."

Amusement dances in his eyes. It's crazy fun, almost silly, that we both landed on the floor at the whim of an infant.

"This is not what I pictured when I put on my tie this morning," he says.

I try to stifle this laugh, but that just converts it into a very unladylike snort.

This makes him cover his mouth to control his amusement. "Is that your laugh?" he asks. "Because I love it."

Now he's charming Dell again, like at the baby

store. He looks at me like I'm an ice cream cone he's more than delighted to lick.

Lying there in his athletic shirt with a faint outline of old spit-up on the shoulder, he seems like any husband, any dad. For just a minute, I think — *I could fall in love with this man.*

"Shall we risk it?" he asks.

I have to shake my thoughts free. It seems as if he knew what I was thinking.

But no, it's just about the baby.

"You want to stand up?" I whisper. "No way!"

"Army crawl it is, then." He starts moving along the floor on his elbows.

This man. So crazy.

He snakes his way toward the door. I follow, my elbows digging into the soft rug. This isn't so bad.

Until I bump the space pod swing.

It turns on in a fanfare of blinking lights and music, like a carnival ride starting up.

"Oh no!" I say, lunging for it, trying to find the off-switch.

"Over there, over there!" Dell hisses, rolling toward it and slapping his hand on the side of the base.

Finally, it's off.

We both turn, breathing hard, to look at the baby

carriage.

Then let out long slow breaths.

She didn't wake.

We crawl to the door.

"Come on," Dell says. "Let's have a nightcap. We could use it."

We arrive in the hall and make our escape.

Bernard is already positioned by the oak bar built into the wall between the living room and the kitchen. "What will it be, sir, madam?" he asks.

This guy is so spooky to know what we talked about. Or else maybe this is part of Dell's routine.

"I'll man the bar," Dell says. "You stay close to the baby's room so you can let us know if she wakes."

Bernard's expression remains neutral, but his nose twitches. "Very well, sir."

"Don't worry," Dell says, waving him off. "I won't get so drunk I can't tend to the child."

"I wasn't concerned for your state," he says, making a meaningful glance at me.

"I'm not one to overindulge," I tell him. "You won't get stuck changing her sticky yellow diapers."

His eyes widen at this unsavory detail, and he turns on his heel.

Dell laughs as he uncorks a decanter. "Oh, you have Bernard on his head!" He pours an inch of amber liquid into a crystal glass. "Are you a brandy drinker?" he asks.

"So upper class," I say, stepping forward. I switch to a false British accent. "Dear Father, put brandy on my teething ring." I take the glass from him.

"Something to keep in mind for Grace," he says with a wink and pours a second glass.

It's so strange to be acting silly with Dell Brant. I keep expecting the spell to break, and the stiff, overbearing version to reappear. He's a Jekyll and Hyde. Or maybe a prince and frog.

"I guess we should have gotten a baby monitor," I say.

Dell takes a sip of his drink. "What does that do?"

"Just transmits noises from the nursery to a handset in another room. So you can hear if she cries."

Dell waves his hand. "Bernard can manage."

"Bernard will have to sleep," I say.

He frowns, as if he hasn't considered that his butler is a normal person who does human things.

"I'm going to let Maximillion out for a little while, if you don't mind," he says.

"Okay."

He carries his drink out to the breakfast nook,

then on to the door to the atrium. I watch from the doorway.

At first Maximillion bounds toward the glass, but when Dell holds up a finger, the dog stops and sits.

Dell nods and tugs on the door handle.

The greyhound walks regally beside Dell as the two of them come back to the sofa. "Sit," Dell says.

The dog obeys, planting himself at the end of the sofa.

"Now we can also take a breather," he says. "It's been quite the hellish day."

He relaxes into the cushions near the dog, reaching out to scratch the dog between his tall pointy ears.

I choose a chair at the other end of the sofa, angled toward them. Dell is acting like his old self again, shoulders square, stiff and formal. I don't see why the dog would bring this out in him.

"Can I call him to me?" I ask. I'm curious about this large lean greyhound. I've never seen one up close. Of course, I've never been to a greyhound race. Our family stuck strictly to quarter horses.

"Sure," Dell says. "He doesn't get to meet many strangers."

I wonder what that means. That no one comes here, or that they don't get around to petting the dog.

I remember what the housekeeper said. He almost never has guests. Maybe he has his trysts elsewhere.

"Come, Maximillion," I say.

The dog stands and trots over, then sits again, eyes on mine.

I reach out a fist for him to sniff, then I pet his head. He ducks a little at first, then allows it.

"Was he mistreated at some point?" I ask. "He's a little skittish."

"Racing is a hard life," Dell says. "Probably someone along the way did not handle him with proper care. He trusts me, but he can still do that with strangers."

Poor puppy. I run my hand under his jaw and cup his long neck. He is so lean and elegant. Like his master. "Is he your first greyhound?"

Dell takes another drink, watching me. I'm not sure why he doesn't answer. Maybe something happened to one of them, and it's a sore point for him.

"No," he finally says. "I've had many."

"Takes a big place," I say. "He's a big dog."

"Actually, racing greyhounds are accustomed to life in crates. So they can live pretty much anywhere."

"Huh." I lean into Maximillion and press my forehead to his. "I guess you're lucky to have an entire room to yourself."

Dell swirls his glass. "So you say they are not good with children. Why is that?"

"I understand most rescues won't give a greyhound to a family with small kids."

"I can't imagine Maximillion hurting anybody," he says defensively.

"He is well trained." I run my hand along his back "Maybe little kids running trigger that urge to chase. Don't they have to wear muzzles during races?"

"Yes, they'll attack each other otherwise." Dell looks thoughtful. "I suppose small children do run a lot, and not all greyhounds are well behaved. I guess as a baby she's fine, though. Right?"

I nod.

After a moment, Maximillion tires of my attention and lies down.

"Have you given a thought to your future if she's yours?" I ask.

He shakes his head. "I don't see that happening. I've asked the building security to review the footage of the cameras."

"You have some here?" My eyes dart to the corners of the room.

"No, and not in my hall either. I don't like giving anyone the opportunity to spy," he says. "But there are some in the lobby and outside the other stairwells. They're just searching for anyone with the carriage. It's such an obvious thing."

True. It should be easy to spot in footage. "How long will that take?"

"I should have had a report already." He tugs out his phone. "We've just been so busy."

He taps a few things. "They found it. Now we'll see. I'll project the footage."

The wooden cap to the arm of the sofa flips down and reveals a compartment. He pulls out a remote. After a moment, the doors to an ornate carved armoire open with an electronic hum. A large television is inside.

When the monitor blinks on, he switches it to an auxiliary mode. For a second, I see the home screen of his phone.

"You play Panda Pop?" I ask, amused.

"You saw that?"

"I did."

"I take it we have two terrible vices in common, then," he says. "Sugar cereal and time-wasting app games."

"I only play it on the subway," I say. "It doesn't require a connection."

"I haven't ridden the subway in a long time," he

says. "Since I acquired a helicopter."

"When do you have time to play?" I ask.

"When my mother calls," he says. "It keeps me from going mad."

My mouth falls open. "You are terrible!"

"I never said otherwise."

The lobby of the building fills the screen with blocky digital footage.

"You're not going to be able to recognize anyone with that," I say.

"Too bad there isn't an 'enhance' mode like on movies," Dell retorts.

The video moves forward in jerky frames.

"There it is!" I say, pointing at the white carriage.

"Looks like a woman pushing it," he says.

We both stand up to walk closer to the screen.

"She's rather stout," I say. "Not your usual type." The woman wears a common khaki trench coat, a scarf, and large sunglasses. She does not look right nor left, but pushes the carriage straight through the foyer.

"I don't have a type," Dell says. "I see no reason to limit myself to anorexic girls."

"Then I stand corrected."

And chagrined. Maybe it was the websites that preferred to show him with the bombshells. I make a mental note to do another search later.

Dell moves the footage frame by frame, peering at the image.

"Do you recognize her?" I ask.

"No," he says. "If she's the mother, I don't think I've bedded her."

He steps back and crosses his arms, the remote tucked inside his hand. "Someone unrelated to me brought the baby."

"But how did she get to this floor?"

"I don't know. This is all they have so far."

"Well," I say, "it does tell us a few things. She didn't use a service elevator or go in a back way like a building worker would."

"Who would do this?" Dell asks. "I thought for sure it would be an employee."

"Does anyone else have one of these?" I remember the elevator card and tug it from my back pocket. I set it on the coffee table.

"Sure. Bernard. Myself. There are a couple extras."

"What about the housekeeper? That shopping lady? The doorman?"

"No," Dell says. "They all have to be keyed in from the bottom floor."

"Did the doorman key this woman in?"

"She didn't even look at him," Dell says. "She went in as if she lived here."

"Does Harry stop people if he doesn't know them?" I ask. "Or does he only speak when someone asks him a question?" I don't know, because he's always known me. I introduced myself when I leased the apartment.

"He's very observant. I think he would address someone who looked out of place."

"But she doesn't," I say. "Her coat is expensive. And her shoes. The scarf and sunglasses make her look sort of famous, kind of Hollywood."

The woman disappears into the elevator. Unfortunately, we can't see what number she pushes, or if the elevator goes directly to the 40th floor. It's not in the range of the shot.

"They've checked all the other floors for this time frame," he says. "But she doesn't come out."

"So she went straight up," I say. "Sounds like she knew where to go. Do all your …" I'm not sure what to call them. "Did all the twenty-five possibilities come up here?"

"None of them," Dell says, turning off the screen and dropping the remote on the table. "I don't bring women up here, ever."

"What about your key cards?" I say, trying to

cover my shock at what he just said. "Are any of them missing?"

"They are in a safe," he says, frowning. He picks up his glass from the coffee table and downs the rest of his drink. "I guess we should go see if any are gone."

He heads out of the living room, and I guess I'm supposed to follow him.

Chapter 19: Dell

Damn distractions. I should have looked at the footage hours ago. But no, I was playing house with Arianna instead of attending to business. Speaking of which, I guess I don't get to go to work tomorrow either. No nanny, no work.

Bloody hell.

I storm down the hall to my master bedroom. Arianna follows. Probably she shouldn't know the location of the safe, but maybe it doesn't matter. She couldn't do anything worse to me than this other woman. Walked right in my building and came straight up to my penthouse.

The safe is a cliché, inside the wall behind a painting. I squeeze the latch beneath the frame and swing the picture aside. Arianna stays discreetly near the doorway as I key in the code. The latch pops and I open it.

There isn't that much here. I keep important

things in a vault at another location. My birth certificate and name change documents. A few jewels, all gifts I never got around to giving. And the codes to the security panel of this penthouse as well as spare elevator key cards.

All are accounted for. I shut the safe. "Nothing missing," I tell her.

"She could know someone who works here," she says. "Someone who maybe waters the plants or cleans the hall outside your penthouse."

"Those are my people," I say.

She stands in the doorway, looking more delectable than she knows in her little flat shoes, fitted jeans, and off-the-shoulder top. More hair has escaped, making the look all the sexier. But her expression shows concern. Her lips are all twisty again.

"It seems like you don't know your staff very well," she says. "So it might be pretty easy for someone to help a friend in trouble sneak a baby up."

I sit on the edge of the bed. I'm tired of thinking about this. And I'm concerned about tomorrow. And every time I look at those bare shoulders, I want to release this frustration between this woman's legs.

"Did you finish your drink?" I ask her.

She steps back. "What?"

"The brandy," I say, my tone harder than I intend.

"You're asking about my alcohol consumption while the fate of that baby is still in the air?" Her voice is all high pitched and angry, like after I called her business a kiddie spa.

"You're touchy," I say. "I'm just checking on your comfort." I pat the bed. "Come here."

Normally I don't bring women to my penthouse. It's too easy for them to try and drop by after their stint is done.

But if they're already here, it's fair game. Like the real estate agent. And the decorator.

I'm determined to turn this situation around with Arianna. She'll be here all night. The baby is sleeping. Maybe a solid orgasm, or two or three, will soften her up enough that she'll stay with the child tomorrow.

But Arianna hasn't moved from the doorway. "I'm not your dog," she says. "Don't pat the damn bed." She steps into the hall. "I'm going to set up near the baby. The reason I'm here. Saving your stupid ass." Then she's gone.

Well, damn. She doesn't operate like most of the women I encounter. They seem intrigued by the idea of a short-term tryst. But I can't even get that far with this one.

There has to be some way to make her crack, see the benefit of making the best of our situation. I'm not a hedonist. I'm all about her pleasure as well as mine.

The unmistakable cry of the baby is faint and distant. I wonder if Arianna woke her on purpose to avoid me.

I stare at the floor, picturing the footage. The trench coat. The scarf. It's like Arianna said. Purposefully Hollywood. Would she know I have this video? That I would see her? If the woman doesn't want the baby, why should I find her?

But she practically dared me to do the DNA, knowing I could. Did she think I would take the baby out of altruism if it wasn't mine? Or did she think the dare was strong enough that I wouldn't bother?

The doctor mentioned some one-day clinic. Maybe it is time to do that. Even if I don't act until I get the official results for court, at least I would know.

Down the hall, the baby's cry persists.

I sit up, wondering if Arianna is struggling. I move out to the hall. The cries are louder here. Despite my reluctance to see her after her attitude, my feet just go.

Inside the baby's room, Arianna is rocking Grace in the dining chair. She has her pulled up close against her chest, both arms holding her in. She watches the baby intently, and only when I'm there a second or two do I catch that she is ever so softly singing to her.

This gets to me, my throat thick. If I thought she was beautiful before, that's nothing compared to how she looks now, maternal and gentle in the soft glow of a table lamp. I can't tell if Grace is asleep again or not. But Arianna seems perfectly happy to rock her regardless.

My shoulder braces up against the door frame as I relax, arms across my chest. I'm content to watch. After a moment, I sense her movements slowing. Then she ever so carefully stands, turning back to the baby bed.

She successfully lays her down without a fresh bout of crying. When she moves toward the door, she finally notices me.

Her soft expression moves to a frown. "Good night," she mouths. Then she scoops up her bag and crosses to the connecting bathroom, leaving the door open.

A light pops on in the room on the other side.

I know she's keeping the door open so she can hear if the baby wakes. But it also enables me to follow her.

She spots me as she sets the bag on the bed. "Mr.

Brant, give me a break. It's late and she'll probably be up every few hours. I will need to sleep while I can."

"I just wanted to make sure she was all right. I should know what sets her off."

"Why?" she fires at me at a rough whisper. "It's not like you'll be handling it."

She's right. I can see I should just punt tonight. Let her sleep. "Thank you for being here," I say. "It's deeply appreciated."

This mollifies her and she turns back to her bag. She pulls out a tiny pair of sleeping shorts and a spaghetti-strap top as thin as thread. My cock stirs so fast I get a head rush. I must see her in this. I simply must.

I let her be, but I'm not giving up yet. She's under my skin now, and I'm determined to get a lot more intimate knowledge before she's gone.

Chapter 20: Arianna

Well, that got him.

I hold the tiny shorts and shirt in my hand. I totally noticed his reaction when I unpacked.

Expectations.

Men are a mess. He begs me to help him. Asks me to do this impossible thing. Then he somehow feels it is a good idea for us to sleep together. I've known him all of what — fifteen hours?

But it was an action-packed day, that's for sure. I'm pretty sure I haven't spent that much time alone with a man, well, ever.

I shove the outfit back in the bag and take out the baggy cotton pants and T-shirt. The safe choice. I kick off my shoes to change.

But then I think of the time with Dell another way. If you divided those fifteen hours into five three-hour dates over two or three weeks, maybe in some warped relationship time, it would make sense that we'd be sleeping together.

But nope. Being stuck all night in Mr. Hottie Cock's penthouse isn't going to change what I want in a sex partner. Besides, Grace is fussy. She has tummy issues, and we have no gas drops. She's also bound to be feeling unease that she's someplace new and unfamiliar.

Surely she misses her mother.

There's a popular theory that even a newborn has a memory. The watery sounds of her mother's voice from inside the womb, the cadence of her speech, the pattern of her heart. The way her footfalls pace themselves. The creak of the door, then three steps down, and a certain space of time before she sits in her car or at a bus stop.

These are all the memories a fetus might have, and when every familiar sound and movement is wiped out, they know it.

Grace has even more memory than that. The smell of a house. The things they cooked. Real voices. Real sights. Real sounds.

All obliterated when she was left at Dell's door.

Thinking of this makes me want to rock her again. To never let her go. But instead I head into the bathroom, careful to leave the light out since the door to the nursery is open, and quietly take off my makeup and brush my teeth.

The penthouse is quiet. It's amazing how silent even a New York apartment can be when you're at the tippy top of the building. No one's heavy footsteps above. No barking dog or loud video games on the other side of the wall.

Too high even for the sounds of the city. Traffic. People. Sirens.

So quiet.

I tiptoe into Grace's room, careful to avoid bumping Dell's space pod swing. I admit to being wrong about it. It is definitely useful.

I peer into the carriage bed. It takes a moment before my eyes focus in on her in the low light.

She's asleep on her back, arms thrown wide. She looks absolutely peaceful. Like she belongs here. I don't know if I even hope for that. Seeing the blocky image of the woman who left her fills me with rage. Who could do that?

I have no doubt Dell's voracious appetite for women means he has no idea what any of them are capable of. He probably barely remembers their names.

But the baby is fine. I should sleep. My footsteps are silent as I head back through the bathroom. This is a terrific setup for a baby and nanny.

My room is lovely in turquoise and gold. It's full of handsome details, including an oak inset in the wall with rounded shelves, currently filled with pretty jade statuettes.

The large window has a seat with gold cushions and a set of shelves built in either side, all stocked with books.

I sit there, perusing the reading options, hoping to get a glimpse of Dell's taste.

They are complete sets of famous series. *Lord of the Rings.* Hardy Boys. All the Stephanie Plum mysteries. Everything by J. K. Rowling. Even *Twilight.*

I pick up one of the vampire books to see if Dell has some unexpected reading habits, but the spine is unbroken. In fact, none of the books have ever been opened.

Bought by a decorator to fill space.

I stick the book back on the shelf and look out onto Central Park at night. The street lamps make the trees and paths look eerie. I pull my feet up and hug my knees. What am I doing here?

I glance at my bag and spot the pink tank and shorts. Maybe all my sex-for-love nonsense is just that — nonsense. I'm going to be thirty in a few short years. I can't wait forever.

I think back on that bulge. He wants me. That's

for sure. He claims he doesn't have a type. So I guess I fit the bill.

I lean my head against the cool glass. There's a whole big world out there. I should figure out who I'm supposed to share mine with. I'm settled. My career is set.

My clock is ticking.

Actually, a clock *is* ticking.

I look around and spot the sound. It's an old-fashioned tabletop grandfather clock. Its pendulum swings back and forth and back and forth. For a moment, I'm mesmerized.

It's out of place here, light wood when the rest is dark. The decorator didn't choose it.

It must actually be Dell's.

He probably picked it up on one of his travels.

I shift it around so I can see the back. I open a little door and can see all the gears moving. There's a little gold plate engraved with a name, address, and phone number.

Barclay McDonald's Clockmaking
5B Adelaide Rd.
Birmingham, Alabama

Wait. Birmingham? Isn't that where that sports team was, the one on the hat that Dell had stashed?

And isn't that where Maximillion raced?

That's too many things to be a coincidence. Dell must be from there. Interesting. He's a southern boy after all.

I turn the clock back around.

Time for bed. I turn out the light and lie on the bed.

A southern boy without a drawl who has a penthouse in Manhattan.

And imagining him curled over me is the last thing on my mind when I fall asleep.

Chapter 21: Dell

I'm not much of a sleeper. I prefer to exist on four hours a night. If I do more, I get sloppy and sluggish. Four hours keeps me knife-sharp and maximizes what I can accomplish.

After leaving Arianna, I fire up the laptop in my room. I review any messages my assistant flagged as important. My VP of Operations took the Tokyo CEO out in my stead. I have to get back to that meeting tomorrow. Missing a second day is not an option.

But I don't have a nanny. Supposedly one is coming for an interview. I'll have to put someone else in charge.

But who? For any task at Brant Financial I would have a whole team.

This is personal. And anyone I hire has to be vetted for confidentiality. I don't like the idea of headlines announcing that Dell Brant dumped some orphan baby into the system. It's total clickbait, and I'm not interested in trying to clean it up.

I ping my social media director to do a sweep of today's publicity references to make sure nothing has gotten out based on Camellia Walsh seeing us. Or any random person who might have recognized me and posted a shot.

I shouldn't be out in public. I can't believe I let that woman convince me to dress down and go out with the baby.

I pluck at the running shirt. Only now do I notice the outline where Grace spit up on me. Great. That's been there all night.

The chair rolls back as I push away from the desk and jerk the shirt over my head. This whole thing is ridiculous. Tomorrow I'm just going to walk away and leave the situation for someone else to handle.

Except, there's the problem again. Who?

I curse not knowing my penthouse staff better. Shannon, having the sick husband. I could help with that. The shopper never even came back. What are her hours? I have no idea.

They also know about the baby.

Sigh. Maybe nobody cares. Maybe I should just have Bernard call around and have someone take her during the day. Maybe I should just call CPS and get it over with. The only qualification I have for being her father is money to support her, even if the DNA is there. I don't have time for an infant.

I kick off the athletic shoes and strip away the jeans. I haven't worn a combination like this in years. My formal dress has been an armor of sorts. If I'm in a full suit worth more than most people make in a month, then no one will guess where I came from. No one will ask ridiculous questions.

Shit.

I'm feeling anxious and out of control. This is not the life I've built. Every company I run, every start-up I fund or buy out, every VP, director, or person of significance in my company is there because they keep everything in my possession running smoothly.

Then this fourteen-pound child mucks all of it up in one day.

I rummage through the closet for athletic wear and pull on a pair of gray shorts with a string tie. No point in a shirt. No one is going to see me.

The athletic shoes go back on. Time to burn some of this angst away. Feel some control.

I head down the hall to the living room. Bernard has taken Maximillion back to the atrium, but I open the door again. "Come, boy," I say. I could use the company. Company that doesn't cry every few hours.

We cross the breakfast nook, pass through the formal dining room, and reach a narrow back hall. At the end is the workout room. Maximillion's nails click on the brushed concrete floor as we cross over to the stereo. I put on some pounding heavy metal and crank the volume until it obliterates all thoughts.

It's a little after midnight. I've just gotten through three sets of push-ups when Maximillion gives out one short warning bark.

I look up.

Arianna is in the doorway, Grace in her arms, wearing long pajama pants and a gray T-shirt that reads "Goddess."

It's not wrong.

But her expression is pure fury.

I jump up. "Is Grace okay?"

"She was perfect," Arianna says, moving forward. "She was just fine. Snoozing away. And so was I." She's close now, and her finger comes out to jab at my chest. "Until. You. Cranked. That. Music."

I glance at the stereo. "Usually no one can hear."

She walks over to one of the walls and smacks it. "This right here is Grace's room."

I hadn't given any thought to what was on the other side. No one ever sleeps here. Bernard is close to the kitchen. My room is way on the end. But she's right. This room would border Grace's.

I head over to the stereo and turn it off. "Sorry. I'm not used to company."

"Well, get used to it," she says. "You're a dad now."

I want to correct her, but in a sense she is right. I am a dad for now. For a few more days. And she's here to help, and I just made things harder.

Grace kicks her legs and looks around. She's wide awake.

"Here, let me take her," I say.

"Damn right you will." She passes the baby to me.

Maximillion lumbers up.

We both look at him, unsure what he will do. He sniffs at my arms, then the baby's feet. Grace spots him and starts to babble happily, reaching out her hand.

"What do you think?" I ask him, kneeling down.

"Are you sure that's a good idea?" Arianna asks.

But Maximillion behaves more unexpectedly than either of us thought. He lays his head in the baby's lap.

"Huh," I say.

Grace instantly grabs his ears and gives a sharp tug.

Arianna lunges forward as if she expects the dog to react. But Maximillion just turns his head and licks the baby's nose.

More happy babbling from the baby.

"Well, okay," Arianna says.

"I don't go to bed for another couple hours," I say. "And I have the magic swing. Go get some more sleep."

But Arianna doesn't leave the room. She plops down on a padded bench by the weights. "This is kinda cute," she says.

I sit on the floor mat, Grace in my lap. Maximillion curls up beside us, his head on my knee, staring at the baby.

Grace thinks he's the best toy ever. She grabs his ears, his nose. She accidentally sticks her finger in his eye, but Maximillion just blinks.

Arianna yawns. "They seem to get along."

"They do," I say, pleased more than I can say.

She lies back on the bench press seat and closes her eyes. I take her in, the belly, the hips, her bare feet on the floor.

I guess very few people see her like this. She's probably a polished, professional owner of an upscale child spa to most of the people in her life. I wonder if she has a best friend, someone she confides in.

Somehow, I don't think so.

There's a loneliness in her. She's driven by work. Surrounded by good people. But all people who work for her.

I make the connection to myself. We're alike.

"That's three things in common," I say softly. Cereal. Time-wasting games. And how we conduct our lives.

I look down at Grace. She's conked out again, her head on Maximillion's long nose, her hands still curled around his ears. His eye shifts to look at me, but he's careful not to disturb her.

"We're their slaves, aren't we?" I ask him.

Ever so gently, I slip a hand beneath the baby and pull her up into my arms. Max follows my lead, slowly pulling back until he is free.

Grace sighs and shifts, then settles closer.

I wonder if Arianna has fallen asleep on the bench. I stand up and walk over.

"Arianna?" I whisper.

She doesn't stir.

I'll come back for her. I carry the baby out of the weight room and through the house. Maximillion trots beside me. I open the door to the atrium, but when I quietly say, "To bed," he simply sits on his haunches and looks pointedly at me, then the baby.

"Fine." I'll get the baby down, deal with the dog, then Arianna.

We head down the hall. Grace's room is still softly lit by the lamp. I set her carefully in the bed and wait a minute to make sure she settles.

Okay.

I head for the door. "Come," I say.

But Maximillion plops down in front of the carriage and refuses to budge.

"Maximillion! Come!" I whisper hoarsely.

He rests his head on his paws and ignores me.

I can't raise my voice, or I'll wake Grace.

"Maximillion," I say again.

Nothing.

Now I'm stuck. I'm not about to lug a full-sized greyhound out of the room. Nor can I use a "command" voice with Grace so close.

"I'm coming back for you," I say to him, although I have no idea what I'll do.

I head back through the house for Arianna. I'm not sure what I'll do with her either. Wake her up? Carry her? Work out around her until she wakes up on her own?

When I return to the weight room, she's curled on her side, knees drawn to her chest. I had no idea the bench press cushion was that comfortable.

I stand over her, unsure. The whole mess is my fault for cranking music at midnight.

The rolled edge of the cushion has formed a little indentation in the side of her head. This can't be a good way to sleep.

I consider shaking her awake. Or I could just carry her to bed.

Which is appealing.

But as I lean down to pick her up, her mouth is just too enticing. I've read the storybooks. There's more than one way to wake up a beautiful slumbering woman.

So I do.

Chapter 22: Arianna

The dream is luscious.

I'm curled up on a soft green lawn. A breeze bends the stalks of a row of tulips. They look like they are leaning in to tell me a secret.

Then I see two shoes. Bright polished men's dress shoes. A perfectly creased cuff lands at precisely the right position. There is no break in the crisply pressed fold. My eyes travel up it, past his knees, to the fly.

There's a bulge there. He's gotten aroused looking at me. Heat courses through my body and I skip ahead to his face.

But he's already bending down, coming for me.

And his lips land on mine.

I fall into the kiss. It's warm and soft and exactly what I've wanted. It tastes faintly of brandy. Smells engulf me. Expensive cologne. A hint of shampoo, something woodsy. Just the faintest whiff of sweat and rubberized plastic, like your hands after holding the handlebars of a bicycle.

The grass is gone. I'm in a black void, spinning. I bring my arms up around the neck of this man in his suit, but I'm surprised to touch skin instead. He's naked now, the suit peeled away just for me.

I hold on to his strong shoulders. The kiss gets deeper, richer, and the sensation of falling is more intense. His tongue enters my mouth and I open for him greedily. It makes sense, the slide into the emptiness and how he fills me.

Then I really am flying, moving through the air, and a bit of scruffy facial hair scrapes against my cheek.

I'm not in a void. I'm in a weight room. And I'm not flying. I'm being carried.

But one part of the dream was right.

I am definitely being kissed.

I pull back. Oh my God. It's Dell.

He looks down at me with a sly smile. "It works on babysitters as well as poisoned princesses," he says.

What!

I kick my legs hard and he lets them go.

His arm shifts me to standing. As soon as I'm on my feet, I push away from him. "Do you always maul girls in their sleep?"

"Only when they are as beautiful as you." His grin tells me he gives zero fucks that I'm upset about this.

I touch my mouth, then check my shirt, my pants.

"You are otherwise unharmed," he assures me. "Unless you'd like me to maul you a bit more."

"No! No, thank you!" God! My hand is still across my mouth. I have to shake my head to get loose of the dream and the blissful feeling. Had Dell done that? Made me feel that way?

Nonsense. Dreams are like that. Distorting reality.

I look around. "Where is Grace?"

"Back in her bed, sound asleep."

"And the dog?"

"Guarding her. I can't get him to leave."

"Really?" I push my hair out of my face, trying to shake the cobwebs of sleep. I'm coming down from the anger now.

Dell isn't trying anything else. I guess he thought it was amusing to kiss me awake.

I walk ahead of him back to Grace's room.

Maximillion is on the floor in front of the carriage. He lifts his head when we walk in.

I peek at Grace. She's asleep and content.

"You didn't give her a bottle or anything?" I ask.

Dell's face is stricken. "Should I have?"

"No, she seems fine. Did you check her diaper?"

Still stricken. "I didn't think to."

She isn't fussy, so I suppose she's all right. "I'm going back to bed," I say.

But then I turn. "Do you always work out in the middle of the night?" I ask.

"I only sleep from two to six," he says.

"That's odd."

He shrugs. "I make up for it on weekends, six hours instead."

"Still odd." I shake my head at him and walk toward the bathroom. I can still feel the plumpness in my lips from his kiss. I touch my mouth.

"Hey, Arianna," he whispers.

I turn. "What?"

"Shall I wake you like that again in the morning?" His grin is pure mischief.

I don't answer, just wave my hand at him and head through the bathroom to my room.

But once I'm settled on the mattress, I can't sleep. I spin around on the bed, my head at the foot, so I can see through the bathroom and into the other room.

Dell is still there, tugging at Max's collar. He pulls

and pulls, but Max won't leave. I cover a laugh with my hand.

His arms bulge with the effort, his chest muscles tight. His belly is flat. The little gray shorts fit tightly over his butt. I lie there, taking him in. No wonder women want a night with him. He's something to behold.

I touch my mouth again. Now that the moment has passed, I'm a little embarrassed at my overreaction to him kissing me to wake me up.

Dell isn't the type to take something by force. He's a charmer. A snake charmer, maybe, but he wants to lure his woman in.

A tendril of desire threads through me as I watch him trying to coerce his dog to move. His back, his shoulders. I feel bold, like I could slip out of this T-shirt and pants and stride over to him in nothing but my panties.

He'd look up, his eyes warm with desire. His hands would trace my body, starting at my ankles, up my calves, and over my knees. His breath would quicken as his fingers slid along my thighs, slipping beneath the edge of my lace panties.

He couldn't stop himself, but would slide a finger inside them. His mouth would take mine, another long, hot, lingering kiss.

His hand would work magic, running along the slit between my legs, then slipping inside.

I suck in a breath and Dell must hear it because he turns in my direction.

Even though he can't possibly see me in the dark, I scramble to move back to my proper place in the bed, my head on the pillow, my legs beneath the sheet.

Then all is quiet and still. My panic settles back into interest. Dell Brant. Nearly naked, just a few yards away.

I want to will him to come check on me, fill the door frame to the bathroom with his bare chest and strong legs. I'd slide over, moving the sheet out of his way.

I can almost feel the weight of him on me. This time his mouth doesn't come in for a kiss, but slips over the peak of a breast, his hot breath teasing my nipple.

I close my eyes, my hand on my own body, wishing it with all my might.

Just before I finally drift off to sleep, I start to rethink my decision to avoid him.

Maybe Dell is a good choice to bump me out of my rut.

To get rid of this self-inflicted ignorance I have

about sex.

To have what other women want from him. A fling. A wild romp. A small piece of his life.

I just might be ready to let this happen.

Chapter 23: Dell

If anybody tries to say I'm not a goddamn gentleman, I'll smash their face.

Between letting the damn dog stay in the baby room and allowing Arianna to go back to sleep — alone — I'm like a bastion of good behavior.

I head back to the weight room to *silently* finish my workout. No music. And apparently no free weights. I heard one clink and decided *nope*. I was not going to be the cause of waking my girls up a second time.

My girls. What the hell was that?

I drop to the mat for fifty more ab crunches. Just because I'm pissed at my brain for thinking that phrase, I add a thirty-pound disc weight to my chest.

These are not my girls. Arianna will jet the moment I hire a real babysitter. Nanny. Whatever.

And Grace. God. She'll be gone as soon as the DNA comes back.

Which needs to happen. Like yesterday.

The sit-ups are grueling, and blissfully obliterate my thoughts for a while. I play AC/DC in my head while I complete another circuit. Silently.

Headphones. I will invest in killer headphones tomorrow.

It's almost two in the morning by the time I kill the lights and walk back through the house. I'll take a quick shower and be in bed right on time.

At least this part of my routine is uninterrupted.

I pause by Grace's room. Maximillion's head lifts, his ear cocked. He's mostly a shadow at the base of the bed.

I slap my leg to call him, but he looks at me and still doesn't budge.

Damn dog. Switched allegiances on me.

Then I see a little movement in the bed. A fist or a foot.

I walk closer.

Grace is lying awake, arms waving, just looking around.

Huh. I didn't know they did that. Just sat around thinking their baby thoughts.

When she sees me, her eyes get big. Then her mouth opens.

I know what's coming.

Before she can let out a wail to wake Arianna, I pick her up.

I know the trouble right away. The smell is terrific.

"You're a real stinker, you know that?" I say.

Maximillion stands up and sniffs the air. He lets out a little dog groan and trots out of the room.

"Man's best friend, eh?" I say after him.

Then to Grace, "You think I can do this?"

She gazes at me with solemn eyes.

"Well, you didn't say no," I say.

I hold her out as we move to the bathroom. I don't want to squish that diaper even more by cradling her.

I peer into Arianna's room. She's asleep on the bed, the sheet kicked off. I use my elbow to close the door so she won't hear us and wake.

It's pretty dim in the bathroom with only the lamp light from the nursery.

"I remember this from when I was a kid," I tell Grace. "Watch and learn."

I set her on the curved mat and pull a towel from the rack.

"Roll it just so," I say, turning the flat towel into an oblong tube. Then I stuff it at the base of the door so light won't leak out beneath it.

I flip on the light. Grace reacts instantly, throwing her arms over her face.

"Oh, sorry, sorry," I say. I glance around, pick up another towel, and cover her eyes. "Better?"

Her arms come down and she wiggles, pulling at the towel like we're about to engage in a game of peekaboo. I guess that's a yes.

The one-piece sleeper looks complicated. There are snaps from her neck down the front. Then they continue down both her legs like the letter Y. I move her feet around, trying to study the pattern. Otherwise I'll never get her back together.

When I'm sure I can replicate the fastenings, I begin unsnapping.

"We're going to follow the example Miss Arianna set," I tell her. She's knocked the towel off her face with her wiggles, but she seems okay with the light now.

I reveal the diaper and keep unsnapping. "Lift. Wipe. Remove diaper. Wipe again. New diaper," I say. "Or is it wipe, then lift?"

My phone is in my room. I can't use the diaper Wiki to refresh my memory.

"How hard can this be?" I ask.

I pull her legs out of the little pants. Immediately I see a problem. Yellow goo everywhere. It's leaked out of the diaper and onto her clothes.

"What sort of cut-rate diapers are these?" I ask. "I'm going to buy this company and force them to redesign."

What a mess. I look around for the wipes. A closed box. Great. I have to let go of Grace to pry them open. By the time I have one, her wiggles have smeared stuff everywhere. And I haven't even opened the diaper yet.

I will not wake Arianna. I will do this.

I pull out three wipes and line them up on the counter. I can only hope they will be enough. I rip off the stick tabs holding the diaper closed and brace myself.

Whoa. It's chaos down there. One wipe barely makes a dent. I drag the trash can out with my foot and drop the wipe in it. A second one means I can see skin.

After the third I feel like I can at least move the diaper. Forget the neat ball Arianna made. I just drop it in the trash.

Grace thinks all this is hilarious, smiling and kicking up a storm. I wrench open the wipe container again and pull out a fourth one.

It takes five wipes to get her clean.

"I should have just dunked you in the sink," I

say.

The new box of diapers is on the corner of the counter, unopened. I pry it open and extract one.

"I assume the fish go in front," I say to her. It's a different brand. Good. The others were substandard.

She doesn't argue about the placement of the fish.

On this supposition, I slide the diaper beneath her.

But the fasteners on this one are different as well. It has Velcro on the tabs. "How many kinds of diapers are there?" I ask.

I look around for a bit of matching Velcro to align with the tab, but there isn't any. It doesn't stick to the white part of the diaper. It doesn't seem to stick anywhere.

"How is this done?" I ask her.

She gurgles with a silly grin.

I push hard on the tab and it makes something approximating a connection to the diaper. I can't put the soiled sleeper back on, so I pull her arms out of it.

Back in her room, Maximillion looks up, sniffing again. He's back at the base of her bed.

"She no longer offends your sensibilities," I say to him. I open the various drawers. The other sleepers have a million snaps as well, so I just grab the

"Genius" shirt and the tights. They are easy, just sliding up her legs with elastic. And the shirt is normal. Really, I don't understand the point of outfits with a thousand snaps.

I pick her up and sit in the chair. "You going to stay up all night?" I ask her.

But she's already heavy in my arms, eyes closing in the dim light.

It won't take long for her to fall asleep.

As we rock, my thoughts drift to Arianna in the next room. Sleeping on my weight bench. The kiss. She'd responded, heavy with sleep. Her eagerness sent my cock raging and promised a good match.

Until she rejected me.

The housekeeper was right. A chair that rocks really helps.

It really makes you sleepy…

Chapter 24: Arianna

I expect to wake to the cries of the baby, so I'm surprised when it's the sun slanting through the blinds that gets me first.

I peer at the grandfather clock on the dresser. It's after eight!

I jump out of bed and hurry through the bathroom to the baby's room. I imagine all sorts of things. That the mother came back and kidnapped her. That she was smothered in the improper bedding. SIDS. A heart defect.

But the sight I find is completely unexpected.

Dell, asleep in the dining chair we moved to the room.

Grace, asleep on his chest.

His bare feet are propped on Max, his dog.

The greyhound looks up at me with weary eyes, as if to say, can I please move now?

"You're a good dog," I say.

Dell snaps awake. He looks around, trying to get his bearings. Grace slides a little, and he tightens his grip on her. "What?"

I watch as it all comes back to him. The baby. The room. Me.

"I'll take her," I say. I reach for Grace and shift her from his chest to my arms.

My skin connects with his, and that fire flares in me. I haven't forgotten my decision from last night. And seeing him there with the baby this morning hasn't hurt his case.

Dell leaps from the chair. "What time is it?"

"A little after eight."

"Shit," he says. "Shit, shit."

He takes off out of the room. I follow him for a few steps, then shrug. He's here. I'm here. It's another day waiting for test results.

Grace stirs as I head back to my own room. I send a quick text to Taylor that I'm still tied up with the baby situation and to hold down the fort. She writes back to say all is well. Every teacher arrived that morning, and Maria is back on organization duties.

I let out a sigh. That's always the big problem, handling any last-minute staff absences. I tell her to use Maria as a floater if needed during the day and that I will be upstairs if anything needs my attention.

When I set down my phone, I feel a sense of accomplishment. Dell's comment yesterday that I had to micromanage my substandard employees was dead wrong. I don't even have to be there today.

"Let's get you a bath," I tell Grace. "Then we'll scare up some breakfast."

Grace gurgles in return. She seems happy this morning. She'll need feeding soon, but if she's content, I'll wait.

We don't have a proper baby tub and she's too small for the regular bathtub, but the sink will work fine. I run the water, waiting for the perfect temperature, humming to Grace.

I set her on the changing pad and pull the "Genius" shirt off.

Wait. She wasn't wearing that last night.

I spot the sleeper on the counter. Obviously she soiled it.

"Did Dell change you last night?" I ask. I'm impressed. He did it without waking anyone or having a cow. Maybe he's going to be all right after all.

Grace babbles in response. I tug off her pants.

Then laugh out loud. The diaper comes off with them. They aren't fastened in any way, just held in place by the leggings.

Dell hadn't attached the Velcro.

"Your daddy is silly," I say before I catch myself. He might not be the father. But Grace takes no notice, happily waving her arms.

I check the water and fill the sink, adding a few drops of baby wash. It suds lightly, and I feel happy and content as I slide Grace into the water.

She loves the feeling, smiling and kicking to make a splash.

"You like that, huh?" I tug a washcloth from the towel rack and smooth it over her soft baby skin.

My throat tightens a little as I realize how good this feels. Maybe being a mother is something I want for myself after all.

Grace beams up at me as I elongate the bath, letting her play. "You need some water toys," I say. It seems like we bought a million things yesterday, but really there was so much more. I wonder if Dell would be up for another trip. We could go to a boutique store this time, since we have all the diapers and basics.

"Let's run up his credit card," I say to her.

She smiles. She agrees wholeheartedly.

Finally the water cools, so I pull her out and dry her off. I take my time giving her lotion and clean clothes, savoring her sweet smell and the quiet peace of a lazy morning.

She looks adorable in the race car romper.

Then my stomach growls. Grace looks up at me as if realizing she is hungry too. Her forehead crumples.

I glance down at my T-shirt and pajama pants. "At least one of us is ready to face the day," I tell her.

But I don't have time to change. We need a bottle before she starts wailing.

I cradle her and pad out into the hall. "Hello?" I call.

Bernard materializes by the kitchen door. "Yes, madam?"

"Are there any bottles ready?" I ask.

"I've kept one on hand," he says. "Let me warm it."

I stay in the hall, jiggling Grace. I wonder if Dell is in his room, or maybe the study. All the bedroom doors are closed other than mine and Grace's.

I walk down to the living room. The study is open, so I cross to peek in.

Light creates a pattern across the enormous oak desk, the conference table, the arrangement of a love seat and two chairs.

But no Dell.

He must be showering or something.

Grace starts to fuss, so I walk with a bouncy step,

keeping her as calm as I can. When we make it to the kitchen, Bernard is just fishing the bottle out of a pan of hot water.

"They make a special machine for heating bottles," I tell him. "We have an industrial-sized one in the day care."

"This is no bother," he says and passes the milk to me.

I test it on my wrist, which seems to annoy him. But he says nothing. It's the perfect temperature. Of course.

I slide the nipple into Grace's mouth and walk to the breakfast nook. Max isn't by the door to his atrium as usual. I peer in. He's completely conked out on a rug near the back wall.

Rough night for him too.

I walk back through the kitchen, where Bernard is mixing eggs. "Omelet, madam?" he asks.

"Sounds great," I say. I'm famished.

"Give me a few minutes."

I pass on through and back to the hall. This time I walk down to the last door, Dell's bedroom. I listen carefully. I can't hear anything.

Huh.

I return to Grace's room to give her the bottle in the chair. Maybe she'll take a nap after this and I can shower. I'm sure I look an absolute fright.

The bottle is just about empty when Bernard appears in the doorway. "Your omelet is in the warmer when you're ready," he says.

I glance down at Grace. She is happy and kicking, nowhere near sleep. I shrug. I can eat an omelet with one hand.

By the time I make it to the breakfast nook, Bernard has already set the table with my omelet, toast, orange juice, and coffee.

"Thank you, Bernard," I say, propping the baby in my arm.

He nods and disappears into the depths of the kitchen.

I attack the egg with a ferocity seconded only by when I pick up the coffee cup. I don't usually take it black, but today it feels perfect. Hot and strong.

When the cup is empty, Bernard is already there with the coffeepot.

How does he do that?

"Has Dell already had breakfast?" I ask.

"Mr. Brant does not eat breakfast at home," Bernard says. "He has a chef at the office."

Or Cap'n Crunch in his desk, I think with an inward smile. "When will he leave?"

Bernard's face is perfectly impassive as he says,

"He left some time ago."

"Oh!" I look down at Grace. It must have been during her bath.

A buzz sounds and Bernard excuses himself and walks away. I'm still reeling from the fact that Dell just left me with this child when Bernard returns with a woman I recognize.

"Ms. Hart?" she asks, confusion on her face as she takes in the baby, my outfit, and my hair.

I stand up quickly. It's Carrie, a sub I use regularly. "Hey," I say. "You're here for the nanny position?"

She nods, her eyes wide. "I didn't realize you'd be here."

"Emergency help," I say. "It was a special situation."

"So you know this young woman?" Bernard asks.

"Yes," I tell him. "She works for me all the time."

"And you think she is good with children?" His expression hasn't changed.

"Um, sure," I say. "She's been a valuable substitute for me for about a year."

Bernard turns to her. "Then you are hired. Can you start immediately?"

Carrie's expression is of shock. She hasn't even said anything. "I think so. I'm not busy today."

"Excellent," Bernard says. "I'll show you to the room."

The room! My stuff is in there.

Bernard leads Carrie down the hall. I look down at Grace. She kicks her little bare feet. What is going on here?

I hurry after them. When I get to the room, I'm aghast. The bed is made. My things are repacked. He must have done it while I ate breakfast.

"This looks good," Carrie says. "Does he want a live-in?"

"He would prefer it," Bernard says.

"We haven't discussed salary," Carrie says.

Bernard tugs a card from his pocket. He hands it to Carrie. "We're currently looking for someone through Monday afternoon, with a move to permanent if everything falls into place."

He points to a number. "This is for the daytime only through Monday."

Carrie nods.

"And this is if you stay here around the clock until Monday."

Her eyebrows lift. "Seriously? That's…" She seems overcome. "Okay. I have an obligation Friday night, but the others I could be here."

"We can accommodate that," Bernard says. He

was obviously given very explicit instructions.

"I will need some things," Carrie says. "I wasn't expecting to start so quickly, and certainly not for overnight."

Bernard glances at me and hesitates. "We can discuss the details shortly," he says. "But there will be an opportunity this afternoon for Mr. Brant to help you settle in."

I want to huff out a loud breath at "settle in." I have no doubt what that means to Dell. I imagine him and Carrie all cozy with Grace late tonight and jealousy blasts through me, hot and unexpected.

Carrie drops her purse on the dresser next to the grandfather clock. She turns to me. "I'll take her," she says. "I can manage from here."

"Her room is through the bathroom," I say, waving my hand lamely. "All her things are there."

Carrie nods. "Thank you, Arianna," she says. She heads into the nursery room.

Bernard stays behind. He pulls another envelope from his pocket. "Dell asked me to give this to you should the new nanny work out." Then he leaves the room.

I sit on the bed, then stand up again, feeling awkward since it belongs to Carrie now.

Maybe I should look at this in my own apartment

downstairs. I walk to my bag, but my curiosity is too strong. I lean against the wall and rip it open.

It's handwritten on heavy textured paper with a monogrammed B at the top.

Arianna,

Thank you for your incredible sacrifice of a day and night of your life for baby Grace. I have made a contribution of $12,000 to the March of Dimes in the name of Del Gato Child Spa.

Dell Brant

Well. That's nice. I can't exactly be mad at him for that, even if he didn't say good-bye.

I fold up the note and tuck it in my bag. I glance at the bathroom, wondering if I should at least change. I've never walked through my building in a T-shirt and pajama bottoms. The Dell Brant Building isn't exactly a freshman dorm.

But everything feels strange now. None of the spaces belong to me, and Dell is no longer here to shepherd me.

So I slip on my shoes, pick up my bag, and head into the hall.

Bernard is already by the door.

"Your assistance has been most appreciated,

madam," he says.

"It's Arianna," I say. "I really prefer Arianna."

"Arianna, then," Bernard says. His formal expressionless face cracks just a bit beneath his gray hair.

I pass through the door and head to the elevator. It's so quiet out here. I press the down button and wait. The elevator is on the ground floor. It will be a minute.

The door to the penthouse has already closed. It's just me and a couple potted plants, plus two chairs along the wall. I walk over to the window to look at the park. It's another sunshiny day. Thursday. At this time yesterday, I had only just met Dell Brant.

And now I don't know him anymore.

My chest aches a little, like I lost something important. I shake it off. That's ridiculous. This was nothing. Just twenty-four hours of an insane panic-driven life. Diapers. Shopping. Midnight dream kisses.

It is over now.

Back to ordinary Arianna.

Chapter 25: Dell

It feels good to be home.

Not at the penthouse, of course. In my office.

My chef-prepared lunch has just been delivered. The Tokyo meeting went well. I've caught up on most of the critical events of yesterday.

I feel in control again.

The baby and Arianna seem like a far-off dream, like a movie I watched once when I was young and impressionable.

It's nothing that affects me now.

The twelve grand for the child spa is worth having a nanny in place. Bernard informed me that the new woman was kind and organized and the place felt as harmonious as could be expected.

All is well.

The first indication that my life has been impacted more than I might be admitting is the unwelcome buzz from my office manager that

Camellia Walsh has arrived and is asking to see me.

"Under no circumstances allow her in here," I say into the intercom. "Put her off."

Camellia. I can still see her hobbling back to her car after breaking her shoe. It was completely unacceptable for her to chase me down like that.

I should face facts. That woman was a tactical error. Most of my weekend women understand me. Short-term trysts. Nice. Neat. Pleasurable.

Then done.

But not her. She has proven too clingy by a long shot. I'm not in the market for a girlfriend or a wife. And even if I was, she wouldn't have made the cut.

That line of thought makes me flash to a vision of Arianna curled up on my weight bench. Other than the kiss, nothing about our time together fit my normal interactions with women. It had all been so — ordinary. Baby shopping. Doctor visit. Assembling a swing and a stroller. Dinner.

But there had been that kiss. The dreamy, half-awake passionate meeting of our mouths. I could still feel her in my arms.

My reverie is disrupted by the abrupt opening of my door.

"Dell Brant, how dare you try to use your secretary to get rid of me!"

Camellia Walsh storms into the office. I stand up, prepared to unleash my displeasure at the interruption, when I see her.

I clamp down my rage. She's a disaster. Mascara down her cheeks. Her hair spilling from an updo. Only her fuchsia knit dress is in perfect order.

"Good grief, Camellia, what's happened to you?"

My assistant pauses to make sure I'm okay with the disruption. I nod as Camellia comes around my desk to lay her tear-streaked face on my shoulder.

I do not want her there. But I act appropriately, patting her back.

"What has happened?" I ask.

Her next words rather confound me.

"The DOMs have rejected me. And I just wanted you! Who cares about those other dirty old men!" Her voice is plaintive, pathetic.

So no one has died. She hasn't been harmed or threatened. I disentangle myself and take a step back.

"Please explain yourself," I say, already impatient. I have no time for games.

"The DOMs said no, but that's not what I want anyway."

I hold up a hand. "What are you talking about?"

She purses her lips. "I thought you knew."

"Is this an S&M thing? I'm not into that." I can

be, actually, but it's not something to share with Camellia.

"No, not that sort of dom," she says, unsure now. Her face is crumpled. She decides to change tactics. "Dell, darling, please say you'll take me out this weekend. Once wasn't enough."

Oh, this is the worst.

"Camellia, I have plans. Perhaps some other time." I return to my chair and pick up my phone. "Now, if you'll excuse me."

She tries to slip into my lap. I'm not sure how to politely retreat. I've met prostitutes who were more subtle than this.

I place my hands on her rather minuscule waist to forcibly remove her from my leg. She had her lowest ribs removed to make her figure more dramatic, and it startles me the same now as it did when she was naked in my limo.

Not that it stopped me then.

When she stands on her own two feet, her eyes flash. "I saw you with that baby," she says, all pretense gone. "You better explain that to me before I use that information against you."

Now we're in a place I'm used to. Cutthroat negotiation. Threats. I've had meetings go this way before. So much more civilized than the head games she was playing before.

"What could possibly be scandalous about a man carrying a child down a New York boulevard?" I ask.

"Whose child?" she asks. She clears away the mascara streaks in two quick swipes with her hand.

"It isn't my place to disclose the private information of a minor," I say.

She swiftly re-pins her hair. She looks nothing like the distraught bombshell who stumbled in.

"I aim to leverage our relationship to get into the DOMs," she says coldly. "So agree to another weekend with me, at least publicly, or I'll go to the worst online gossip sites about your secret love child."

"I don't do second weekends," I say.

"I know," she shoots back. "That's why it's sure to get me in."

Despite playing ignorant earlier about this DOM group, I have a rough idea of what she's talking about. A certain subset of my former lovers gather to drink and no doubt speak of me with sarcasm and disdain. It's fine. Amusing, really.

"Why do you want to associate with the other women I've slept with?" I ask.

She arranges her face into the classic expression of a beatific upper-class wife, pleasant and neutral. "It's social security for aging divorcées," she says.

"Now what will it be?"

"No deal," I say, waving her off. "Do your worst about the child. You'll only embarrass yourself."

"We'll see about that." She huffs out an unhappy breath and turns on her heel.

I picture Arianna rolling her eyes at the woman and have to smile at my computer monitor. The door closes behind her.

But she has reminded me of a task I should do today. The DNA test. The one-day non-court-admissible one. At least I would know. If it turns out Grace is not mine, I can let her go right now. The official one is pointless.

I type in the Google search to find a clinic nearby. I'll need the child of course for another swab. Perhaps I'll have the nanny bring her separately so we aren't seen together again.

But as I scan the list, I think about how Grace reacted in the doctor's office. Her screams. The upset. She was inconsolable for an hour. I can't do that to her again, even if it won't involve a needle jab.

I close the window. I have a nanny in place until Monday. The child will no longer be a bother to me.

I will just let her be.

Chapter 26: Arianna

If I admit it to myself, I know that I spent more time in the front foyer of the child spa than usual as five o'clock rolled around.

Normally I greet the mothers back in the secure area as they pick up their children.

But today I want by the windows. To spot Dell.

There, I've said it. In my head. But I said it.

Of course, I see nothing. I don't even know when he normally comes home. Maybe he stays at work until late.

I tug at the cool blue-green scarf around my neck. I've worn my favorite outfit, a smooth floral dress in shades of aqua and teal. It accentuates my boobs, which I know he liked. Covers my flaws, mainly the exceedingly curvy hips.

As if he'd see the dress anyway. As if he'd notice.

I'm a mess.

Taylor looks at me sympathetically more than

once when I turn from the windows. "Maybe you should have just let her stay here," she says.

I'm annoyed that she's figured me out. "She's a cute baby," I say sharply. "I just miss her, is all."

"But not him," she says. "Not him at all."

"Why don't you take off a little early?" I suggest.

"There's still some kids," she says.

"That's okay."

She opens the drawer where she stores her purse. "I didn't mean anything by what I said."

"It's quite all right. See you tomorrow."

"Okay." She tucks a long strand of blond hair behind her ear nervously as she pushes through the door. She probably thinks she's upset me enough to fire her. I wouldn't. I'm just annoyed I'm so obvious.

I lean against the desk. At least now I can stare out the windows without feeling self-conscious.

A familiar stroller appears. I stand up straight. It's Carrie. With Grace!

I race to the door and push it open.

"Hey!" I say. "How is it going with her?"

Carrie smiles and stops in front of our window. "Super great. She's such an easy baby!"

"Have you burped her? It's like a drunk man belching."

Carrie laughs. "It is! In fact, I was just running

down to the pharmacy to pick up some drops. Dell didn't have any."

My face freezes. Dell. First name already.

"Yes, we forgot. Me and Dell. When we were shopping. Yesterday. Together." I fumble with my words.

Carrie tilts her head. She looks adorable with her pixie haircut and cute little jeans and soft clingy tank. Dell is totally going to fall for her. She probably won't put him off.

"Well, I thought it might be helpful to have some on hand," she says. "Thank you so much for thinking of me for this opportunity." She leans in close. "Do you know the situation? All Bernard said was that this was full-time until Monday. Then they would make a decision about keeping me on."

I twist the scarf uncomfortably. "Did you talk to Dell about it?"

She shakes her head. "I haven't met him yet. How is he? The rumors aren't very kind."

My relief and my ire rise up simultaneously. He isn't terrible! Okay, maybe he is. Should I scare her off from him? Or be honest?

"He's all right," I finally say.

"I looked him up on my phone. He's gorgeous as hell." She gives me a conspiratorial smile. "I bet it was tempting."

"Not really," I say. "He sleeps with a different woman every few days."

She straightens up. "Really? That's pretty awful."

I shrug. "It's how he operates."

Grace starts to kick up a fuss, so I bend down to look at her. She's strapped in, her stocking feet rising and falling, her face scrunched up.

"I should get walking. She likes it best when we're on the move." Carrie rolls the stroller forward. "So nice running into you. Thanks again!"

I watch her push through the crowd. I want to call out, "I chose that stroller, dammit!" But I don't. I just turn back to the child spa and head into the foyer.

I won't think about Carrie and Dell together tonight. About her thinking he is gorgeous. About what he might think of her.

I made my bed. And I stayed in it rather than going to his.

Now I have to live with it.

That evening drags. It's me, Netflix, and a pint of Ben & Jerry's Chunky Monkey.

Sometimes I swear I can hear Grace's small cry, even though thirty-six floors separate my apartment from the penthouse. Just wishful thinking.

The next morning, Taylor isn't in more than five

minutes when she calls me up front. "I had a late-night message for you on the voice mail," she says. "You might want to listen to it yourself."

I take the portable headset from her.

The voice is rich and low. I'd know it anywhere. Dell.

"Arianna," he says. "I've just been informed that the new babysitter, I'm sorry, the new nanny cannot be here tonight. I would very much like to discuss your availability to help us. I would be most grateful." He rattles off a number to contact him.

I type the digits into my phone contacts and hand the headset back.

"You going to do it?" Taylor asks.

I raise my eyebrows and give her a stern I'm-your-boss look. But then I relent. "Of course I am."

I buzz my way back into the security of the back of the child spa. The universe has given me a second chance with Dell Brant, and I'm not going to blow it this time.

During lunch, I go back to my own apartment to make the call. I'm pleased when it's Dell himself who answers, not an assistant.

"Arianna," he says. "Thank you so much for sending Carrie. She's amazing."

And cute. And confident. And hopefully not in

your bed last night. "She is," I say. "I'm glad she's working out."

"Except for tonight. She had plans and I really could use you. I'm not used to this father thing."

His voice is like melted velvet. There is seriously nobody who could say no to that.

"Not a problem," I say. "What time do you want me to come up?"

"Carrie is leaving around five. I'd give me no more than an hour alone with Grace before I botch something."

I smile inside. Like that diaper. I wonder if Carrie showed him how to fasten them properly. She may have already convinced him to pick up cloth ones. I was just waiting for Monday to suggest things like that.

"I'll be up there," I say.

"You want Bernard to bring down an elevator card?" Dell asks. I can actually feel his voice sliding down my body. Yes, yes, I'm definitely ready for more.

"I'll just tell Harry," I say, singing a little inside that he'd offer.

"Very well. See you tonight."

The call ends. I hold on to the phone for a moment, letting my anticipation wash over me. I'm doing this. The fling thing. With Dell, master of weekend one-offs.

And I'm totally fine with it. Screw the love part. Screw complications.

I'm ready to see what I've been missing. With a master.

Now, what to wear?

Chapter 27: Dell

I clip on a set of silver cuff links. The tux is new, another original by a local designer. I'll be expected to pose for pictures in it. She'll want the suit to be seen. It's fine. It's always fine. Part of the lifestyle.

I heard the door buzz a half hour ago. Should be Arianna. I'm sure she's down in Grace's room so that she and Carrie can have a changing of the guard.

This isn't so hard. Nannies. Babysitters. There are many good ones to be found.

I check the mirror. Everything is classic. Black tux. White shirt with pleats, bow tie in a burnt-red color. Perfect pants crease. Something about the vest is signature to this designer, but the detail is too subtle for me to recognize.

I head out of the bedroom. Down the hall, the door to Grace's room stands open.

Bernard appears. "Sir, Miss Carrie has taken her leave. Madam Arianna is here now."

An irate voice comes from the room. "Why is Carrie a 'miss' and I am a 'madam'? It's Arianna." A smile forms on my lips.

"You better not answer that," I tell Bernard. "It's a trap."

Arianna appears at the doorway with Grace in her arms. My eyes want to pop out of my skull. She wears a ribbed tank top that makes her breasts look so perfect and so round that I actually salivate. Then jeans again, low on her hips, leaving a tempting inch of creamy skin exposed below the hem of the shirt.

She's wearing a bra, which is clear from the straps that show beside the top of the tank. But it can't be much of one. As she watches me watch her, the nipples harden and make themselves known.

It's hard to control the stirring in my cock.

Bernard murmurs, "I'll take my leave," and turns on his heel.

When I get back to Arianna's expression, it has completely changed.

"You're in a tux," she says. Her voice is filled with disbelief.

"Of course," I say. "That's why I needed a babysitter."

Her eyebrows shoot up.

"Nanny," I correct. "Sorry."

She clamps her jaw a moment. Then she says, "I'm neither a babysitter nor a nanny. I thought I was helping you."

"You are!" Shit, I've pissed her off. "You are saving my skin."

"Where are you going?" she demands. "Please tell me it's a charity event where you are saving thousands of dying children by donating a ridiculous sum of money."

"Actually, you've nailed it. Well, adults too. It's a famine something."

"Famine something?" she repeats, taking a step toward me. Her eyes flash. God, I love it when she's angry. Little sparks fly right off her.

"I don't recall the charity," I say. "But you're right. It's for a good cause."

She lets out a huff and steps back. "Fine. But don't be out late." Her demand sounds so much like an angry mother of a teen that I have to work hard not to smile while I'm being chastised.

"Scout's honor," I say, holding up both hands.

"You don't even know the scout salute," she says. "You were probably never a scout."

"That's where you're wrong," I say, putting three fingers to an imaginary cap. "I just…outgrew it." Actually, I had to quit when I took on a second shift after school at the racetrack to help out with bills. But I won't tell her that.

She seems taken aback. "Oh! Well, I stand corrected." She turns back to Grace's room, her anger melting into something else, something I can't quite put my finger on. Disappointment, maybe. Or resignation.

"Hey," I say. "I mean it. You're saving me. A third time."

She nods. "Have a good night."

She kneels by the fancy swing and sets Grace in it. The baby instantly reaches up for the lighted toys.

I watch them interact for a moment, an uncomfortable feeling settling over me.

But it's Friday, and I'm expected at the charity dinner. And in precisely thirty-four minutes, I'm supposed to be picking up a perfectly lovely young woman named Meredith Sing.

Arianna doesn't look up. Eventually I turn away.

"Bernard, is the car downstairs?" I ask. Meredith is in midtown, so it will take a while to get there.

"Yes," he says, stepping from the kitchen.

I cross through to the breakfast nook, then the atrium. As soon as I open the door, Maximillion darts out without paying me the least bit of attention. I watch as he takes off across the house.

Back to the baby's room. I see how it is. Carrie showed abject fear of the dog, so we've kept him locked up. But no doubt he's figured out the kinder, gentler, more dog-friendly Arianna has arrived.

They can manage him. I move on to the door. I'm three minutes ahead of schedule. It's a good place to be.

The drive to her building is typical weekend fare, busy and irritating.

Meredith herself is pleasant, smelling of lilacs as she enters the limo. She wears a long slim wine-colored dress, backless, fitted from neck to ankle. A long slit allows her to walk, and I appreciate a generous reveal of her slender leg as she steps in and slides onto the seat.

I pass her a vodka and cranberry, a drink I noticed she ordered from the bar at the last Met gala. It's where I first spotted her.

"Thank you," she says, lifting it as if in a toast. "You are both handsome and observant."

"When it's important," I say.

But instead of considering my next point of pre-conquest banter, I recall those same words from Arianna, inside the baby superstore. When I noticed the baby bucket seats.

"What's in your glass?" Meredith asks.

"Brandy," I say.

"I hear brandy kisses are the best," she says coyly, taking a sip of her own drink. Her eyes watch me from over the rim.

Usually that's my cue. I would normally say, "Shall we test that theory?" And then scoot closer.

And the night would begin in earnest.

But I don't. I just nod. "I can pour you one if you like."

She hesitates. "I'm fine with this," she says. The coy look is gone.

I don't know this woman well. She doesn't seem the social climber type, like Camellia. But she's no innocent ingénue either. She's the daughter of a prominent developer in upstate New York.

That's all I was told by Ram, the friend who filled me in when I asked who she was.

The venue isn't far from her building, so we arrive before we can even finish the drinks. Meredith sets hers carefully in a cup holder and waits for the driver to open the door.

She's cooled, and I find I don't particularly care. We exit the limo and are greeted by a doorman.

"This way, sir," he says.

Limos line all the curbs. Otherwise this part of town is quite deserted. No place to escape to, no good bars, no nightlife.

Just this night with a tepid date I have no interest in warming up.

My memory flashes to Arianna, the tank top, those jeans, that strip of skin.

And as we pause to have our photo made just inside the overdecorated foyer, I realize maybe I should have just stayed home.

Chapter 28: Arianna

"Men are pigs," I tell Grace as I change her into the lion sleeper. I fluff the mane on her hood. "This outfit is perfect. You can eat them alive."

I pick her up from the bed. "You ready for bottle and sleepytimes?"

Her slate blue eyes watch me with wonder. It's probably just the sloppy topknot I stuck my hair in after Dell left.

"My hair looks like a poodle, doesn't it?" I ask her, pressing on the errant curls popping out all over. "Well, it's not like it matters. Nobody is going to notice."

We move to the dining chair still sitting near the white carriage. I half expected Dell to order a proper rocking chair. But it's still not Monday. He's obviously still planning to send Grace away if she turns out not to be his.

I guess he has to. She belongs to somebody. No

telling who the real father is. The mother doesn't want her. Social services will have to figure it all out.

Grace settles in my arms with the bottle. My heart squeezes for her. How could anybody not want this sweet girl? She's no trouble, really, at least not any more than any baby. Once you learn to burp her properly, anyway.

"You do belch like an old man," I say.

She smiles around her bottle, then resumes sucking.

"I wonder if I could take you," I say.

I know it's a ridiculous thought. There's a lot to it. Approval to foster. Classes to take. Inspections. Certifications. By the time I would be eligible, Grace would be settled with some other family.

Unless Dell just gave her to me.

The idea takes hold. I could move Maria. Open a third baby room. Gosh, where? I'd have to rearrange.

My head starts buzzing. I could do this.

Screw men. Screw Dell. I could be her mom right now.

Why does my life have to revolve around some traditional structure? Screw marriage. Screw nuclear families. None of the families at my spa are set up the old-fashioned way. Every kid is a half-step-something.

By the time Grace has finished the bottle and I've

turned her on my thighs for a good burp, I've come up with a little speech for Dell. The last thing I want is for him to call CPS before I can let him know I want her.

I mentally rearrange my house, moving things out of the extra bedroom for a nursery.

For the first time in a long time, I feel energized, excited. Like there's a reason I'm here.

"It's for you," I tell Grace. "Everything I've gone through so far has brought me to you. My parents. The nannies. Opening a day care." My throat chokes up with emotion.

Grace responds by falling asleep in my lap. I kiss her fuzzy head. At first I think I'll just hold her until Dell gets home, but my energy is too much. I want to pace, think, plan. I lay her in the carriage.

Maximillion, who has planted himself at my feet, walks with me in circles around the room.

"What do you think, Max?" I ask. "Is this a good idea? Do you think Dell will do it?"

"Will I do what?"

I halt. Dell is at the door!

"What are you doing here?" I ask. "It's too early for you to be back."

He tugs at his bow tie and slides it out of his collar. "This gala was more lame than most."

"Think of the children!" I say.

He laughs, a low throaty sound. "They got their money."

I want to ask if his date was lame too, but I don't. I can't needle him. I have a bigger purpose now. A more important one.

"So what are you asking my dog if I will do?"

His eyes take me in, jeans, shirt, resting on my tank top. Crap. My "seduce Dell" outfit is the totally wrong thing now that I've switched to "prove I'm mother material."

I take a step back. "It's about Grace," I say.

"What about her?" His eyes flicker to my face briefly, but he can't hold it. They go back to the flimsy bra and too-tight shirt combo that took me a half hour of changing clothes to get right.

I resist the urge to cross my arms over my chest and turn to my bag. "This might not be the best time to discuss it. Grace is down. You handled her fine the other night. Carrie can cover things again in the morning." I pick up my leather duffel.

"That looks like you were planning to stay the night," Dell says.

"More like I was planning on having to go to sleep while waiting up on you," I shoot back. "And I didn't. So good night!"

"Arianna, drop the bag." His voice is so authoritative that my arms actually set it down.

Then I'm annoyed with myself for falling for whatever voice wizardry he just pulled and bend over for it again.

"Just…come," he says. "Let's talk away from the baby."

Well, he has a point about that. I straighten and cast a glance back at the carriage. Max has set up his guard on the floor beside it.

"All right," I say. Maybe it is time to discuss it, pokey nipples or not. Maybe he'll be distracted enough by them to just say yes.

We walk to the living room. Bernard is by the bar. "Shall I make drinks or will you mix them yourself?" he asks.

"Two brandies," Dell says to him.

A few hours ago, I would be disappointed not to already be in his bedroom. But I imagine he's already gotten his jollies on one woman tonight. I'm not interested in making it a double.

Dell settles on the sofa, unbuttoning his tux shirt. Then he stands up again, stripping off the jacket. "Not a fan of this designer," he says. "This feels like a straitjacket."

Bernard sets the drinks on the coffee table and

takes the jacket from Dell.

"Anything else, sir?"

Dell waves him off. He picks up the glasses and passes one to me.

I decide to avoid the nearness of the sofa and return to the chair I sat on before.

His gaze flickers, but he lets it go. "So what is this about Grace?"

I gulp a mouthful of brandy as I figure out my first words.

The fire, followed by a warm calm feeling, is so wonderful, I take another.

Now Dell's face is full of amusement. "Was she that tough tonight?" He seems to decide that this conversation will be frivolous, and relaxes back on the cushions.

After my second gulp of liquor, I just blurt it out.

"I want her."

Now Dell's head snaps around. "What do you mean?"

"Grace. I want to be her mother. I know I'm not kin or official and I don't have a home study or approval to adopt, but I'm sure we can work something out between us. Your lawyers and my lawyers."

He sets his glass on the table. "And you decided

this when?"

"A little while ago." My voice is less steady now. "I missed her yesterday. And today. And last night. When I saw her again, I just knew." I hold the glass in my lap. "We're right for each other. She came to me for a reason."

Dell leans forward, his elbows on his knees. When he speaks again, his tone sends a chill through me. "She came to you because *I* brought her. Me. She is mine. She will remain mine until I decide that she is not."

My belly quakes a little but I won't let him intimidate me. "But you were so put out by her. She inconvenienced you."

"It's all settled now. Carrie is a great nanny. We have three days until the test results. Just leave it be."

The timbre of his voice rattles the crystals in a bowl on the coffee table.

But it doesn't rattle me.

"You should think of her future if she's not yours." And maybe even if she is, I think, but I don't dare say it. "I can care for her."

"You work full-time and you live alone." He barks this out like an accusation.

"So do you," I shoot back. "At least when I work, she'll be with me. I'll open a new baby room.

Make sure she has the best teacher in the city. She won't be stuck with a nanny."

"She won't have a father."

"I'll get married eventually." I assume. I haven't exactly had many prospects.

Dell stands up and walks to the huge windows looking out over the park.

I sit, gripping the glass. The air conditioner kicks on and I shiver in my tank top. Or maybe it's just the chill coming off Dell. I didn't think he'd put up this much of a fight.

"There is the issue of her mother," he says finally. "Once we know who she is, we can move forward."

There was that *we* again. My heart hammers. It sounds like he's including me in his plans.

I set the drink down and head over to stand beside him at the window. "Did you make any progress these past two days?"

"Not on the footage. She's like a ghost. She appears in the foyer, never comes out anywhere, and we never see her again."

I think for a minute. "So she comes up wearing one outfit, drops off the carriage, and then changes so she isn't recognized when she leaves."

"Or goes to work," he says. "I haven't ruled out that it was someone on staff."

"Has someone reviewed the employment records? Was anyone pregnant?"

"Only two maternity leaves, and both are happy moms showing their babies off on social media," he says. "With terrible privacy settings, I might add."

"Well, it could be that someone who works here dropped off a baby who belongs to someone else." This prospect excites me. We have abandonment. A case to adopt. I could get her!

"And that is almost impossible to follow up on," Dell says. "There are three hundred employees here. They each know dozens, if not hundreds, of people."

I see what he means. A rabbit hole. A wild goose chase.

"So what's next?" I ask.

"Wait for the test."

This makes sense. He seems calmer now, so I take the risk of touching his arm. His dress shirt is soft and well made, the muscle beneath it hard and unyielding. He continues looking out on the darkened park.

"So why did you come home so early?" I ask. He wasn't gone even two hours.

"Wasn't up for it," he says. "Too much going on at home."

"It wasn't that woman from the other day, was

it?" I ask. "The one who broke her shoe?"

He snorts. "No. Although she did visit me yesterday." He shakes his head. "That was unpleasant."

"Did she confront you about the baby?" I was worried about that.

"She did, actually."

"Well, what did she say?" My anger rises. I won't have some society tart tramping around talking about Grace!

"Just wanted to go out again. Said she'd keep quiet about the baby if I was seen with her again." He turns to me. "She kept going on and on about some group that wouldn't accept her."

I inhale sharply. "The list? The one you only get on if they are seen out with you?"

His eyes search mine as if seeking an answer there. "You know about this?"

Now I stutter. I only heard about it from Red Dress, when I stopped her from coming up to Dell. "I've heard."

"Don't tell me you want on it too."

"No!" I say, my voice shrill. "I barely know anything. It's just a silly rumor." I think fast. "You own the building. People talked about you when the deal first went through."

Dell sighs and turns back to the bar. "I sent her on her way. I'm not going to worry about it."

I stay by the window as he pulls a fresh glass and pours another drink. "Damn, this night was something," he says.

"You want to talk about it?" I don't really want to hear about some woman who didn't work out for him, but I want him to trust me. To feel like I'm the right person to take care of Grace.

He perches on the arm of the sofa. "It's nothing. Tell me how it went with our wayward daughter."

The phrase, and the way he says it, warms me to the core. I can almost imagine the impossible. Dell, me, and Grace, having a cozy evening. Spoon-feeding her baby cereal. Laughing as it dribbles out of her mouth. Dell and I kissing over the high chair.

"Arianna?"

I manage to recover. "She was great. She's a perfect baby. We played a little. Sang some songs. She got a bottle and went right to sleep."

Dell takes a sip. "You make it sound so easy."

"Well, I'm around a lot of babies," I say. "It's what I do."

"It is," he says. Then he tips his head to the side. "And why does Arianna Hart tend to babies?" he asks. "What in her upbringing led her to this profession?"

He scrutinizes me for a moment.

This sounds like an interview, and he told me it was an important skill, critical to success in anything.

So I treat it that way.

"I was raised by nannies," I say. "My parents wanted me to major in prelaw, but while I was at Brown, I just didn't feel called to that sort of work. I felt around a little, then just settled on a liberal arts degree."

He frowns at this. "Not business?"

I shake my head. "I would have had to totally regroup and start again to go that direction. It was easy just to build on my core classes and graduate."

"Grad school?"

"No, I had capital. A trust fund. When I graduated, I cashed it in and hired a financial manager to help me formulate a business plan for the child spa."

"Is it turning a profit?"

This makes me smile. "Since year two. It's easy if you charge as much as I do. I just had to impress parents with a facility like none other. They assume that if you can do that, you'll hire the proper help. In reality, it's the other way around. Spaces are easy. People are the real asset."

He raises his eyebrow at that. "So you trained them to be what you wanted."

"It's like you said. The interview tells you everything. Even if they botch it." I walk over to an armchair and sit down. "I don't look for the same qualities you do. But I can spot what I need."

"Fascinating." He stands up, considering this. "So it doesn't matter if they put on a good front when you bring them in. You care more about their interior lives. Their motives, not their ability to impress."

"Something like that," I say. I turn to watch him walk around the room, looking at his own walls and fireplace and art as if he's never seen them before.

"All right," he says. "I think we can form a partnership on this. I provide the stability and proper upbringing for Grace, and you do the nurturing."

My heart beats in my throat. "So you think I can adopt her?"

He turns suddenly. "I don't know about that. We should wait on Monday before discussing legalities."

Right. The DNA test.

"Are you saying there is a different plan if she's yours than if she's not? Because I'm here either way."

"Just for the paperwork," he says. His eyes fall back on my chest, lingering. "Need a refill?"

My heart races for a different reason now. Dell is

acting differently. Like we're on the same level. I'm no longer just a babysitter.

And he finds that really hot.

But I'm not so sure anymore. If I can get Grace, maybe I should hold back from Dell. I can't be a drunk hookup.

"Actually, I'm good," I say. "Should I check on her? I can just sleep on the bed in her room. The other one is Carrie's now."

But he's closed in already. "I can think of a better place for you to sleep."

Chapter 29: Dell

This woman is way more than I bargained for. Damn smart. Crazy sexy. Owner of the world's most perfect breasts.

I'm done talking about business. And babies.

I couldn't get away from Meredith fast enough. I kept fumbling, making it obvious my mind was elsewhere.

And now I'm here.

Arianna plucks at her shirt. She has to know what it's doing to me. Each perfect globe is punctuated by a sharply delineated nipple. I could take it in my mouth through the flimsy fabric.

I plan to.

She hesitates after my line about where to sleep, her eyes big and round. She looks incredibly innocent, like she isn't twenty-seven and surely intimately acquainted with what I'm after.

I give her no time to think of some way to say

no. My mouth is on hers, and it's as sweet and yielding as I remember.

Desire blasts through me like a flash fire. It's fueled by all the images of her that played through my head at dinner, culminating in me just walking out. Meredith stayed behind, cozying up to some hedge fund investor as soon as she sensed I had cooled.

Fine by me.

My palm presses against the back of Arianna's head, fingers working their way into the funny twist of her hair. It loosens easily, and soon her curls cascade down.

I touch them, soft and wild. I want to touch all of her, taste her, worship her.

I walk her back to the sofa, my arm around her waist. Then we're down, her lying beneath me.

The position is too tempting. I'm raging for her, my tongue teasing the inside of her mouth, my cock pressed against her soft thighs. But she's dressed. Jeans. Shirt. Bra.

I thread my fingers through a strap. Expertly, I drag one side down her arm, then the other. I reach beneath her and find the hook. In one swift movement, I've pulled it free, dragging it from under her shirt.

She gasps against my mouth, but I don't release

her. I won't stop tasting her until I've moved to the next part of her body to savor.

My hand slides up her shirt, greedy to touch what I've recently freed. Her nipple beneath the thin stretchy fabric of her shirt is hard and pebbled. I roll it between my fingers.

Arianna lets out a whimpering groan and lifts her hips to mine. I grind against her. Yes, she knows where this is headed. At last.

My mouth moves down her jaw, her neck, her shoulder. Over the tank top, my breath is hot. My teeth find that wayward nipple and I take it in my mouth. The fabric is nothing, heating up with my breath.

Her hands are in my hair, her body moving rhythmically beneath mine. She's so ready. So ready.

I shift my face up to near her ear. "Shall we retire to my room?"

Her eyes meet mine, and I see uncertainty there. I slip my hand along her body, cupping her breast, then down to the strip of belly exposed above her jeans. When my fingers come in contact with her skin, she draws in a quaking breath.

Finally, she nods. I shift away, standing, and take her hand to help her up. We've just passed the front door when we hear it.

Cries.

"Oh! Grace!" Arianna says. She rushes past me to the nursery.

I follow her, cursing the situation. I need a night nanny so I can seduce the babysitter.

Nanny. Friend. Whatever.

I run my hand through my hair with frustration. How are second children ever conceived?

Max is in the room, standing up. He looks at me with disapproving eyes, as if he knows what I'm thinking.

Arianna has the baby in her arms, up on her shoulder. She pats her back.

"Shh, shh, baby girl," she says. "You're okay. I'm here. I'm here."

Her breasts sway as she moves, and my mind struggles with competing feelings.

"I think it's gas again," she says. "It'll take some time for me to help her work it out."

Great. I nod and sit on the bed for a moment. Arianna eases into the chair, laying Grace across her thighs.

I can't watch. It's torture. Those breasts. Those thighs. I want to fling myself back on the bed.

"I'm going to change," I tell her. She nods, her eyes on the baby.

The hall feels ten miles long. When I arrive in my bedroom, I kick off my shoes and strip off my shirt. Shit. My raging hard-on won't go down. I have to peel the suit pants off over it.

I survey the tent in my boxers ruefully. "Give it up," I tell it. "You're screwed."

Or not screwed, as it were.

I don't even bother to pick up after myself, leaving tux parts strewn across the floor like a college kid after a kegger.

Nothing about this night has gone as planned.

Or this week.

I don't know if I should go help her, or let her do her thing. My boxers aren't exactly containing this one-eyed jack. I don't want to frighten the kid.

What the hell am I supposed to do?

I head into the bathroom and brush my teeth. I could go work out, I guess.

But I'm not up for it. I don't want to let this go.

I want her.

I pace around thinking about puppies and cemeteries, and puppies in cemeteries, until my boxers somewhat resemble a normal state.

Probably taking one look at her will send it off again.

When I make it back to Grace's room, she's

bending over the carriage.

Maximillion has settled back on the rug, head on his paws.

I stand next to her. Grace is asleep again, arms thrown out.

"Get it out?" I whisper. It's very strange to be discussing body functions of babies while trying to have sex with a woman.

"Not as well as I would like," she says, her forehead scrunched. "Her belly is hard."

"We should have gotten those drops," I say, feeling pretty pleased that I even know about them.

"We do. Carrie got them. I gave her some." She pats Grace's belly. The child's mouth pouts even in her sleep.

"Do we need to take her to urgent care?" I ask. "Call someone?" I won't stand for her feeling pain.

"It's a normal thing," Arianna says. "But we might try switching formulas. Some babies are sensitive to certain kinds."

My shoulders relax. That's an easy fix. "I'll send the shopper out tomorrow."

"I can do it," Arianna says. "It's a Saturday. I'm off. I'd like to look them over and decide."

I won't argue with that. I doubt my shopper knows much about the intricacies of baby formula and digestion.

"I should sleep in here," she says. "She might wake up again."

The boxers resume their normal shape entirely now.

"I'll stay with you."

She gives me a weak smile. "You should sleep," she says. "You need your six hours on the weekends, remember. It's already after midnight."

Damn, that woman has a good memory.

"All right," I say. "Just wake me if you need me. I'll leave my door open." Hopefully she gets all the opportunities that entails.

But her gaze is back on the baby. "Okay. We'll be here."

And with that, I let her be.

It's about as honorable as I get.

Chapter 30: Arianna

When I peer into Dell's bedroom door early Saturday morning, he's up and on his computer.

"Knock, knock," I say. I've dressed before coming down the hall, this time in a more respectable top, a flowing short-sleeved tunic in the same slate blue as my employees' smocks. I often wear it when we do events so that I both match and set myself apart from my staff.

He looks up, his hair playfully tousled, his chest bare. He wears more than last night, at least, a pair of running shorts pulled over the gray boxers that are seared in my memory after he appeared in them last night.

"Already been out?" I ask. As I get closer, I can see a sheen of sweat across his shoulders. I have to force myself to drag my eyes from it.

"Yes. I do some great thinking while running," he says. "I came in and started looking immediately."

I lean in beside him, assuming whatever it is will be no secret from me.

"My staff was able to confirm that twenty-three of the twenty-five potential mothers were not pregnant this year. Recent photos, news links."

"But not the last two," I say.

"Right. They've gone missing for almost a year."

"Do they show back up?" I ask.

"One does," he says. "And look at the before and after."

He pulls up two photos of a tall blond woman.

The first shows a bright, vibrant thirtysomething in stylish clothes, waving to a crowd from a red carpet. She's with an extremely handsome man.

"The Emmy Awards," he says. "Early last fall. She would have been about one month pregnant. Might not even know it yet."

His mouse hovers over the second image. Same woman, but completely different look. Tired, haggard, sad. Her hair shows dark roots. Her clothes are baggy. The caption says her name is Winnie Simmons.

"When is that one?" I ask.

"Two weeks ago."

"Wow," I say. "Something definitely happened."

"I've been reading," he says. "You can't get your hair dyed while you're pregnant."

"You're not supposed to," I say. "But people do. Generally, though, women who are planning to get pregnant will revert to their natural color."

"Exactly," he says. "She didn't plan it."

"Was she the sort of woman who would sacrifice her looks for a pregnancy?" I ask.

"Maybe," he says. "She was a kind woman. Thoughtful. We spent a week in Paris just before this. So the timing is good."

I look at the vibrant picture, jealousy slicing through me. So she got a whole week with him. In Paris, no less.

I think about last night and what I could have done differently. I could have gone to him. When Grace went back to sleep, there would have been time.

But I have a bigger purpose now. I want her. I want this baby.

I'm not going to throw that away if he decides to discard me and blow me off like that girl who lost her shoe.

"Where is she now?" I ask.

"Chicago," he says. "I've already got my pilot filing a flight plan."

"Wait, you're going?" I can't hide my shock. "I thought you were waiting on DNA."

"I was," he says. "But look at this." He pulls up another picture. It's the haggard version of the woman again, but this time, she's standing in front of a very well-known location. Radio City Music Hall.

I gasp. "She was here?"

"Four days ago," he says. "That puts her right here in town to leave Grace with me."

"But why the big secret?" I ask. "Why not just bring her over?"

He pushes back from the computer. "That's the million-dollar question."

"You think if you just confront her, she'll spill?"

He kicks off his running shoes. "I'm banking on it. When I show up with Grace, she'll know she's busted."

"You're taking Grace?"

He slides his running shorts down his legs. "Hell, yes. Carrie can take care of her on the trip."

There's a quick knock on the door. "Did I hear my name?"

"Come in," Dell says. "You may need to rush home to pack."

"Pack for what?" Carrie asks. She comes in, halting when she sees me. Then Dell, wearing nothing but gray boxers and socks. "Oh!"

"Arianna spent the night to help with Grace since

you couldn't. I'm taking the baby to Chicago."

"Today?" Carrie looks from Dell to me.

"Today," he says. "I can only really spare the time on a weekend."

Her eyebrows knit together. "And you want me to go?"

"Yes, that was the deal. Days and nights until Monday."

She frowns. "I didn't know we'd be traveling."

"It's a private plane," Dell says. "Easy and quick."

The color drains from her face. "I can't do that."

Dell pauses in the middle of pulling off his socks. I was wondering exactly how bare he was going to go with both of us in the room.

"Why not?"

Carrie twists her hands. "I'm...afraid of flying."

Dell stands, tossing his socks toward the closet. "And you were going to tell me this when?"

Carrie's face is contorted. "I didn't think it would come up! You'd travel. I'd stay with the baby."

He waves her off. "You'll just have to get over it. Take a Xanax or something."

Carrie looks panicked. "I'm working on it. But I can't just...go. Not with a baby too!" She gestures to me. "Take Arianna."

Now it's my turn to stand a little straighter.

"It's the weekend," Carrie says. "It will be a fun little trip for you!"

Dell turns to me. "You up for it?"

The last four days flash before my eyes. Grace. Dell. Shopping. Kissing. Bare chests.

But what else do I say? I want the time with Grace. "Of course."

"All right," Dell says. "Carrie, we'll let you know when we return. Probably late tomorrow night."

Carrie's relief is evident. "I'll be here the minute you call," she says. "Thank you."

"I'm going to shower," Dell says, dropping his boxers to the floor. He faces me. "Can you be packed and ready in an hour?"

"Uh…yes, sure." I'm surprised my mouth works at all. Dell is standing naked before both of us. He's glorious.

"Good. I'll be out shortly." He strides into his bathroom. After a moment, we hear the sounds of the shower.

Carrie and I turn to look at each other.

"Does he always do that?" Carrie asks. She's fanning herself with her hand.

"Not when I'm around," I say. Frankly, I'm relieved it's a first for her too.

"This might be a very interesting job," she says.

I turn back to the bathroom. I don't say it, but I think to myself, this could be a very interesting trip.

Chapter 31: Dell

When I get out of the shower, Carrie is watching the baby and Arianna has gone to pack.

This will be quite the journey. Me, Arianna, the baby. I have no idea how the confrontation with Winnie will go. I'm stunned by how she changed. At first I thought it was some trick of the tabloid. But image after image showed the dramatic transformation.

Did something that led her to give up the child cause it? Or just the act of relinquishing her?

I start to question the wisdom of taking the child to her. What if she wants her back? At least I have handled my end of the DNA. This could set up legal standing for me. Between her not informing me about the child's birth and the subsequent abandonment, I stand a good chance at full custody.

Winnie will have lawyers too, of course, and good ones. She is a Hollywood darling. She enjoys having public flings with the A-listers.

I was just a small side trip. Our week in Paris was actually partly for her to come in contact with an actor there. Perhaps the one she attended the Emmys with a week later.

I didn't follow up. I was in France to conduct business with the Duke of Attenbury, a grizzled beast of a man who had a wife he didn't deserve. She was considerably older than my usual tryst, almost fifty, and I didn't normally go near married women.

But something about her elegance intrigued me. She was shockingly naive about pleasure. I was happy to show her. As I told Arianna, I didn't have a type. The Duchess had already raised four children. The oldest was almost thirty. Older than Arianna.

Perhaps I should stick to post-reproductive-age women from now on. Surely would save me my current hassle.

Which led me to another line of thought. Birth control.

I am a strict condom user except in very specific circumstances. So in order for Grace to have come from me, I must have missed a failure on that front.

Of course I wasn't in the habit of checking them after the fact.

Bernard has already taken out my bags. They are

partially packed, and stacks of clothing are on the bed awaiting confirmation of my preferred state of dress for the trip. There are jeans and designer shirts, suits and jackets, and even, I notice with a smile, a few combinations of jeans and athletic shirts.

I pick those up, plus a few of the more casual of the dress shirts, and place them in the bag. Then I head down to the nursery to see how Carrie might be coming on packing Grace.

The two of them are on a blanket spread on the floor. Carrie is showing Grace how to hold up her head. Grace is paying her no mind, her head bobbing up and down until it thunks heavily.

"She getting it?" I ask.

Carrie glances up. "She hasn't done this a lot," she says. "Spent a lot of time on her back or being carried."

Grace starts to fuss, so Carrie rolls her over.

"What do you make of that?" I ask.

"Someone who doesn't know much about taking care of babies," Carrie says. "Either ignorant of it and without resources to find out. Or who just didn't care."

"Will she catch up?"

Carrie picks Grace up and lets her stand on her legs, much like Arianna did on the first day. "Oh, easily. She'll strengthen those neck muscles in a few weeks."

"Good." I roll up the sleeves to the dress shirt. "How is her tummy?"

"Aren't you the attentive father!" She helps Grace bounce up and down, making the baby laugh. "All good today. Activity like this helps. It could all boil down to the same thing, not enough of the right kind of movement. Her bowels could just be sluggish."

Well, all right, then. I nod at her briskly. "I'll leave you experts to it, then," I say.

"Bernard is looking for some bags to pack her things," Carrie says. "Just two days' worth?"

"Make it three just in case," I say. "But I expect to be back tomorrow."

Carrie nods, making silly faces at Grace. "Okay, Dada!" she says, as if she is speaking for the child. We never did correct her on this or explain the situation. No point doing it now.

The front door slams, so I know it isn't Bernard who closed it.

Arianna bursts into the room, looking flushed. "Okay, I'm here. Packed. I managed to race down to the store and pick up another type of formula."

She stops when she sees me. "Oh, hello, Dell."

"We're fine on time," I say to her. "Did Bernard get your bags?"

"Didn't see him," she says, patting her leather duffel. "This is all I brought."

"That's it?"

"Should I bring an evening gown?" Arianna juts out her hip just like that first day we met. She looks young and fresh in bright pink shorts and a light flowered peasant top. Between her beauty and her sass, I have to struggle to keep myself under wraps.

"We can pick one up if we need it," I say, then realize both Arianna and Carrie are staring at me. "There are shops in Chicago."

"I'm the nanny," Arianna says, bending down and scooping up Grace. "We stay home while the crazy people party, don't we?" She blows air on the baby's neck, causing Grace to laugh like mad.

She's right. She's there for the baby, although the urge to see her in something decadent and glittery is strong.

"Here's the new formula." Arianna digs a canister from her duffel. "It should get us through."

I leave Carrie and Arianna to their duties and head to the living room to brief Bernard.

After a moment, Carrie and Arianna bang down the hall with the baby and all their bags. Bernard rushes forward to help them. Arianna has Grace tucked back inside a purple wrap.

"Should we bring the stroller?" I ask. "The car seat?"

"Definitely the car seat," Arianna says. "We'll drive somewhere once we're there."

"It's in the car," Bernard says.

"She'll need some bottles made up," Carrie says. "I'll go do it."

Bernard looks stricken that someone else will be in his kitchen, but he is laden with all the bags.

"Here, Bernard," I say. "I'll take care of these. See to the bottles."

He nods and leaves them at my feet. I shake my head. Four people to take care of a baby and still we can't get it done.

Chapter 32: Arianna

I really truly have no idea what to expect from this trip.

The plane is luxurious, gray and black with red bits just like Dell's living room. Four heavy loungers surround a circular table. A long sofa lines the side wall. There's crystal and glass and a huge flat-screen television. For some reason I picture it all shattering in a rough landing.

Maybe I just expect this whole plan to crash and burn.

Grace's car seat is strapped to a chair. The vibration of the plane has lulled her to sleep.

Dell works from a laptop at the table. I've stretched out on the sofa, fretting that I've brought all the wrong clothes. I was so caught up in looking the part of the kind, involved mother that I didn't even think about what would happen if we were forced to drag Grace to a fancy dinner. Or had to track down this Winnie person at a gala or the opera.

Too late now. Like Dell said, I can always shop.

But everything is harder with a baby. We can't exactly lug her baby bucket to a theater, or plunk it down at a five-hundred-dollar-per-plate fund-raiser. I picture trying on dresses with her crying at my feet.

Arrgh! Why did I agree to do this?

I roll on my side, watching Dell work. He's both professional and laid back in jeans and a button-down shirt with the sleeves rolled up. He's very intent on whatever he's reviewing. I can stare at him without him noticing a thing.

His profile is striking, and his eyebrows make his expression seem like he is always brooding. Unless he smiles. Which is rare. But when he does, it's like the sun rising. You can't help but smile back.

His hair is perfectly cut, clean over his ears. A bit more sideburn than you might expect. The top of his hair falls in a perfect wave over his head. He doesn't seem like he'd be fussy or use a lot of product. I'm thinking he just has the very best hair stylist who created a cut that suited his hair exactly.

That's what Dell would do.

I look around the airplane. Like his house, everything is perfect and in its place. I'm surprised he didn't have Bernard come along, but maybe that's their agreement. Bernard belongs to the penthouse.

I should sleep. There is no telling what Grace will be like, sleeping in hotels, going new places. She might be fussier, harder to settle. This might be the only rest I really get.

Eventually the rumbling of the plane gets me too, as I wake up when a young woman shakes my arm. "Time to buckle in for landing," she says.

I nod and sit up. I have a light blanket over me and a pillow under my head. "Thank you," I tell her.

Dell is standing near the front wall, a phone to his ear. I wonder how he gets a signal up here. It must be satellite or something. I check my phone and realize he has wireless Internet access for the plane. Of course he does.

The young woman takes the pillow and blanket away as I move to the seat beside Grace to strap in. She approaches Dell, but he waves her off and nods.

His voice is just a murmur, but I can catch a few words. "Try to make sure she doesn't leave." And "Half an hour at most."

I wonder if he means Winnie. Nerves flutter through my belly as I think about confronting her. I search for her on my phone and pull up several pictures, comparing them to Grace. The coloring is right. But Grace is just too little to show any likeness.

Dell sits in the lounger across from me and fastens his buckle. "Winnie is home right now," he says. "I spoke to a mutual friend who was able to contact her."

"Are you going to let her know you're on the way?" I ask.

"No. If she's the mother, she won't let me in. I don't know what she'll do."

He looks over at Grace.

When the landing gear comes down, she startles awake. Her eyes are wide, and her face moves side to side in a panic.

"You're okay," I say. "I'm here. Dell too."

She fixes on my face a moment, and I think she'll stay calm. Then she opens her mouth and wails.

"Should I take her out?" I ask. "We're about to land."

"I don't know. I guess moms on regular airlines just hold their babies in their laps."

That's true. I lean over and pop the harness. Grace comes to me eagerly, settling down as soon as I cradle her. I check her diaper. A little wet, but nothing major.

"You think she'll need a bottle before landing?" Dell asks.

"We'll be fine," I say. "It can wait."

"We'll be on the tarmac a few minutes before we're cleared."

"We can give it to her then." I jiggle Grace on my lap, pleased at how Dell and I problem-solve together. He could just ignore us, or care little for how the baby is faring. But he pays attention. He wants her happy.

He's already got many of the fathers from my child spa beat.

The next half hour is a bit of a rush. Landing. Getting a bottle. Loading into a car to drive across the airfield to the main road. I've ridden in private planes before, but Dell has every part of the journey planned to the minute.

When we're in the back of a black Mercedes, Grace strapped into her seat between us, I finally ask him, "Do you know what you're going to say?"

"Not a clue," he says. "It will take all my self-control not to throttle her."

"It might not be her," I say. "You can't assume anything going in."

He sighs. "I know. It just all lines up. The timing. The travel."

"Did she ever say anything about not wanting children?" I ask.

"It didn't exactly come up."

"And…" I don't know how to put this delicately.

"No protection?"

"Of course I did. I always do. It must have broken or malfunctioned."

"Was it hot there? Maybe it degraded?"

"There is no point speculating on that point. If any of this is true, we have to assume that there was a mishap." His tone is curt.

"All right," I say. "So how is this going to go? We walk up to her house and ring the doorbell. Hold up the baby and say, 'Remember her?'"

He glances over at me. "We should have gotten you some sort of nanny uniform," he says. "You look too much like a pretty girlfriend."

My heart stutters at that. "Is that bad?"

"Winnie is the jealous type," he says. "Not that she has any claim to me. But she just doesn't like to be confronted with competition."

"But you guys were only together for a week!"

"I'm just explaining her to you."

"Maybe I shouldn't go in."

He looks down at Grace. "No, if there is a confrontation, or a difficulty, I want you to be able to get Grace out of there. Even if I need to stay and handle it."

"How will I know that you want me to do that?" I picture the woman collapsing in tears, or coming after us with a fireplace poker. My stomach flips.

"It'll be obvious," he says. "The driver will be out with the car should you need to escape whatever transpires."

When we slow before a giant iron fence, I realize we won't be ringing any doorbell, and this woman won't be answering her own door.

We approach the gate. Dell leans forward to speak to the driver.

"There should be a pot of flowers on the seat. When you ring her, hold them up and say it is a delivery."

Huh. He's thought this through.

"Will do," the man says. He wears a flat-topped cap and has a bushy mustache. His accent is thick. India, I think. He catches me looking at him in the rearview mirror and smiles.

The window goes down and he presses a button. The flowers are bright white with red accents. Easy to see on a video.

"Hello?" It's a man's voice.

"Flower delivery," the driver says. He shows them.

There's a pause. "Come on through," the voice says.

The big gates open.

"Wow, it's just as easy as it is in the movies," I say. "What's the point of having a gate if anyone can fake their way in?"

"I happen to know Winnie's weakness," Dell says. "She can't resist flowers. And you never know when some are coming. It's not like pizza or a plumber, which you call yourself."

All true.

The driver sets the flowers down and we cruise up a steep incline to the front of the house. It's enormous and sprawling, surrounded with rockwork and strange, angular trees.

"Should I leave her in the bucket?" I ask.

"No, let's take her out," Dell says. "I don't want Winnie to see her until the right moment."

"Isn't her butler or whatever just going to answer? We won't see her."

"I can talk my way in once we're there," Dell says. "And if it's flowers, she might come."

The old Winnie might have come, I think, but I don't say that to Dell. The new Winnie, after whatever she's gone through, might not be so willing.

We pull in front of the door.

"Well, here goes nothing," I say, unbuckling Grace.

"I'll carry the flowers," Dell says. "You stay to

the side with your back to me."

"How will I know when to turn around?" I ask.

"You'll know."

I'm not so sure, but I pull Grace out of the car seat. The driver has opened my door. He holds the flowers.

Dell comes around and takes them. We walk up to the tall double doors.

My heart thuds. I don't know what I want to have happen. It to be her. Not her. Nobody home. I'm not sure!

Dell rings the doorbell. He has the flowers in front of his face.

The door opens. A man's voice. "Thank you," he says.

Then Dell. "Actually, I'm not a delivery man. I'm a friend of Winnie. Can I give them to her myself? She's been out of pocket lately."

There's a pause. I want to turn around terribly.

"Let me check with her," the man says. "What is your name?"

"Dell Brant."

"Come inside."

What now? Should I go in? How do I keep my back to them?

"This is my nanny," Dell says. "Come along,

Arianna."

Okay, so I do go in.

I turn. The man is dark-skinned and tall. Puerto Rican. I place his accent now.

I keep my head down and follow them inside. There's a huge foyer with tall round walls. Three doorways lead off from it.

We're ushered to the right. Inside is a parlor with an African theme. Tall plants. Black and tan pillows on rich brown furniture.

"Wait here a moment," the man says.

When he's gone, Dell and I survey the room.

"You go over there by the window," he says, pointing behind a black baby-grand piano. "Just be looking out and listen."

"Okay," I say. "I'll try to keep her quiet."

Grace is absorbed in looking at all the contrasting patterns in the room. I take her over to the window. She seems content to stare out.

I don't remember the last time I felt this anxious.

The clack of shoes on tile heralds the woman's arrival. I stay turned away.

Dell greets her. "Winnie, how lovely to see you! I brought your favorite."

"Dell Brant," she says. "What a strange surprise. They are beautiful."

A few more steps, then quiet again.

"How have you been?" she asks. "God, I haven't heard from you in what — a year?"

Either she's an actress or it's not her. I'm anxious to hear how Dell handles her.

"I bought a new place in Manhattan," he says smoothly. "Had to buy the building so they couldn't kick me out as riffraff."

Her laughter is deep. "I doubt there are many willing to call you that to your face."

They go on reminiscing about France, and my arms grow heavy. I don't think it's her. She's too easygoing, too light. I want to turn around. They must be facing away for her not to notice me.

Grace makes a funny gurgle.

"Oh!" the woman says. "You brought someone!"

"Yes, sorry," Dell says. "It's my nanny. Arianna? This is Winnie."

He was right. I do know when to turn around.

I take a deep breath and face them.

"Oh, look at that sweet baby!" Winnie says.

She looks better than her pictures, her blond hair recolored. Her outfit flows around her, looking stylized rather than sloppy. She stands and walks over in tall clunky heels.

"Who is this sweet thing?" she asks, bending

down to get close to Grace. The baby reaches out to grab her nose.

She turns to Dell. "Did you finally knock up the wrong girl?"

I look up and meet his gaze. His lips are pressed together. "A family situation," he says. "We were traveling in Chicago, and thought we'd stop by. Seemed you'd disappeared for a while and I wanted to ensure myself of your good health in person."

He walks over to us and wraps an arm around her shoulders.

"Well, I did have a bit of a tough year," she says. "Lymphoma."

"I'm sorry to hear it," Dell says.

"Well, thankfully the new chemo lets you keep your hair." She flips a bit of it with her hand. "But the rest of me looks a bit used up. And the steroids did their number." She presses her hand against her belly.

"You look ravishing," Dell says. "And I'm pleased you've beat the bastard."

Winnie laughs again. "Well, thank you for the flowers. And the visit." She smacks him on the back. "But call ahead next time, you hear? We can make an afternoon of it."

She walks Dell to the door. She never even greeted me herself, only the baby. Typical. I'm relegated to the servant treatment.

I'm glad she's not Grace's mother.

As we load up into the car, I try to let it all go. Grace fusses as I buckle her in, so I take out a single-serve packet of formula and make a quick room-temperature bottle.

"What now?" I ask Dell. I wonder if we'll just fly back tonight and this will be the end.

"We regroup," he says. "There is still one more of the twenty-five to consider." He swipes his phone. "You got a passport?"

Chapter 33: Dell

"Passport?" Her voice is high-pitched. "Why would I need a passport?"

The Mercedes pulls away from Winnie's house.

"She got me thinking," I say. "She disappeared and it didn't hit the tabloids until she resurfaced. Anyone could do that. A year is long enough to have a child and have no one notice."

"Okay," she says. "I guess you are thinking about number twenty-five?"

"I didn't consider her before because of her age. But I suppose anything is possible."

Arianna looks down at Grace. "How old is she?"

"Her fiftieth-birthday celebration is this weekend." I don't mention that number twenty-five is actually a Duchess with a very terrible husband.

"When is the party?"

"Tomorrow night. We should arrive in Paris around nine a.m. their time. That gives us enough time to get you a dress and drive out to their estate."

"Dell," she says. "This is outrageous. We can't fly to France. Why not wait on the DNA?"

I know she's talking common sense, and I can't put my finger exactly on why this is important. Because of the party? Or the husband?

"It is extremely difficult to get anywhere near this couple," I tell her. "I only met them before due to a business transaction that led to an invitation to their castle."

"Castle?" she squeaks. "Couple? She's married?"

I've said too much. A decade of high-stakes business has helped me not a whit when it comes to holding my cards with her.

"I recognize that this constitutes a black mark on my character," I say.

She holds up a hand. "Your character is already coal to me. But the husband. Won't he kill you? Does he know?"

"I highly doubt it," I say. "He had two of his mistresses at the dinner table. The Duchess is a lovely woman. Kind. Gentle. Deserving of so much better."

She snorts. "Right. Black-hearted you."

"Deserved," I say. "But the point is, she also represents the 'almost' in my 'almost always' use of birth control."

Now Arianna's eyes go huge. "You didn't protect herself with her?"

I don't know how to explain this. How the Duchess and I had a connection. That she held up beautifully in the face of her husband's flaunting of the young women he was bedding right there in their home.

She was so lovely. And innocent, in her way. She'd had no lover other than her husband, and knew very little of all the pleasure to be had.

For three days we ran amok in their castle while he drank with his business partners and showed off the girls he kept dressed like harlots.

She thought herself far past childbearing years. Going bareback was a treat for me, a gift she could give to me.

But now, I had to wonder.

"I did not," I say. Best to keep it simple. "She thought herself past the point of risk and had not had any sort of relationship for many years."

Arianna's face falls at that. I think she can picture it.

"It's probably safe to say, however, that I overstayed my welcome at the time and would not be welcomed back."

"But you were invited to the party," she says.

This is the next scary part. "I'm not exactly invited," I say.

"What!" Arianna exclaims. "How are we going to get in?"

"Same way I got to Winnie," I say.

"On good looks and luck?" she demands.

"It's gotten me this far."

She sits back against the seat, her eyes staring up at the ceiling.

"Look, I can go alone," I say. "Maybe dragging the baby there isn't a good idea."

But she turns to me. "Actually, no, it's a great idea. The Duke may have disliked a man he suspected was wooing his wife, but he probably won't feel any threat by a married man with a baby."

She has a point. "So you're getting upgraded from babysitter?"

Arianna reaches across the car seat to bop me on the shoulder. "Nanny."

"Hero," I say. "You are nothing short of a beautiful, smart, lifesaving hero."

"I *would* look good in a Wonder Woman costume," she says.

And I can't even answer, with the images going through my head after that.

Chapter 34: Arianna

Dell's plane can't make international flights, so we have to book an overnighter on a commercial airline. It's apparently not easy on such short notice. He decides to use his plane to fly to any airport with seats.

We end up in Philadelphia.

Grace is holding up well. When we're finally in a row on the commercial plane, Grace asleep between us, I decide it's time to plan.

"So we need to have a real strategy this time," I say. "You might be able to woo a former lover with flowers, but if I'm picturing this right, some huge party with limos and valets and a security detail with a guest list, you can't just waltz in there."

"Especially with a baby," he says.

He's right on that. We need a nanny for the nanny.

"How big is this castle?" I ask. "How many

bedrooms?"

"I didn't exactly count them," he says. "But maybe twenty."

"So probably some of the guests are staying with them?"

"I would assume so. It's really out in the country. It will be an hour's drive to the nearest inn."

This makes me laugh. I picture us in a coach going to the ball. "So let's go early. Before the security detail is checking a list. When families with their nannies would still be arriving to stay with them and prepare for the party."

Dell nods. "I like this plan. Then we can catch the Duchess without being surrounded by a million people."

"But we can use the chaos to help us get in," I continue.

"All right," he says, leaning back against the headrest. "We're in business. I guess this will be our only objective, so we'll just get another overnight flight back after the party."

I look down at Grace. "That will be awfully hard on her," I say. "We can stay one night."

He glances over at me. "But you'll miss work Monday."

"It's fine. It's more about you having to wait

another day on the DNA."

His gaze moves down to Grace, asleep in her bucket. "If we're right on this, the test won't matter. We'll already know."

A wave of affection passes over me for both Dell and the baby. They're both caught up in this craziness.

"I still think you should get a dress for the party," he says.

"In case we can't find her before it starts?" I ask.

"So I can see how beautiful you look." His eyes are on me. I remember our interrupted night, how I had agreed to go to his bedroom.

But that was before. Now I want Grace as my own.

It's so risky to let myself fall for him. He'll just leave me, and that will make me an ex, rather than the woman who has always cared for his daughter.

It's hard for me to say this, but I do. "I'm guessing you probably mix business and pleasure all the time," I tell him. "But I don't." I turn my gaze to Grace. "She's more important than all the rest of us put together."

I can't look at him. I just keep my eyes on the baby. As long as I do that, I'll be able to resist Dell Brant in all his glorious smolder.

He doesn't answer. The flight attendants pass

through, offering drinks and magazines. They fuss over Grace, say how beautiful she is, how sweet.

I organize her things around me so I can help her the moment she wakes up. Bottles with water. Formula to mix. Pacifiers. Clean diapers. Wipes. I'll take care of her, no matter how this turns out.

The night grows late and black. Dell sleeps, his arm curled over the canopy of the car seat. I long to take his hand in mine, but instead examine every finger, each perfect nail. I remember his touch, the passion in his kiss. It's no wonder that women swoon for him right and left.

I wish I had the luxury to do that. I've never felt so much yearning for it. All my notions that held me apart from all the boys I'd known as a teen and young woman seem silly now.

This is the real deal. Family. Faithfulness. Love.

I just can't get it all in the same package with Dell. He wants his wine, women, and song.

But I'll take the next best thing. The baby is all the benefit without any of the hurt.

Grace stirs and yawns. I pick up the bottle of water and the formula, ready to mix in a hurry.

But she settles back in. I poke her diaper to make sure it isn't too puffy. I don't want a big leak job in her car seat on a transatlantic fight.

All is well.

I'm tired. Bone tired, actually. My head leans against the side of the seat. I'll just sleep a little.

Just a tiny bit.

Chapter 35: Dell

A bump on the flight wakes Arianna, and she instantly reaches for Grace.

When she sees the car seat is empty, she sits up, frantic, looking around.

"Hey," I say. "She's fine."

I push down the folding canopy of the bucket seat, revealing Grace, lying in my lap.

"She got bored after her bottle," I say. "We've been discussing global economics."

Grace waves her arms. Arianna glances around, realizing the bottle and formula pack in her lap are gone.

"You fed her? Did she cry? I didn't wake up," she says.

"I caught her before she ramped up." I lift the screen over the window. "We're almost to dry land."

She leans over to peer out. I can smell her floral shampoo, subtle and light. It's been a difficulty, watching her sleep so close to me, knowing she has chosen to hold herself apart. I'm not used to failing at a conquest, but then, I've never had to try with an infant in tow.

"How much longer?" she asks.

I free a hand from under the baby and power up the screen on the back of the seat in front of us. After a few moments, an image of a map and plane with a little dotted line appears. We're almost at the end of it.

"Less than an hour," I tell her.

She glances down at her clothes and tries to smooth a wrinkle in her shirt. "Where are we going to put ourselves together before heading to the estate?" she asks.

"We have a hotel in Paris," I say. "We'll find suitable clothes there, repack, and take a car to the castle."

"Sounds good." She seems relieved. "We'll have to hustle."

The sun is just a small ball, half hidden by the horizon. "It's barely dawn here. We have all morning."

She reaches over for Grace and squeezes her little hand. "If only you could tell us, little one," she says. "Is this your first time in France, or are we back to the place where you were born?"

Her question gets to me. We don't know. She may have made a flight just like this less than a week ago. Maybe she jets all over the world. She has no way to communicate that to us.

Grace turns to the sound of Arianna's voice, her eyes seeking. I lift her a little, so she can get a good look. When Grace sees her, her tiny mouth breaks out in a beauteous smile.

Arianna's eyes tear up. The baby's fingers clasp one of hers.

It's one of those moments people talk about. The bond between a parent and a child. Commercials make you relive it. Greeting cards extoll it. It's the gold standard of feel-good movies.

And now, I get it.

Arianna looks up to me, overcome. A rush of emotion courses through me. It's like the world manipulated its own events to bring us to this moment. This gaze. This connection.

I'm starting to wonder if when the time comes, I will be able to let either of them go.

Chapter 36: Arianna

The hotel is one of the best in the world, near the end of the Champs-Élysées.

"I've never stayed here," I tell Dell. "Even my father wasn't at this level."

This pleases him. I can see it in his subdued smile. The valet opens our car door as the doorman rolls a cart. We wouldn't have had much except for Grace. Between her bags and car seat and accompanying accessories, we don't look like this trip was unplanned.

There is no check-in for us here. Apparently Dell is well known. We are whisked up a side elevator and directed to a suite.

When the door opens, I have to catch my breath.

"It's stunning," I tell Dell.

The entire suite is decked in gold and white. A breeze enters through the open windows, stirring diaphanous curtains.

"I always feel a certain peace, just walking in here," he says.

"I get it," I say. "I feel it too."

Grace starts to wail.

"The baby, not so much," I add, laughing.

Dell sets the bucket on the sofa and I unlatch her. "Come on, sugarplum," I say. "Let's get your diaper changed."

Our bags are already in the bedroom.

That's when I realize, there is only one bedroom.

I glance around. I guess it doesn't matter. We're not staying here. At least I don't think we are. I got the impression it was a long drive to the castle.

A castle. I slide a fresh diaper under Grace. "You really are going to be a princess!" I tell her.

Then stop.

Actually, if she is the daughter of a Duchess, what does that make her?

I have no idea.

I hear unfamiliar voices in the other room. I quickly fix Grace up and head back. Two men are there with a rolling rack covered in black vinyl.

"There she is!" one says. He's tall and thin, with skinny jeans rolled up at the ankle.

"She is soooo divine," the other adds. He's shorter but just as lean, hair pulled back in a ponytail.

I think they are talking about Grace, but then they both circle me.

"Red?" Ponytail asks.

"God, no, she's too innocent," the tall one says.

"Cool blue," the first counters.

"Possibly."

"We could go for broke," the other says.

They stop each other and say simultaneously, "White."

They scurry to the rack and unzip the cover. Beneath are at least two dozen gowns and several suits.

The tall guy removes a black tux and smacks it against Dell's chest. "Here you go," he says, not giving Dell even a passing glance.

"Paul-Simon, lay it on me," Ponytail says.

"On it," the tall man, apparently Paul-Simon, responds. He pulls a long white gown from the rack. It's stunning, sheer on top with beadwork that is sparse, then gets thicker until it forms a solid middle and falls in a sheath with a terrific slit up the leg so I can walk.

"So you," Paul-Simon says.

"So innocent, yet so seductive," Ponytail says.

Paul-Simon turns to Dell. "Take the baby."

Ponytail leans down to finally acknowledge

Grace. "Aren't you a lovely baby girlie whirlie poo?"

Dell steps forward to take her. "Arianna, these pushy bastards are Paul-Simon and Michel. They usually take great care of me."

"Today, we could not care less," Paul-Simon says. "You have brought us a woman."

"You know, he has dated a few," I tell them.

Michel slaps his knee. "Oh, I love her. Love. Her."

"So real," Paul-Simon says. "Just so so real."

"Now let's see it on you!" Michel says, pushing me toward the bedroom. He turns back to Paul-Simon. "Please say you brought shoes. Spikes. Size six."

"I did," Paul-Simon says.

I fear they are going to make me strip in front of them, but Michel lays the dress on the bed. "No bra," he says. "Support is built in." Then he assesses me. "Although these sisters are on fire!" He stares at my boobs. "How much support do you have now?" He approaches, feeling for the bra straps on my shoulders.

"That's it? You have natural flotation," he says. "Heavenly. You'll be fine. Unzip, slide up from the bottom, and call me to snuggle you in."

He leaves the room, ponytail swinging.

Whew.

Okay.

I strip out of my clothes and pick up the dress. It weighs a ton with all the beads. After a struggle, I get it unzipped.

I unhook my bra and drop it to the bed.

The dress shimmers with every movement as I open it wide and step my feet in. I lift it up. The top is thin and sheer, and it takes a moment for me to fit my arms through tiny sleeves in the fragile fabric. When I have it in place, I move to the door.

The dress is far too long and I have to work not to trip. I peek into the living room and say, "Ready."

The two men are clucking over Grace. Dell has her turned out in his arms to face them.

"Yes!" Michel says. "Let me zip you."

He comes into the room. "Oh, look at that cleavage. Nobody is going to stop staring at your girls."

I glance down. Holy moly. That's a lot of boob action.

Michel comes behind me. "I'm just going to give these a little bit of lift." He reaches inside the dress and slides his hand around to the front. "Just a little boop!" he says, pushing my breast from beneath. "And now the other! Boop!"

I have to laugh. His rearrangement is about as impersonal as getting an exam at the ob-gyn.

Then the sound of a zipper. The dress seals around me like Saran Wrap.

"Come see," Michel says, gesturing to a triple-paned mirror in the corner of the room.

I step toward it. The dress is stunning. I see what he means about innocent and seductive. It's like a trick of the light. At first glance it is all opaque. But then you see a shadow. You stare a moment and realize you're seeing full cleavage, breasts pushed high and on display.

For a boob man like Dell, this is going to kill him.

"I love it," I say.

He hurries to the door. "Shoes! Shoes!"

Paul-Simon comes in and squeals when he sees me. "Divine! Like an angel walking!" He kneels before me and holds out a crystal-encrusted stiletto.

I slip my foot in. It's not comfortable. Stilettos never are. But it fits. When both are on, the hem of the dress just grazes the floor.

"Perfection," Michel says. "We are in the presence of transcendence."

"Okay, guys," I say. "That's enough."

"It will never be enough," Paul-Simon says, all serious. "There will never be a more perfect dress for a woman."

"Now get it off her before the lowly man-bear sees it," Michel says.

"He can't see? It's not like it's a wedding dress," I say.

"Uggh," Paul-Simon says. "Do not speak to us of such trivialities. We are outfitting you for something so much more important."

"A birthday party?" I say.

"The celebration of a Duchess," Michel says. "At the Castle Attenbury."

"Way better than a wedding," Paul-Simon says. "Those just end in misery and broken dreams."

"But royalty is forever," Michel says. "And you will outshine them all."

I kick off the shoes. "Thank you for finding it for me." I hadn't had a personal shopper since I left home. And Paul-Simon and Michel were way more fun than the stuffy women my mother arranged for me.

"Delighted," Michel says. "Please post pictures."

"Especially ones the tabloids will steal," Paul-Simon says. "Feel free to tag us."

Crazy boys. Michel unzips the gown. The two of them discreetly head out while I change.

I decide to take this moment to go ahead and

shower and prepare for this trip. It's nice to know I have a dress in case we do stay for the party.

When I come out, fresh in a sundress and hair that is temporarily blow-dried into submission, the men are gone.

Dell stands by the windows, holding Grace. She is half-asleep, her eyes heavy.

"I can take her now," I say. "You can get ready to go."

"I guess we did spend all night on a plane," he says. He passes Grace to me and runs a hand through his hair. "I'll be quick."

Two new garment bags hang near the front door. His suit and my dress, I presume.

I walk along the windows with Grace. "Too bad we don't get to stay here longer," I say to her. "It's very beautiful."

She's in her "This princess will save you" onesie, which doesn't seem very appropriate for a castle. Or maybe it is.

Still, I pull out the sweet yellow dress Dell bought for her. "Let's pretty you up," I say.

Her eyes are even heavier as I change her. By the time she's all buttoned up, she's out.

Dell emerges from the bedroom, his hair wet and shiny. "We should go," he says. "It's a two-hour drive and we want to be well ahead of the party."

He calls downstairs and the porter arrives to move out all the things we just brought up. Within minutes, we are in the backseat again, Grace between us.

It takes over half an hour just to clear Paris, then we're driving through the country. I sit back. I've been working nonstop for six years, afraid to leave my new business for even a day.

And now I'm in France.

"Have you been here since last year?" I ask him.

He shakes his head no. "I got caught up in the rat race." He stares out the window. I wonder if he's thinking of his time here a year ago. Winnie, then the Duchess. I didn't peg Dell as being sentimental.

We stop for lunch at a small cafe in a tiny town en route. The proprietor, a stout woman with red cheeks, plays peekaboo with Grace, fluttering a white cloth over the baby seat and pulling it away.

As we grow closer to the castle, I start to feel anxiety. Is it possible to get arrested for trespassing in France? Are there separate laws for nobility?

My shoulders tense up. I feel like I do when I have to face an angry family who discovers that they aren't going to get into my child spa after all, that their child has aged out before ever finding a spot.

I let out a long breath, trying to calm myself. It will be okay. This is Dell's issue, not mine.

Can she take the baby? Will she see Grace and decide she can't live without her after all?

"Ready for this?" Dell asks.

I nod. In the distance, I can see a large structure sitting on a hill. Land stretches out around it. It's like a city to itself.

"Is that it?" I ask.

"Yes," he says. "They don't live here year-round, just summer. I understand it's impossible to keep warm in the winter."

He banters on about the layout, the seasons, and how most of the people in the area work seasonally at the castle. The Duke likes to create an air of historic aristocracy, and actually holds an annual ball.

That word makes me snap to him. "This isn't a ball, is it?"

"No, just a party. But there will be music and dancing. Balls are very structured, so I hear."

"Have you been to one?"

"No," he says. "I'm not exactly high on the Duke's list of favorites."

"Does he know about the Duchess?"

"No," Dell says quickly. "And I'm pretty sure he'd shoot me, or have someone shoot me, if he did."

Fear blossoms through me. "Then why are we going there?" I glance down at Grace. "With proof of what you did?"

"He won't know. I just want answers. For her."

Our eyes clash. I settle down a notch, but I feel grossly out of my element here. I don't take risks. I've had a safety net beneath me my whole life. Wealth. Privilege.

Now I am walking a tightrope over a ravine.

Dell reaches across the baby seat to squeeze my arm. "This will be fine. We are all civilized people." He reaches in his pocket. "That reminds me."

He has a small velvet pouch in his hand. He opens the drawstring and drops an enormous diamond solitaire ring into his palm.

He looks at it a moment, watching the light twinkle through it. Then he holds it out to me. "You're my wife, remember?"

I'm speechless as I reach for it. Instead of passing it to me, though, he holds my hand with both of his and slips it on my finger. "Until death by a Duke's shotgun we do part," he says.

"Not funny," I say, but I do laugh.

I look at my hand. The ring is gorgeous, round and as wide as my finger. "It's a very nice fake," I say.

"Not a fake," he says.

"You just have five-carat diamond rings lying around?" My hand feels heavy with it on.

"I had a jeweler send along a selection to the hotel in Paris," he says. "I chose one while you were showering."

"Oh," I say. "Will you return it when we go back?"

He shrugs. "I'll keep it as an investment, perhaps."

It's hard to pull my eyes from it. I see why newly engaged girls take pictures for social media. It's such a beautiful thing. Wearing a ring like this makes you feel like a princess.

The road meanders as it approaches the castle grounds. Dell releases me and I lay my hand inside the baby seat next to Grace. I have to be strong, at least for her. This is her legacy, her story that we're unfolding.

We won't let it be just about her abandonment. We want to know the truth.

The driver takes us through the opening in the low stone wall that runs around the entire structure. I half expect to see a moat and a drawbridge, but there is simply a circle drive. There are a few cars already lining it, glossy paint jobs, impressive emblems. Ahead of us, a catering truck makes the circle and is directed by a man dressed in white to a small road that goes around the side.

"This is it," Dell tells the driver. "Park close. If you see us come out, pick us up immediately."

The man nods.

A valet approaches and opens my door. I step out.

He asks us something in French. It's been years since I took any of it, and I stare at him blankly.

"Americans," he says, switching to English. "Are you guests of the castle for tonight?"

"Yes," I say. Dell is removing Grace from her seat.

"Do you have bags?"

I glance at Dell. If we have to leave quickly, we can't lose all of Grace's things!

"Let us get settled first," Dell says. "We have some concerns that the baby will disturb others. We may go somewhere else."

Good call, I think. I'm relieved he's thought some of this through.

"Very well," the man says. "Come with me and I will take you to greet the Duke."

I want to cry, "No!" but Dell just nods at the man and takes my arm. Grace is cradled in his elbow.

My nerves are a wreck as we walk up the steps to

the main doors. I have no idea what is going to happen.

"Please let me know how to announce you to the Duke," he says.

"The Captain and Mistress of the Berry River," Dell says with flourish. "From Manhattan," he adds when the valet snaps his head around.

I try to contain my giggle. At least he wasn't Cap'n Crunch.

"Very well," the man says.

We enter a monstrous room with a soaring ceiling, incredible stone stairs leading up on either side. Beyond is another unbelievably large room. The ballroom, I assume. It could be nothing else. Tables are being set up inside.

The valet leads us to the right, down a corridor.

The ceiling is still impossibly high, and each doorway towers over my head.

We pause before a set of open double doors. I get a small peek inside as the valet motions for us to stay and steps forward.

"The Captain of the Berry River and his Mistress, of Manhattan," the man says.

Now we're both trying not to laugh. Grace waves her arms, excited by our barely contained mirth.

"What in the world?" a voice calls.

"Let's hope his wife is with him," Dell whispers. "Lock in on her expression."

But when we step through, there are only three men.

One, a burly man with a bushy beard, is staring at the door. "Are you shitting me?" he says.

His gaze locks on Dell, then his eyes go cold. "You were not invited," he says. "Leave before I have you thrown out."

"Philippe, how is that for a greeting? We may have deals to manage in the future." Dell steps forward, extending his hand.

"You are to address him as the Duke," one of the other men says. "And you are unwelcome here, Dell Brant."

I shiver. It's like we've stepped into medieval times. And not the hokey restaurant.

Grace doesn't like the sound of these voices, and puckers up and cries.

"When did you acquire a child?" the Duke asks, glancing at me. "Ah, I see. Well, go on, then. Children are not permitted at tonight's festivities."

The valet takes my arm to lead me out, and the two men with the Duke step forward to make sure Dell follows.

"Might we have a word with the Duchess before

we go?" Dell asks. "To wish her a happy fiftieth? We did fly all the way from New York."

The Duke hesitates. "She's seeing to the party. I'll send your regards." He waves us on. "Now please go before you make a scene on her day."

By the time we've reached the hall, two more men are standing outside to escort us. The Duke must have somehow alerted security.

The sun blasts down on us as we are ushered down the steps. The two men and the valet wait at the top, ensuring we actually leave.

"Well, that was a bust," I say as the driver comes around.

"It was," Dell says. "We'll go to the inn and regroup."

The drive back through the countryside is pretty, but long. Grace is fussy, still unsettled by the loud angry voices. I pat her leg and continuously place a pacifier in her mouth since I can't pick her up.

We arrive at the inn, a small rambling place with only forty rooms. Quite a number of the guests are clearly attending the party, as the women are already fussing with elaborate hairdos that don't match their casual outfits, and everyone seems to be on edge.

"Thank you for finding a room for us," Dell tells the woman at the desk. "It looks quite busy here."

"One of the busiest weekends of the year," she says. "For the party of the Duchess."

"I heard," he says. "Our driver can manage our bags."

"Oh good," she says. "There are a lot of people here who are used to being waited on. Our poor porters are really having a time of it."

"Well, don't worry about us," he says.

"It'll be quiet here in a few hours," she adds. "The entire place will be off to the party."

Dell accepts an old-fashioned key. He looks at it, amused. "Been a long time since I've had something other than a key card," he says.

"We like to retain some Old World charm," she says. "But you'll find a large safe in your closet you can program for your valuables."

He looks at the key again. "Thanks."

The elevator looks like it was built before elevators were invented, so we take the stairs to the third floor.

Once we're settled, I collapse back on the bed. "Well, we didn't get shot," I say.

Dell sets the baby seat beside me. "I see you had a high bar for success."

I laugh. "I didn't know what to think."

He pulls Grace out of her seat and sets her on his

lap. "Well, baby, I guess we'll never know if you were the daughter of a Duchess."

I roll over to move close to them. "It doesn't matter. She's a princess to us."

Chapter 37: Dell

The inn starts to empty out at dusk. Arianna and I watch them head out, car by car, from a porch swing at the front of the building.

"Look at the dresses," Arianna says. "Look at the hair!" She seems stunned by all the elegance and beauty walking by. She has no idea she has them all beat.

"I didn't even get to see the gown Paul-Simon and Michel chose for you," I say.

Arianna feeds Grace her last bottle of the evening. She's been sleeping better, long stretches of six hours. Even on the plane she only woke once.

"Well, she's out," Arianna says, setting the bottle between us.

"No sailor burp?" I ask.

"She's doing better on this formula," she says. "I'll pat her a little but try not to wake her."

Another problem solved. I assume others will

arise. This teething thing everyone talks about. It sounds abominable. Walking. Falling. Nursery school. Her first boyfriend.

I'll kill him. Murder him with my bare hands if he so much as touches her.

"What's got you so worked up?" Arianna asks. She gestures to my balled-up fists.

"Nothing," I say. "I arranged for dinner in our room. Might as well make it a nice night since we're missing the big soirée."

"That sounds wonderful," she says. "I feel like we've been on the run for days."

She hesitates, then asks, "So if the Duke doesn't know about you and the Duchess, why did he kick you out?"

"He wanted me to buy a business he had plunged into fatal debt. I refused."

"So just business?"

"Just business."

A young woman with a white apron steps out. "Your dinner is in your room when you are ready," she says.

We stand up. "Thank you," I tell her.

I take the baby from Grace. We head up the back stairs.

The room looks magical, just as I asked. White

lights are strung throughout it. The window is open wide to the approaching night, the breeze blowing the curtains. A table is set nearby, two chairs and candles.

"I thought this might be the best we can do since we're miles from anywhere and have a baby," I say.

Arianna turns to me. Her sundress whirls in pale yellow. It makes her look like a goddess. The curls she meticulously straightened at the hotel in Paris this morning have fought back and won, framing her face with tendrils.

"It's beautiful!" she says, slipping into a chair. "Oh!"

I set the baby in her bucket on a small sofa in the corner of the room. It's definitely no suite, with little space for walking around. But it's not an impersonal hotel either. The walls have blue and gold wallpaper. The frame around the window is hand carved.

Women like these details, I know. Especially someone like Arianna. She appreciates everything. I want to give her things that make her feel that joy.

I pour each of us a glass of wine.

Arianna's face is awash with happiness. "This is the best night I've had in a while," she says. "Everything looks perfect." She picks up her knife and fork. "And I'm starving!"

I am too, but not in the way that she means. The

candlelight kisses her skin, accentuating her cheekbones, catching highlights in her hair.

The shadows are deep across her collarbone, down in that cleavage of the sundress.

But she's gotten determined to keep herself away. I should respect that. I *will* respect that.

I drag my attention to the food. Prime rib. Roasted potatoes. A salad made of just avocado and tomatoes. It's all delicious. The food. The company. The view.

There is a harmony here with Arianna, the baby sleeping in her little bucket, her tummy free from the pains she once felt. I'm content. It's unfamiliar. Suspect. After chasing dreams all these years, why would I feel it now? I haven't acquired any tricky new company. No new start-up I have purchased has gone public.

And yet. I feel it. A release of that ache I felt after leaving Alabama. That need that drove me to get out of there, away from cleaning up after dirty grounds at greyhound races.

Away from my father. His constant reminders that I would come to nothing, be nothing, do nothing.

"Hey," Arianna says. "You okay?"

I adjust my expression. Obviously my boardroom face is not fooling her tonight.

"I'm fine. How is the food?"

"Swoonworthy," she says. "I just want this moment to freeze. I could stay right here for at least a year."

"And let your child spa run itself?" I tease.

She laughs. "They can handle it. They're good people and I have plenty of them."

"You could probably increase profits if you cut back on your staff," I say. "Sounds like you might have a few more than you need."

She stabs the air in front of my face with her fork. "No. No. No. My spa is not about profits. Sure, I want to support myself, but I don't want anyone who works for me to feel like they don't have time to nurture the children in their care. They can't be overburdened. I won't let them burn out. I take care of them. They take care of the babies."

"All right," I say. "So what made you choose this model over the capitalist one?"

She stabs a bit of avocado and twirls it on the plate. "I wasn't nurtured. My power parents left me to be raised by nannies."

"Were they horrible caregivers?"

"Some were. Some were good. It was hit or miss, and I don't want that for these children. My spa is expensive to hit the right demographic. And I have amazing staff so I can keep their lives from being like mine."

"But your day care ends at kindergarten, right?"

She frowns. "Yes."

"So then they have to make their own way."

Her shoulders droop a little. "They do."

"So why not expand? See them all the way to adulthood. Elementary. High school. The whole experience."

"It's tricky," she says. "There's accreditation. There's space. I can't expand easily. Real estate is rare and expensive. I have to be in the right location to reach the right parents, but then I'm locked into spaces that are too small."

"Surely Manhattan isn't the only place where rich kids get neglected. Expand somewhere else. Try your model where space isn't an issue, and work on the other pieces. Accreditation. Reputation. The business model."

Her eyes flash. "It's a big dream."

"All dreams should be so big," he says.

She tilts her head. "What about your dreams? What made Dell become a cutthroat investor and collector of start-ups?"

I take a sip of wine. "I don't talk about my past. But I do like where I am now. I can go for any opportunity I see. Airlines. Professional sports teams. Entertainment conglomerates." I lean forward. "If I want it, I can get it."

She sits back, eyeing me curiously. "What does Dell the human need?"

I'm done tiptoeing around this particular issue. I set down my glass and eye her steadily, piercingly.

"What I need right now is you."

Chapter 38: Arianna

My fork stills. I have known that Dell wanted to add me to his conquests.

At first, I wanted it too. But then I wasn't sure. Now, he's got me locked in his gaze and I'm certain I can resist.

My eyes travel over to the bed, only a few feet away.

And there's only one bed. I'm so tempted.

I set down the utensil and take another drink of wine. After another intense few seconds, Dell releases me from his attention and resumes his meal.

"You know," he says after a moment, "it's a shame I didn't get to see that dress."

I sigh with relief that he's changed the subject.

"It is very beautiful," I tell him. "I'm not sure I'll have any occasion to wear it back home." I don't add that I'm never invited to charity galas anymore, not since I started my own business and broke the trust-fund mold.

Dell looks around, gesturing at the room. "Why can't this be your occasion?"

The room is dazzling, classic, beautifully appointed, and softly aglow with the strings of light. A flash of boldness streaks through me. "All right," I say, setting my napkin on the table. "But only if you wear the tux."

"Fair enough," he says. "You take the bathroom and I'll change out here."

My heart hammers as I cross the room to the garment bag hanging by the door.

I can't believe I'm doing this. But Dell asked. And it *is* a shame I can't wear the dress to anything fancy.

Phony baloney, I tell myself as I close the door to the bathroom. I'm going back on everything I decided two nights ago. To adopt Grace. Be a mom.

But, the devil on my other shoulder argues, why can't I be a mom and a lover?

I stare at myself in the mirror. *Arianna, you're crazy.*

Stop. Just get dressed.

My curls are back. So much for my elaborate blowout this morning. I wet my fingers and smash them down. They spring back within seconds, like that's their superpower.

I tug the sundress over my head. I have a strapless bra beneath it, and I strip that away, rubbing at the marks on my skin. The new dress has support built in, so Michel said. Doesn't matter. The way the sheer part dips in the front, the beadwork creating a pattern that exposes me down the middle, there is no bra that would work.

I kick off my shoes. At first I think I'm screwed. Without the stilettos I'll trip all over myself walking back to the room.

Then I see them, sparkling at the base of the bag. Paul-Simon and Michel thought of everything.

I look at my underwear. They are plain cotton, pale yellow. Not a match at all.

I frown at them. I probably have some silkier ones in my bag. Out there.

Not going to help me in here.

Shoot.

I don't know what Dell is going to see. But I can't handle the dowdy panties beneath this kill-them-dead dress. So I slip them off and fold them inside the sundress.

Now, I'm naked.

I hear Dell moving around the room. I wonder about his state of dress. I guess guys don't ever worry about their underwear matching their outfit. Double standard.

I remember him in the gray boxers, and then him taking them off right in front of both me and Carrie. My cheeks get hot. I wouldn't mind seeing that again.

Would I?

Dell's attitude felt like a seduction, but then, we weren't exactly moving to sexytimes. We were getting dressed.

And there is the issue of a baby in the room. She could wake up at any time.

I can't worry about these things. I said I would put on the dress, so I'll put on the dress.

The gown slides off the hanger. I catch it with my arm, still astonished at how heavy it is.

One of the folds catches on the back of my hand, and I realize I'm still wearing the diamond solitaire Dell gave me in the car. His "investment" ring. No use taking it off now. It suits the dress.

I step into the gown and shimmy it up over my hips. This might be a lot harder without Michel to help. I slide my arms through the sheer top. My boobs don't look anything like they did before.

I reach inside through the neckline and push up on them, like Michel had. Now they press in the right spot. The support lifts.

Now for the zipper.

I reach low and manage to get it partway up my back. Then I reach from above, but I can't quite snag it. Dang it. How can I make an entrance if I can't get in the dress?

I turn my back to the mirror so I can see how far I have to go.

It's still an entire hand's width away. Dang it.

I crack the door open an inch. "I can't get the zipper, but I don't want you to see the dress!" I say.

Dell is near the bed in pants and a partially buttoned shirt. His grin is infectious as he approaches the door. "How about you just put your back to the door and I promise not to peek at more than I have to?"

"Okay," I say. I face away.

I feel a tug and hear a little zip, and then the dress is completely closed.

"Thank you!" I say.

"Anytime," Dell responds. "And I do mean *any* time."

I laugh a little as I close the door. Dang, that man is charming. Would he really be a total ass the day after? I mean, he spent a week with Winnie, and they talked to each other just fine.

I think about seven full days in Dell's arms, and I

feel lightheaded. And the Duchess, devouring him in every one of those bedrooms.

Surprisingly, I don't feel jealousy. I'm the one who is here now. Maybe this night could turn into a week. Maybe a month. Maybe there is something different here. Maybe it can last.

Maybe I've had too much wine.

I turn back to the mirror. God, this dress. I know where Dell's eyes will go first. The cleavage. Then the roundness of my breasts. This gown is perfect for a boob man. Then my waist, which looks like an hourglass.

"Not bad," I whisper to the mirror. "Not bad at all."

I fuss with my hair a few more minutes, trying to make it into something more than a mass of curls. But without a straightener or gel or conditioning spray, I'm pretty much as is. Finally I just let it go. His eyes aren't going to go above the neckline anyway.

I crack the door. "You ready?" I ask.

"I was born ready," he says.

Oh, Dell. I almost trip when I remember the shoes. I duck back inside and slide them on my feet. Now I'm really ready.

I push the door open and step out, imagining I'm a model on a runway, as if that could ever happen to a frumpy riot-haired practically thirty-year-old like me.

Dell turns, then freezes, then his mouth opens, then closes.

Finally, he speaks. "Arianna, it's…"

And apparently words fail him again.

"It's your thing, isn't it?" I ask. I cup both of my breasts and push them even more tightly together than the dress does. "Look what it does to my boobs!"

Dell stutters a bit more. I stop examining my crazy cleavage and look up at him. He seems paralyzed or something.

"Are you okay?"

He forces himself to recover. "I am. I am." He grabs his lapel in both hands and tugs, as if pulling himself together. "That dress is, like, I don't know, maybe…"

"Divine?" I offer, quoting Paul-Simon and Michel. "Transcendent?"

Dell nods. "I never want to see you wear anything else again. Ever."

"Might be hard to do my job in these," I say. I move my leg to show the shoes, revealing the slit up to my thigh.

"Oh, that's…" he falters again. "Yes. Shoes. Very tall."

I draw my leg back. "Are you sure you're all right, Dell?" He's always been so smooth. I can't imagine he's been rendered speechless by a dress.

"Yes," he says. "I'm fine. Some music?"

"Dancing?" I ask. "Like at a ball?"

"Why not?" he says, picking up his phone from the table. "We'll keep it low for Grace."

I glance over at the baby seat. Grace is still very much asleep.

A slow jazz number begins. Dell holds out his hand. "May I have this dance?"

"I'm not sure you were added to my dance card," I say. "Is your family born of nobility?"

"Not a blue blood among us," Dell says. "Only rakes and scoundrels."

I pretend to tear up a piece of paper. "Well, then, seduce me, O rake and scoundrel." I step closer and Dell takes me into his arms.

His mouth moves close to my ear. "I plan to."

My body shivers. His hand is warm and strong, holding mine. His other hand is low on my back, his fingers trailing down. Everything tingles. The roots of my hair. My cheek, so near his. My hip, which connects with his when we step. My feet, slipping across the hardwood floor in time with his.

And everything in between.

It's like I'm waking up from an extraordinarily long slumber. I remember, now, his kiss on the weight bench. I felt the same way. Like Sleeping Beauty must have. Awake. Really, truly awake for the first time in one hundred years.

There isn't much room for dancing, so we shift back and forth across the small space. Each point of contact sets me on fire. I can't believe I feel this way. I can't believe such an intensity for another person exists.

Suddenly it all makes sense. Trysts. Suicide pacts. Till death do us part. Who wouldn't want to feel like this?

One song ends and the next seamlessly begins. Still we move.

"You have no idea how much I want you right now," Dell says.

"I feel the same," I say.

"You had reservations before."

"I don't now."

In the moment, there is no room for doubt. His body, his need, his desire consumes me. He dances us closer to the bed. "I would like to revise my former statement," he says against my ear.

"What is that?" I can barely get the words out, I'm so overcome.

"I don't want you to wear this all the time."

"No?"

I feel air on my back. He's unzipped the gown.

"I want to see you without it."

His arms slide down mine, and I realize the dress is going with it. He lets go of my wrists, and the gown puddles to the floor.

I'm naked beneath it. Only the stilettos remain.

"My God," he breathes, extending my arms, looking at me, every inch.

He kneels before me in the tux, the suit I haven't even had a chance to compliment him on. His hands wrap around my ankles, thumbs bumping over the fragile bones.

They slide up my shins, his fingers surrounding my calves.

Then up to my knees.

My breath catches as his touch slips across my thighs. He grazes the space between them lightly then passes on by, skimming my hips and reaching behind to cup both soft round cheeks.

"Exquisite," he says, lingering a moment. His face is near my belly button. I can feel his word against my skin.

As he stands, his hands move with him, up and around to my breasts.

He exhales, his thumbs tracing the circles that surround my nipples. He's reverent, like he's holding a chalice.

Then he towers above me, his hands on my jaw and the back of my hair, and he kisses my mouth, hungry, urgent, devouring.

I fall into him, tasting his lips, wine and spices and vinaigrette. His tongue explores me like it did that night on his sofa. Only I'm naked now, the breeze from the window brushing against my skin. Everything is heightened.

His hands clutch at my skull, fingers tangled in my hair. He kisses me as though there are no kisses left in the world, and we must hang on to this one.

My tender nipples brush against his suit, and I'm overwhelmed by my vulnerability and his control over me. But I want it. I want to lose sight of everything I thought before. I just want to be taken and feel all of it without worrying about boundaries and consequences and tomorrows.

This is worth it.

His arm slides beneath my knees and I'm in his arms. He sets me on the bed. He hasn't broken the kiss.

When I'm lying there, he releases me and reaches for the stilettos. He takes off one, then the other.

He unbuckles, unsnaps, unzips. The suit jacket drifts down, then the pants. I hear the thud of shoes.

He strips away the tie and the shirt. Now it's just the boxers like before, though these are light blue, fitted, hugging the erection that is perfectly delineated by the fabric.

I look up at his face. He kneels on the bed and bends down. "Now I will do it all again with my mouth."

His lips caress mine for a moment. Then he trails them down my jaw and across my shoulders.

He pauses by the swell of my breast. Both hands take me in his palms, lifting the soft mounds. His tongue circles wide, then closes in until the nipple slides into his mouth.

Sparks fly from my body. I can't contain the feeling. Heat rises from low in my belly. I want him down there. I want him everywhere.

But Dell takes his time, first with one, then the other. I'm left panting, wanting him to go lower, needing more. Frenzied.

He grazes my ribs, dipping his tongue into my belly button. His hands move to my thighs, and when he slides my knees apart, I'm eager to comply.

He hovers, his breath hot against those tender places. My need pulses there, like a heartbeat, like life itself.

When his tongue slips between my folds, I lurch up to him. I want it hard, grinding, endless. Dell senses my need and spreads me wide with his fingers, delving so deeply I cry out.

"Shhh," he reminds me. Yes. Grace. I cover my mouth with my arm.

Dell returns to his touching, his licking, sucking against me. No one has ever done this to me, never, and I'm overcome. And coming. It's nothing like what I've experienced by myself. I can't predict what he'll do, what will happen next.

The urgency builds on itself, like a top that's being wound up. It's unlike anything I've ever known. I sink my teeth into my arm, my other hand grasping the bedcovers. It's so intense, so much, so hard to manage, demanding and insistent.

It peaks. It holds there. I'm on the brink, hovering, waiting to fall.

Then it all just lets go.

I feel like a star has exploded. A bright flash, an internal combustion, then the showering trickle of light.

I drop my arm to the bed. Dell is still there, his fingers massaging me, his tongue gentle now.

I'm lost. I'm wrung out. After a moment, he

moves upward, his hand on my cheek. "Doing all right?" he asks.

I nod.

He lies beside me, an arm thrown over his forehead.

I'm not sure what that means. Is that all he wanted?

"Dell?" I lean up on one elbow to look down at him.

"You didn't wake Grace," he says. "Impressive."

I lay my head on his shoulder. Maybe he doesn't want me after all. Maybe after seeing me, he figured he'd get me off and be done.

A tear slips out of my eye and slides across his chest.

He lifts his head. "You okay?"

I don't know what to say. That he just completely turned me inside out and now I can't handle that this is it?

So I don't say anything at all.

Chapter 39: Dell

Damn. I don't know what to do here.

She's crying on my chest and I'm not sure why. She seemed to enjoy it. Watching her orgasm was like a high for me. She really turned herself over to my care. Totally let go. That doesn't happen often with women who are more concerned about what they will get for an exchange than just falling into it.

But I saw the deal when I was down there. Or felt it, rather.

She's a virgin. Totally intact. So intact she couldn't have shoved so much as a finger vibrator up there.

It's a lot to grapple with.

"Hey," I say. "I'm more than happy to do that again. You tell me when you're ready."

But this makes things worse. She sobs a little and hits my chest.

Oh boy. Okay.

I try to think my way around this. I'm so hot for her my cock could reach the goddamn moon. But she works downstairs. She knows the nanny.

She loves Grace.

She's a damn virgin.

It all makes sense now. Why she held back. Why she wasn't willing to trade a fling with me for a future with the baby.

Thing is, I believe her now. And I'm on board.

My dick, not so much. But I control it. It doesn't control me.

"Arianna?" I say. "Come here."

She's already in my arms, but I lift her higher so her head is tucked against my neck.

"I thought you wanted to do this," she says. She's trying to sound normal, but the quavering in her voice gives her away.

"I do," I say. "I can't even tell you how much I do. I'd rather shoot off my damn dick than not do it."

I can feel her expression shift, even though I can't see her face. "Then why?"

I could tell her the easy answer. That she's a virgin. That if she's saved it this long, she should just hold out for Mr. Right, not Mr. Asshole.

But she deserves more of an answer than that. And I don't even know where to begin.

"Is it because I'm not like your society women?" she asks. "I have no idea what I'm doing?"

"No," I say quickly. "That's just fun and games for them. You're just…different."

"Different bad or different good?" she asks.

"Different perfect," I say.

She's quiet for a minute and I think we've gotten past it. My cock hasn't, still standing at perfect attention. In the hazy light of the strings overhead, I can see every delectable inch of her. And that part of my brain is directly wired to the part that wants to slam into her.

But it won't.

"Is it because I know about Birmingham?" she asks.

Now I get still. "What do you know?" Has she hired her own investigator? Have I missed something? God damn it. I never should have left the purge to those incompetent fools.

"Of course," she says. "I saw the shirt. And Max is from there. And the clock."

My jaw tenses. That damn clock. I was a sentimental jerk to keep it. Shit. Shit. Shit. The name on it would tell her everything. Obviously it has.

Because otherwise, Hasmund McDonald just disappears at age twenty-three.

Yeah, Hasmund. Thanks, Mom and Pop. They gave me a name so rare anyone could find me by Googling my first name alone.

She'd find dozens of pictures of me and the dogs at the racetrack. I was the photogs' favorite kennel mucker, big cheesy-ass smile, Raggedy Ann freckles, and Alfalfa cowlick. Right as the Internet kicked into gear.

"I guess you're curious about how a guy goes from cleaning dog kennels to Fortune 500 companies," I say.

This startles her. I can feel it ripple through her body. "You used to clean dog kennels?"

I clamp my jaw. I don't know anything anymore. What she knows. Doesn't know. What she's after. Blackmail to get Grace?

"Dell, hey," she says. "You're going completely tense."

She sits up and looks at me. "I think it's amazing that you built your empire from nothing. That's a hell of a lot more impressive than cashing in a trust fund."

I force myself to relax. This is Arianna. The crusader who wants to save every rich child from a lonely childhood. She wouldn't blackmail anybody.

"Tell me," she says gently. "Who is Barclay McDonald?"

The idea that someone would know, that I could talk about the ghosts from my past, is inviting. It's been forever since I've spoken any of their names. Some of them were good people.

"He was my grandfather," I say.

"Oh!" she sits up more. Her breasts sway before my face and I feel momentarily lost with the need to feel them again. "As in the grandfather with your grandmother Grace?"

I drag my view from her breasts to her face. "Yes. It is."

"Oh, tell me about her!"

I drag my gaze from her chest again. "My father's mother. She was a typical housewife. She kept me when I was little. Loved me to the moon and back."

"So your grandfather made clocks?"

"He did. They never had a lot of money. It wasn't exactly a booming business. But they got by."

"The clock in your room is amazing."

"Yes, he made a few of his own. If I could go back, I would have advised him to go upscale and serve the interior designer market, but back then all I knew were greyhounds."

"You said you had greyhounds before Max. You had them as a kid, then?" Her face is full of excitement. She's enjoying hearing my story.

It all just tumbles out, like a great purge.

"My parents worked at the Birmingham Racetrack. Dad helped in concessions. Mom cleaned. I generally mucked the area where they let the dogs relieve themselves when they were out of their kennels."

"A productive job for a boy."

She's being kind.

"It was a shit job."

She laughs. "It is. I didn't have a job. In fact, I've never had a job with a boss."

"Be glad," I say. "It's nothing but misery."

"So how did you work your way up from poop to hot shit?" she says.

I tug on her ear. "Not funny."

"Is too," she says.

The moment earlier seems to be forgotten. At least for now.

"What I really wanted to be was a lead-out," I say.

"A what?"

"The lead-out is usually a teenaged boy who leads the dogs out on the track and into the starting box."

"Wouldn't the trainer do that?" she asks.

"Too low a job for them," I say. "But perfect for a young strong boy who is great with the dogs."

"I take it you never got to be a lead-out," she says.

"No. Those jobs kept going to rich kids whose fathers were in racing or owned dogs. Even though I was perfect for it. Even though I would have done it for free."

"I can see how that would motivate you." She tilts her head. "I looked you up pretty thoroughly when you bought my building," she says. "I was worried about redevelopment and having my business evicted. I never saw anything about dog racing."

"You won't," I say. "I had it all purged."

"You purged the Internet?"

"No, just anything connected to me." I hesitate. "I changed my name."

Now she sits all the way up. "Get out of town! What did it used to be?"

I don't think I'm going to give that up. "Let's just say that Dell Brant suited my brand better than Old McDonald."

"Tell me your old first name," she says. "Or I will tickle you."

She throws her leg over me, her fingers running up and down my sides. "Tell Arianna!"

I'm not the least bit ticklish, but the sight of her naked body straddling mine is way more than I can handle. "Okay, okay!" I say. "Hasmund."

She stills. "What?"

"Hasmund."

"Spell that."

"I'm not going to spell it!"

She looks thoughtful. "Is that even a name?"

"Not that I know of."

"Huh."

Her warm, wet body parts are against my belly, her breasts hovering over my face. I can't take it.

"Arianna," I say, "I have to move you, or I'm not going to be able to control myself whatsoever."

She flattens her palms against my chest, as if she can stop me from shifting her away. "Why is that?" she asks. "Why do you need control? I'm right here. Totally naked. I've said yes."

Her throat bobs. She's going to get upset again.

"You haven't done this before," I say. "And I've got too many feelings about you to just take something that precious."

She moves her arms to cross in front of her chest, as if she's suddenly shy. "How did you know that?"

"I felt it. That is one intact hymen you have there."

Her lips press together. "I had some pretty

screwed-up ideas about sex and love," she says. "I don't know. There's just all these husbands at my spa, fathers even, and they are all just looking for their next poke. I wanted something more."

"So you chose me."

She opens her mouth to say something, then closes it again.

"Arianna," I say. "Are you sure?"

She melts a little, the stiffness in her body starting to give a little. "Yes," she says. "A thousand million times yes."

I grasp her waist and lift her off me. "Then it will just have to be a thousand million times worth it."

Chapter 40: Arianna

Dell shifts me on my back. Now that we've settled this matter — again — I'm nervous. It's time to just do this.

He peels off his boxers. I can see him now, and not the way he was before the shower with Carrie in the room.

He's monstrous. It comes at me like it has a mind of its own.

"Um, birth control," I say. "Unless Grace needs a sibling, like now."

He laughs. "Got it." He pads over to his bag.

"You brought condoms?" I ask. "Did you plan this?"

He tears open a square package. "Think about it. I always plan this."

Okay, true.

He leans down to kiss my mouth. I relax into it, thinking about all the other kisses. The wake-up. The sofa. And earlier tonight, as we began.

I like them all. But this one has so much more to say. "I'll take care of you." And "I'll be careful."

His hand moves down my body, touching, cupping, massaging. He reaches between my legs again. I don't think his fingers will match the skill of his mouth, but I'm wrong. His thumb finds a spot and whoa, I'm soaring again, that familiar need winding up.

The room swirls around me, like I'm drunk. But it's just him, Dell, and the magic of his fingers. Soon I'm breathing hard, and I want to spread for him again. I want to feel that starburst a second time.

He shifts over me, the weight of him solid. I feel him, but don't overthink it, caught up in the shower of sensation of his hand.

"Talk to me if I should adjust," he says, and I just nod because I don't want him to change a thing.

But suddenly there's pressure added in, and I clutch his back. I'm caught between the pleasure of his hand, and the thick filling of him inside me. There's a sharp pain, like a hard pinch, and I gasp.

He pauses. "You okay?"

I nod. Now it all mixes together. Pain and arousal. Discomfort and bliss.

Dell starts to move over me. I love the slide of

his body across mine. His fingers continue their pattern, pushing me higher. Slowly, the ache fades out, and I'm left with him, shifting above me, and his hand, slow and careful.

"I'm good," I tell him. "It's good now."

His finger moves more swiftly and I can scarcely breathe. The star is getting brighter and fuller and I'm so ready for it to burst.

The sensations are even more overwhelming than the first time, with the combination of his muscles working over mine, his hand, plus the fullness inside me.

"Come for me, Arianna," he says. "Come for me right now."

His words split me open just as the light bursts. I hear him groaning, his thrusts more fervent, and the pleasure just goes on and on. It's not just a single explosion, but a continuum, like the end of a fireworks display. Shower after shower after shower.

Finally, they settle. I gasp for breath, trying to hold on to the feeling, not wanting it to end.

But something new spreads through me. A flood of peace, contentment, quiet joy.

"Holy shit," I say. "Is it always like this?"

Dell laughs, low and throaty. "No."

"Different worse or different better?"

"Different perfect."

He slides away for a moment and my body shivers. Then he's back, pulling back the covers, sliding me beneath them.

I'm wrapped up with him, his arms tight around my shoulders, across my chest.

"Do you always sleep with them afterward?" I ask. I can't help it.

"No," he says again.

"Do you ever?"

"Arianna, let's sleep."

"Can we do it again in the morning?"

This makes him laugh. "We can do it as many times as you want."

He falls asleep quickly, but I feel like I have coffee in my veins. Why didn't I do this before? I clutch his arm. He's amazing. He's perfect.

I look up at the lights strung over my head and think, this is a wonder. If there is no other night with Dell, if this is it, I will not regret it. It was magical. France. The food. The lights. The room. Even the baby.

And Dell. Dell. Dell. Dell.

It's probably the endorphins, but I'm totally in love with Hasmund McDonald.

Chapter 41: Dell

Arianna gets her wish in the wee hours of the morning. I get up and feed the baby, change her, and settle her back to sleep around five. I kill the lights too, to make sure they don't keep her up.

Then I start kissing the sleeping form in my bed.

I start with her knees, nibbling at the edges. Then up her thighs. She sighs and adjusts, parting them for me.

I thought so.

I slip a finger inside her. She's still incredibly slick and wet.

"Hey, beautiful," I say in her ear.

She stirs a little, and I caress her sweet clit, that perfect nub that was a cinch to find. I add a second finger, and now she moans. She's coming awake.

My mouth lowers to hers. She murmurs a little, then her hand comes around to the back of my neck.

I move over her. The condom is already in place,

as I'm not wasting any time on this one. When her eyes open, she sucks in a breath. "It's not a dream," she says.

"Total reality," I say. Now that I have her, I pour on the sensation down below. My mouth takes her nipple in my mouth, and I tug.

"Oh my God," she says, her hips bucking upward like they're pulled by a string.

And they are. Mine. I own her.

"Dell, oh Dell, oh Dell," she murmurs. I capture her mouth before she stirs our baby.

When I'm sure she can't cry out, I plunge into her. She gasps against me, but holds silent. Unlike last night, when she held still, anxious about how the pain and pleasure might compete, this morning, she's wild. Her hands grab my ass, shoving me into her.

Her breasts bounce, creating a sweet friction against my chest.

I want her to know more, feel more, so I slide my hands behind her back and twist us around.

Now she's on top of me, straddling my cock.

She sucks in a breath, looking down. "This is more," she whispers.

Her hands grip the pillows on either side of my head.

"More how?" I don't get a lot of honest sex talk

from the women I have trysts with.

"You're farther in," she says. "I feel it in new places."

I lean back, my hands behind my head. "Do what you like, then."

She concentrates for a moment, shifting her hips, making little gyrating circles that make me have to summon some resolve to stop me from slamming into her.

"I like this," she says. "Whew. Wow."

I watch her face shift expressions, her body jolting with each newly discovered point of pleasure. Her breasts shift over me like two suns rising. Eventually I can't manage the temptation and hold each glorious one, thumbing the nipples.

"I want to go fast," she says. "Like really fast. Will that hurt you?"

I place my hands on her hips. "Try me."

Her body begins to pulse over mine. Damn, that's good. I help her, urging her faster.

She moves her hand to her mouth to stay quiet. I can feel the tension in her, muscles tightening around me.

I move even faster, harder, until I'm not sure I'll make it a minute more, clamping down on my control.

She squeals a little, sounds escaping, and collapses on my chest. She'll be spent, so I go ahead and let loose inside her, pumping, grinding, loving every stroke.

I bring us both down slowly. She sighs against my neck. "I just want to do it again," she says against my cheek.

"I am at your service," I say. Damn, she's a wonder.

But after a few minutes of holding on to each other, the first peek of sun spills through the still-open window.

As soon as a beam hits the baby bed, Grace lets out a lusty cry.

"At least she waited," Arianna whispers.

"She did us a solid on that."

"And she's probably done more than a solid in her diaper."

I have to laugh. From pillow talk to potty humor. Parenthood.

Arianna gets up and picks up Grace. Her body is rosy in the low light. Something about her naked form holding the infant stirs me like nothing else has. I don't care what dolled-up high-end stylist does your hair or what six-figure Paris-designed gown you don, there is simply no more beautiful sight than what I'm looking at now.

She turns, patting the baby so she's calm before she tries to change her. I see a sparkle on her finger and realize she is still wearing the ring I put on her finger yesterday.

And it looks exactly right.

Chapter 42: Arianna

We've all gotten showered, dressed, and had a quick breakfast at the table in our room when there's a knock.

Dell checks his watch. "The driver's a little early. I'll tell him to take the things we've already packed."

He opens the door. But it's not our driver from yesterday. It's the woman from the front desk.

"Mr. Brant," she says. "Your presence is requested in one of our cottages. Your wife and the baby too."

Dell stares her down. "Who sent you?"

"I'm not at liberty to say," she says. "It's just for a visit."

"If it's just a visit, then you can tell us who it is," he insists.

I guess he's afraid the Duke is back with his gun after all.

The woman looks both ways down the hall, then

leans in. "It's the Duchess, sir."

"Of Attenbury?" Dell doesn't disguise his surprise.

She nods. "Can I take you there?"

Dell motions for me to bring the baby. I snatch up the diaper bag and heft Grace on my shoulder.

We exit the back of the inn and cross a landscaped courtyard. Beyond a gate is a small pond with three cottages.

"It's the one in the middle," the woman says. "She is expecting you."

When she is out of earshot, I ask Dell, "You think the Duchess knows we showed up at her house?"

"Looks like it," he says. "And she wants to see the baby."

My heart hammers in my throat. This is it. What we came for.

Dell knocks on the door. After a moment, it opens. It's a young woman, maybe twenty. "Come in," she says.

After we pass through, she leaves the cottage, closing the door behind her.

The inside is rustic and charming. A braided rug beneath a coffee table. Well-worn floral sofa and Queen Anne chairs.

In one of them is a woman, regal, fair-haired, and thin. She has that air about her you expect in those who know their station in life.

"Dell," she says. "So good of you to come."

She doesn't take her eyes off him, as if looking anywhere else will spoil the illusion that he is alone and there just for her.

Dell walks up and bows. "Duchess," he says.

She lifts her hand and he kisses the back of it.

"My husband informed me you tried to crash my party," she says. "I thought it very dashing of you. But of course you brought a wife."

Only then does she look to me. When her eyes meet mine, I bow too. I'm not sure if I'm supposed to, or if Dell was being gallant, but I err on the safe side.

She turns her attention back to Dell. "What have you named your child?" she asks.

"Grace," Dell says. "For my grandmother."

"Lovely," she says. "I suppose you are here because you think I am her mother."

What? She's not? I glance at Dell to see if he is registering any shock, but he has his boardroom face on.

He bows again. "When I looked upon her beauty, I knew she could be none other than yours."

"Still the charmer," she says, relaxing a little. "What a whirlwind few days we had. I will never forget them."

Dell gestures to the baby. "And now they live on."

Her face remains neutral. "Who is this woman you've married? I saw no mention of it in the press."

He pauses. "Arianna," he says. "She's the perfect mother."

"You can't have known her long," the Duchess says. "Yet you know this about her?"

I'm aghast he hasn't corrected her about our marriage, but I say nothing. She still hasn't admitted to being the mother.

"I know her," Dell says. "And there is none like her."

The Duchess watches him a few moments more. Then she says, "That is good enough for me." She rises and goes to a small rolltop desk in the corner. She withdraws a long envelope.

"You'll find in here a certificate listing the baby's date and place of birth in a very small Russian village. The mother is documented officially as one Galina Popov. She was a local girl who died in a car accident around the time I arrived. Her mother assisted in the delivery of the baby and agreed to list her. You are named as the father. This ensures she could easily become an American even though she was born in Russia."

"What is her official name?" Dell asks.

"Galina Brant." The Duchess passes the envelope to Dell. "But it is of no consequence. Change it as you like."

"How did you hide your condition?" Dell asks.

"It is not so hard to disappear on an extended holiday when you serve no purpose past your provision of heirs," she says. "With my children grown, no one even noticed, other than Christmas, which was covered with minimal fuss. Everyone has their lives, you know."

I can't imagine not being missed for a year. It's terrible.

"Who brought her to New York?" Dell asks.

"I have no idea," the Duchess says. "I had it arranged. I never saw the baby. I would not allow myself to fall in love with her. I wanted more for her than to suffer as the object of derision and scorn."

Only now does her gaze shift to the bundle in my arms. "However, I should like to see her just this once."

I hesitate only for a moment. Then I walk up to her and hold out the baby.

The Duchess takes her. "I have three grandchildren. I never would have dreamed for a moment I could still conceive. But it had been a decade since the opportunity could have arisen."

My empathy rises for this woman. She is admired and envied throughout the country. But she is lonely.

The woman examines the child. Grace looks at her with a solemn expression. There is still no resemblance, but when she is older, it will most certainly be there.

"You can use the birth certificate or burn it," she tells Dell. "It was not officially registered. Your lawyers there will do what is necessary, will they not?"

He nods.

"All right, then." She presses a long kiss into one of the baby's cheeks, then the other, then passes her back to me. "It is done. I trust you will keep this secret to your grave. We cannot upset the balance of heirs." She gives a sardonic laugh. "As if anything passes through the females, even today."

She stands and kisses both of Dell's cheeks. "Love her. I could not be more pleased to see you have settled your philandering ways."

Then she turns to me. "Raise her as your own." She tilts her head at Dell. "And keep him too busy to wander."

She kisses both of my cheeks as well. Then she leaves the room.

Dell and I exit the cottage. Neither of us speak, as if struck dumb by the Duchess, her confession, and the necessity of her sacrifice.

Chapter 43: Dell

When Arianna and I get back to our room, I know we should discuss what has just happened. It's difficult to process all that has transpired in the past few hours.

Few days, even.

Arianna seems subdued, slowly packing all of Grace's things and preparing the diaper bag for the trip home.

I'm not sure what is getting her the most. Seeing Grace's mother or the events of last night. She's different.

I fear she regrets everything.

And of course, there is Grace. Arianna wants her. She has said so. But she is my child. The DNA will confirm it, but of course it isn't necessary now. We know.

"Should we talk about this?" I ask her as she zips the garment bag around the incredible white dress she wore last night.

"What is there to discuss?" she says. "Grace is yours. You already have her room all set up. You have a perfect nanny."

So she does have regrets. She's cutting herself out of the picture.

I shove my own things willy-nilly in bags.

Willy-nilly.

My grandmother used to say that.

She is long gone, but I wonder what she would think of what I've become. "Always cherish the important things," she would say.

She just never said what those were.

I've lived my life surrounded by the things I've earned.

But maybe there is more, things that can't be bought or sold.

Only freely given.

The driver arrives to take our bags. The opportunity to talk more about the Duchess has ended. We seem to have nothing else to discuss, and the drive passes in silence other than occasional comments about Grace's hunger, or the need to stop and change her.

Then we're at an airport. Then our seats. Always surrounded by people, strangers, making it impossible to talk about anything. The secret is too big to risk.

And then, we're back in New York.

And home.

Arianna does not want to speak to me. She is impatient to get back to her life, her routine.

It seems that this time the weekend fling was orchestrated by the woman, and it's her decision to end it. The child is not adoptable, so there is nothing else for her to do with me.

The tables have turned.

Chapter 44: Arianna

We make it back to the Dell Brant Building around midnight Monday. I've missed a day at the child spa. Dell missed the DNA test. Not that it matters.

We know who she belongs to. And it will never be me.

I'm not sure what will happen next. The driver helps us load our things in the elevator. The night doorman tips his hat and codes the elevator for the fortieth floor.

When the door closes, Dell pushes number four.

My floor.

Grace is asleep in the bucket. Carrie is in the penthouse, ready to handle her. Dell has already extended her nanny job. I heard him speak to her on his plane.

I guess this is what the morning after feels like. The awkward separation. The "I'll call you."

Except Dell never does.

I want to remind him what the Duchess said to me. To take care of Grace. Raise her as my own.

But that promise was based on a lie. I'm not Dell's wife. I'm not his anything. Not even the babysitter.

As the elevator opens to my floor, I pull off the diamond ring. "I guess the ruse is over," I say, passing it to Dell. "It worked."

He takes the ring and stares at it.

I shoulder my duffel. I'm tired. I want to sleep.

I step out of the elevator.

"Arianna, wait!" Dell says.

I turn, expectant.

He holds up the garment bag with the white gown. "This is yours."

I deflate inside. I want to tell him to keep it. Shove it somewhere. Up his ass, maybe. But I reach out and take it from him. "Thanks."

The driver hits a button and the door closes. I keep standing there, waiting, wishing it would open again.

What did I expect?

I trudge back to my apartment. This is the worst. Only when you soar can you crash this hard.

When I step inside my apartment, there is a white

envelope on the floor, slid beneath the door.

I set down my duffel and toss the garment bag across the back of the sofa.

Inside the envelope is a card.

Congratulations! You have been accepted into the DOMs. Our next gathering of Dell Brant's exes will be held at the La Feria bar on the Upper West Side, August 3 at 2 p.m. sharp. Don't worry about recognizing us. We will recognize you.

Oh. My. God.

One. How did they know?

Two. What the hell? I don't want in their little group!

I storm to my bed and flop down on it. I don't know what to do first. Laugh? Cry? Hit things?

Luckily, exhaustion wins. I'm out before I can do any of those.

I wake to my phone alarm, reminding me it's time to start my Tuesday.

Might as well get up and begin the first day of my post-Dell life. There will be many more. In fact, all my days will be post-Dell. Because Dell is Dell.

I spot the DOMs card again. What a crock.

No way.

If I'm a Dell ex, I'll do it alone.

***

A week passes. It's horrible. I wonder how Grace is doing. Carrie hasn't walked by the front of the spa. Nor has Dell. I stopped watching for them around Friday.

I try to move on. I find an adoption agency that accepts single mothers, but toss the packet after attending the first meeting. That doesn't feel right either. The only baby I want to adopt is Grace.

On Wednesday, Taylor buzzes me to the front with the emergency *get here right now* pattern.

I sprint to the foyer and burst through the door in a complete panic. I have no idea what to expect. A fire? A crazed parent? Did Dell finally evict me?

But it's Bernard. He's holding Grace at arm's length. She is screaming at the top of her lungs. Her diaper has leaked all over her outfit with yellow ooze.

Taylor looks relieved to see me. "He wouldn't talk to anyone but you," she says.

"That's all right. Just fine," I say. I reach in a drawer for a signature Del Gato Child Spa burp cloth and wrap Grace's bottom. Then I take her from Bernard.

"What is going on? Where's Carrie? And Dell?"

Bernard's normally placid face is full of terror. "She quit. He left. Madam Arianna, this is NOT in my contract!"

I cuddle Grace against my cheek. "Shush now, baby girl. You're okay."

"He left no instructions. Gave me no assistance!" Bernard's voice is full of anguish and confusion. "I have a mind to give notice!"

"You're all right, Bernard," I say in the same soothing tone I'm using with Grace. "Let's go back and get the baby cleaned up. Would you like a cup of hot tea?"

"I might," he says, wringing his hands as he follows me down the hall. "I had no idea what to do. She was screaming and smelling and screaming."

I buzz us into the diaper room. "Sit right there, Bernard," I say, pointing to a pristine white chair.

Penelope jumps from her stool. "What's going on?"

"Can you fetch Bernard some tea from the break room?" I ask her. "He's had a rough morning."

She takes off as I lay Grace down on the changing pad. "How is Gracie-boo?" I ask. "Bad morning for you too?"

She reaches up with her hands to touch my face. Her eyes are wet with tears.

I sweep away the outfit, a pink one I don't recognize, and the soiled diaper. I change her and pull a Del Gato Child Spa onesie from the cabinet. When she is settled, I turn to Bernard.

He sits, stiff as a board, looking anywhere but at us. He seems unhappy that he lost his calm facade.

Penelope returns with the tea. She passes it to him and I suggest she check on the baby rooms. She happily heads out again.

"So start at the beginning," I say, picking up Grace. She's happy now that she's dry and changed. I could squeeze her forever.

"Mr. Brant has not been the same since returning from France," Bernard says. "He will mind me saying it, but I can't help it. He's been terribly unpleasant, disorganized, and out of routine."

"Do you know why?"

"No one has the slightest clue. I even spoke to the housekeeper about it, and you should know I am not one to gossip with the help." He holds the string of his tea bag, bobbing it up and down.

Grace babbles and I rub her back, shushing her. I'm anxious to hear what Bernard has to say about Dell.

"Then he lost his temper with Miss Carrie this morning, and she said that was one too many times, and up and quit." Bernard's face contorts. "She handed the baby to me! ME!" He is overcome and can't manage the tea anymore. I step forward and take it before he spills it on his hands.

"I tried to pass the baby back to Dell, but then HE left." His hand flutters before his eyes as if he's shielding them from a bright light. "I'm too old for this."

"You're not too old," I argue.

"I am very set in my ways," he says. "I simply cannot go through the process of finding another position. Bachelors are very hard to train."

"Where is Dell now?" I ask.

"His office, I assume," Bernard says. "He won't take any calls, though."

We could go there, I think, but maybe that isn't productive. He probably has layers of security and assistants.

"Let's just go back to the penthouse," I say. "I'll stay with you until Dell returns."

He calms considerably at that. "I'll be happy to warm the bottles. I do that well."

"You do," I say. "You make the very best bottles."

Penelope walks in during that last line and turns right around and heads out again. We can't hog the diaper room much longer. Someone will need it.

"Let's go, Bernard," I say. "Take your tea."

He picks up the mug. I leave Grace's dirty outfit on the counter. Someone else can handle it.

Bernard seems to pull himself together on the ride up. "I'm dreadfully sorry for inconveniencing you, Madam Arianna."

"Just Arianna," I say, still smarting that I'm a madam to Carrie's miss.

"Yes, of course. Arianna."

He buzzes us into the penthouse.

Longing hits me like a brick wall when we step inside. The smells, the perfect room. The sofa where I agreed to go to his bedroom, before Grace interrupted.

"I'll take it from here," I tell Bernard, and head down the hall to the nursery.

It's been transformed. The big bed is gone, as well as all the old furniture. The set I saw in the baby superstore is here. The crib. Changing table. And a real rocker.

He chose the set I loved.

I sit in the new chair. There are toys. Dozens of them. Stuffed animals and a baby gym and even the soft lamb I saw that day. I pick it up and hand it to Grace. Her arms wave excitedly.

Everything is the same soft green. "I love it in here," I tell Grace.

Out of curiosity, I stand up and cross into the bathroom. There are more baby items here as well. A wipe warmer. A baby bathtub. A little net with baby water toys inside.

Then I visit the adjoining room. It's the same, the bed and books and dresser.

But the clock. It's gone.

"Your father is very strange and secretive," I say to Grace.

I'm so happy to hold her, so overcome. I go back to the rocker and cradle her in my arms. "If I could stay here forever, I totally would," I tell her. "If only you could be mine."

After Max howls for half an hour, Bernard relents and lets the dog come to the nursery to lie on the rug at our feet. The three of us spend hours playing with toys. I practice teaching Grace to say "dog" although she just babbles.

Bernard brings me lunch in the nursery and a bottle for Grace. He seems to be able to predict when she'll want one. Carrie must have established a routine.

Carrie. She's good. One of the best nanny candidates I know. What happened?

When Grace goes down for a nap in her beautiful crib, I close the door and dial her number.

She answers on the second ring.

"Arianna, I know why you're calling. I just couldn't take it anymore. Not one more minute."

I glance over at Grace to make sure she's good and out. "What happened?"

"He was awful. Just awful. I didn't know him well before you two left town, but the Dell I saw when he got back was unbearable. You'll never get anyone to nanny for him if he's like that."

"What did he do?"

"Just charged around like an angry bull. I couldn't do anything right. I didn't hold her right. She was hungry. She was wet. She shouldn't be crying. Why isn't she sleeping? I simply could not take it."

I don't know what to say. I know Carrie is a good caregiver. I've seen it myself.

"Did you get an idea of what made him act that way? He wasn't like that on the trip."

Of course, I was screwing him. Maybe that helped.

"No clue, Arianna," she says. "All I know is that nothing I did could measure up to some impossible standard in his head. So I quit."

"Okay, Carrie. This doesn't impact the work you

do for me. I think you're great."

"Good. Thank you. Good luck."

I shove the phone in my pocket.

So weird. Why was Dell so mad? Because Grace was his? Did he not want her after all? I'll speak to him. Maybe we can work out an arrangement where she lives with me. He can visit her when it suits him. Like he did with his dog Max. Morning breakfast and a few commands in the evening.

I'll do anything he wants to keep her.

The afternoon passes slowly. My anxiety rises as the clock ticks and a confrontation with Dell seems imminent. I rehearse my speech. Honoring the Duchess's wishes. Keep custody informal. I'll just be downstairs.

Five o'clock comes and goes. I wonder if I'll need to stay the night. Great, I get to babysit for another one of his dates. He can initiate another member into the DOMs.

Still, I grit my teeth and decide to stick it out. I have a higher purpose now. The baby is more important.

Grace and I do tummy time on her new play mat. She's already holding her head up better. Occasionally she tips to one side as though she's ready to roll over. I can't wait to see her first milestones.

Seven o'clock.

I decide I'll have to take Grace with me downstairs to get my overnight bag. If Dell has skipped town rather than face his obligations, I'll bring her with me to the spa tomorrow. I'll use the wrap and wear her.

Moms have carried babies in the fields for centuries. I can haul her to my stupidly easy job. With Maria as a floater and Taylor taking more responsibility during my absences, I'm needed a lot less than I was.

I've just shoved a fresh diaper and a travel pack of wipes in my purse to take with me when I hear the front door open.

"Good evening, sir," I hear Bernard say. "I trust your day went well."

"Where's the baby?" Dell asks. "Did she cry all day or did that nanny actually do something for once?"

"Actually…" Bernard says, but trails off.

Dell is coming down the hall. His stomping footsteps could be heard on Mars.

He walks in talking, his voice gruff, as if he's continuing a conversation. "And furthermore, I take great offense at you threatening to leave a vulnerable baby without a proper —" He sees me and cuts off.

I'm shocked at him. He's nothing like the Dell I knew. His hair is askew, as if he's been unable to stop running his hands through it all day. He has no tie. A few buttons are undone.

I don't think he shaved today. Or possibly yesterday or the day before.

I'm okay with that. It's sexy.

Just not Dell.

"Are you okay?" I ask. "You look like you've been through the mill."

He backs away. "What are you doing here?"

"You ran off your nanny and Bernard needed help."

Dell continues walking back until he hits the far wall. "Bernard, I did not authorize you to contact this — this woman!"

Wow. I've been downgraded from babysitter even. I'm just a gender.

My practiced speech goes out the window. I'm as angry as I've ever been.

"What did I do to you?" I shout. "Other than help? Saved you when Grace arrived. Got you set up with what you needed. Got you a nanny. Which you then ran off. Went all over the godforsaken globe to find her mother!"

I want to add "slept with you," but I know the

butler is near.

"You are an ass!" I say. "Worse than an ass! You kick the people who try to help!"

Grace begins crying from her crib. "And now we've upset the baby!"

I head over to her. "Shush now, sweet girl," I say. "I'm here."

But she won't stop, her face quickly blooming red. I pick her up. What am I supposed to do now? I can't leave her with him.

I hold Grace on my shoulder, patting her back. I have nothing else to say to Dell at the moment. I'll talk to him when he is calm. Maybe after his brandy. Or a good night's sleep, more than four measly hours.

I refuse to face him, walking in bouncy steps to settle Grace. I can't think about what will happen to her if I'm not here to help.

"Arianna," he says, and his voice is so different, so broken, that I whirl around.

"Dell?"

He drops into a chair by the door. He leans forward, his head in his hands.

Something is definitely wrong.

I relent and move closer to him.

He still doesn't look up.

"Hey." I kneel down, the baby close to my chest.

"What's happened? Did the Duchess contact you again? Does she want the baby back? Has that Camellia woman blackmailed you?"

He shakes his head. "No. I just can't have you here. It's too hard."

Really? Uggh.

I stand up, my concern evaporating.

"What is hard, Dell? Having an ex around? Does it cramp your bachelor style? Nobody's stopping you from screwing every debutante in town. I'm not stopping you. I just want Grace."

He barks out a rueful laugh. "Grace. Right. That's all you ever wanted. You were even willing to sacrifice your high and mighty Brown University cherry to get her."

I want to slap him, hurt him the way he's hurting me. But I have the baby. All I can do is back away.

"You are awful," I say. "Horrible and disgusting. I should have called CPS on the first day."

"Would have saved me a lot of trouble," he says, his voice bitter. "I wouldn't have fallen in love with her, and I wouldn't have fallen in love with you."

For a moment, I'm sure the ground has fallen from beneath my feet.

"What did you say?"

"You heard me," he says. "But it's pointless. You

want the baby. So just go. Take her to the fourth floor. Raise her. Just do what you have to do. I just can't see you. I can't stand all the things we could have been."

He stands up. Heads for the door. "I'll draw up some paperwork. Shared custody. Whatever is necessary." He looks back at me. He's in control now, his decision made. His face has returned to the boardroom mask. "I will provide for her."

"Dell! Wait!"

My god. He's just assuming everything! My mind is reeling. Dell Brant? In love? With me?

"What else do you want?" he asks. "I've given you everything."

"No, you haven't," I say. I walk up to him, slowly, as if I'm wading through a dream.

We're close now. I can smell him, woodsy aftershave and expensive fabric. He might look a wreck, but he's still Dell underneath.

His gaze levels me. I could shrink back from his stiffness, his professional distance. But I don't.

His voice is gruff. "What, then?" he asks. "Is your trust fund insufficient?"

"Cap'n Crunch," I say.

"What?"

"Cap'n Crunch," I repeat.

"Bernard can fetch it for —"

"Every day," I cut in. "Every morning. And I want you to pour it for me. Not Bernard. And one day, we'll introduce our favorite cereal to Grace."

I look down at Grace. "And I want you to promise never to poison her with the peanut butter flavor —"

I can't say more, because Dell is kissing me. He's heard what I've said. And he's understood.

I've cut through his boardroom facade, his game face, his layers.

He keeps kissing me, my face, my shoulder, then Grace's head. She laughs at this, reaching up for him.

"I love you, Dell Brant," I say, then whisper, "Hasmund McDonald."

He groans, but keeps kissing us, me, then the baby, then me again. "I should never have told you that."

I press my palm against his cheek. "I am proud to be the keeper of your secrets," I say, then look down at Grace. "And hers."

"And I want to be the man you trust."

"I will work on that," I say. "Just don't give me any reason to doubt you."

"I never will."

He kisses me then, and it's a different sort of kiss.

It's a kiss that tells me that he's accepted my gift. My innocence, long delayed, slain into submission by his seduction.

And he's accepted the gift of Grace. The baby he had no idea was his from the woman who had never truly known passion until he showed her.

The kiss goes on and on. It's not the first kiss, my wake from slumber. And it's not the second kiss, thwarted by circumstance.

And it's not the kiss that said yes to giving in to passion, growing up, and trusting that he was not the man my father was, or his father was, or any of those sperm donors at my child spa.

And it won't be the last kiss. Definitely not that.

It's a kiss that says we'll have a lifetime of them. And Cap'n Crunch. Panda Pop on phone calls. Dog walks. Late-night workouts with earbuds.

Grace protests being squished between us. We laugh and look down at her. Max jumps up now that the angry voices are gone, his tail going nuts in a happy wag.

This is what a family looks like. Maybe not the way anyone would have planned. Maybe not the most traditional. But forged in fire and burning brightly in love.

Epilogue: The DOMs

The La Feria bar is far seedier than I expected. When I open the door, it's so dark inside that I can only make out the colors on the jukebox and a blinking red exit sign in the back.

When my eyes adjust, I look over the tables. I expect to see Camellia Walsh. Actresses. Society women. I don't expect to see Winnie.

Now I know how the DOMs figured me out.

She holds out her hands as she comes forward. "Arianna," she says. "You made it."

She wears a loose floral outfit that flutters as she walks. Her hair is not as blond as before, as if she's transitioning it back to her natural color. She grasps my hands and leads me to a tall table with a half dozen other women.

Camellia isn't there. I recognize a few faces from press photos back when I was stalking Dell.

"We've sent you six invitations over the past four

months," Winnie asks. "What made you accept it this time?"

I slide onto a stool. "Morbid curiosity," I say. "I'm surprised you're still meeting."

A slender brunette speaks up. "We assumed he'd come back around eventually. We never thought your single motherhood would be such a draw. But Dell gets bored quickly."

I'm amused that the world has fallen for that ruse. My obscurity made it easy to pretend Grace was mine first and Dell's second. This ensured no one ever connected the dots back to the Duchess. Nobody cared who my baby daddy was. I wasn't interesting enough for speculation.

And as for Dell getting bored, not happening anytime soon. We just discovered the dark thrill of spreader bars. On him.

"You might want to find another bachelor," I say. "Or membership is going to die off."

"Oh, really?" the brunette says. "You think you've landed him?"

I pull my left hand out from beneath the table and casually tap my nails against the surface. The diamond solitaire from Paris catches the neon from a beer sign on the wall.

"Shit," whispers a fortysomething women with

boobs that rival mine. "A wedding will keep him off the market for at least six months."

The brunette holds up a palm. "This group is not about Dell Brant per se," she says. "Our mission continues."

Now she has my interest. "What is the mission of the DOMs? What does it even stand for?"

"Dirty Old Mistresses," Winnie says. "Isn't that a hoot? We're all discarded lovers of powerful men. We help each other get invitations to events where we can stay in contact with the right sort of prospects."

My jaw falls open. "And Dell was your quality control?"

"Exactly," Boob Woman says. "Not all of his exes made the cut. His track record isn't perfect."

"But he met women in the right places," the brunette says. "Between all of us, we could get into most any charity event or fund-raiser. Where the big fish swim." She glances down at my ring. "Sadly, you are currently not eligible for membership."

Fine by me. "Isn't this whole thing sort of manipulative?" I ask.

Winnie picks up her drink. "It's tough out there, Arianna. We've been discarded." She holds up her glass to the others. "But we will stick together."

"'Till marriage we do part," a blonde says.

"And divorce gets us back together," Boob Woman adds.

They clink their glasses.

"Don't forget about us," the brunette says. "We'll find another method of recruiting members while you have your hold on Dell."

"But remember, we'll be here if you need us," Winnie says.

"*When* you need us," the brunette amends.

I smile at them and slide off the chair, then turn for one last question.

"Camellia Walsh," I say. "Is she in your group?"

There's a collective groan.

"Girls like Camellia make the rest of us look bad," Winnie says. "We're not gold diggers. We just want to make sure we can survive and flourish, no matter the whims of the men."

"Well, good luck," I tell them. I guess it's good they have each other. I know most of what they say is true. I see it at the child spa all the time. Last month, for the first time, we had two couples marry each other's exes. The kids didn't even have to switch rooms. Only the billing information changed.

So the DOMs are right about that. It *can* be tough out there. Happiness is rare. True love even rarer.

I exit the bar, blinking in the bright light of a

brilliant fall day. Two blocks down, I turn and head to a small park. There's a figure there in a ball cap, Mets jacket, and jeans.

Dell. My lover. My future husband.

He's pushing Grace in one of the bucket swings. She laughs in a bright blue coat with the words "Future CEO" across the front. It's a sample. He bought a children's line from some manufacturer and made them change all the logos on the girls' wear.

Max bounds around the park, chasing birds and leaping around like a squirrel. Every time Grace sees him, she lets out her little baby laugh.

Dell spots me. "How did it go?"

"I got kicked out," I say. "It's only for single ladies looking for their next love affair."

"Huh," he says. "That figures." He leans down to kiss me. "You feel better now that you know?"

"Sure." I watch Grace's beaming face as she moves forward and back in the swing.

"You going to the spa now? It's your day to work."

Dell and I have both gone part-time, alternating days off so we don't need a nanny. "It's nice outside," I say. "I think I'll just stay here with you two."

"Sounds good to me," Dell says.

Grace babbles a little more. According to the

birth certificate, she is eight months old today. We have kept her middle name Galina to honor the family who holds her secret. We hold out hope that one day, when she is grown, the Duchess will be able to acknowledge the daughter we have raised on her behalf.

But for now, it's just the three of us.

A beautiful baby.

A much more chilled-out mom.

And the single dad who taught me to dream big, love hard, and never be afraid to create your own definition of being *on top*.

Also by JJ Knight

The UNCAGED LOVE Series
The FIGHT FOR HER Series

www.jjknight.com

Made in the USA
Monee, IL
08 February 2024

53161299R00216